**In the camp of a murderous cult,
a prisoner is tied upright to a pole—
Captain Gringo!**

To the sound of a throbbing drum, a figure moves out into the ruddy firelight. The natives gasp in awe—and so does Gringo. He hadn't expected a naked lady wrapped in the coils of the biggest snake in the world. It darts out its tongue to touch Captain Gringo's knee. Sliding round and round, it unwinds from the black girl's hips and begins climbing him and his post like a stripe going up a barber pole. Its ugly head confronts him and its darting tongue explores his face. He's done for—and he knows it, but, damn it, if they want him dead, they'll have to do it right. He's not about to be swallowed whole by a goddamned animated sausage!

Novels by Ramsay Thorne

Published by
WARNER BOOKS

Renegade # 5

MACUMBA KILLER

by
Ramsay Thorne

WARNER BOOKS

A Warner Communications Company

WARNER BOOKS EDITION

Cover design by Gene Light

Cover art by George Gross

Warner Books, Inc., 666 Fifth Avenue, New York, N.Y. 10103

Ⓦ A Warner Communications Company

Printed in the United States of America

First Printing: October, 1980

10 9 8 7 6 5 4 3

Renegade # 5

MACUMBA KILLER

Chapter One

The machine gun stuttered hysterically at the jungle wall across the clearing as a long ragged line of eerie figures left the cover of the tree line. The sun hung low above the treetops to the west. The sky was a big, inverted bowl of blood. Everything was bathed in a hellfire-red light. But it wasn't the lighting that had the plantation guards so frightened. It was the ominous silent calm of the attacking skirmish line. They didn't shout; they didn't run; they didn't wave their machetes. They just kept coming as the machine gun hosed them down with hot lead.

One of the guards stared stupidly as he clicked his empty revolver at the oncoming line. Then he gasped, *"Nombre de Dios! Vamanos, muchachos!"* and, suiting action to his words, ran like hell.

The machine-gun crew was made of sterner stuff. El Patron had assured them the marvelous new weapon would stop anything that walked this earth, and in God's truth, it fired awesomely. But there was something wrong. Something that hadn't been included in the book of instructions that came with the new machine gun. The ragged line from the jungle, for some strange reason, kept coming!

They didn't charge. They weren't even walking fast. The red-lit figures almost *strolled* across the ploughed red soil, holding their machetes as if they were sleepy peones moving into the fields to start another weary day, cutting cane. But there was no cane to cut. The only and too obvious targets of those ruby-gleaming blades were the frightened men around the machine gun, and the machine gun wasn't stopping the advance enough to matter!

Oh, some of the oddly detached attackers were going down. The gunner grunted in satisfaction as he saw one man stagger and fall. But then, to his horror, the man got up again, picked up his fallen machete, and kept coming!

The belt man sobbed, "It's no use! I told you ordinary bullets can't stop a *zombi!*" But the gunner groaned, "Shut up, and feed this gun! There is no such thing as a zombi, damn your eyes!"

But in truth, he was frightened to the point of wetting his own pants as he swung the muzzle back and forth at what was now almost point-blank range. If the attackers were not zombies, they certainly looked and acted like zombies. Like the gunner and his comrades, the attackers were that West Indian mélange of Hispanic-Indian-African that results in a curiously raceless breed of tawny dark men dressed in white cotton and straw.

The people coming at him were neither larger nor smaller than the ones he was used to fighting. They didn't look particularly fierce. Their faces, as they came nearer in the ruby light, were devoid of any expression at all. They looked half-asleep, or, *Madre de Dios—dead!*

"To your left!" the belt man sobbed, and the gunner swung his muzzle to cover a large, more Negroid man bearing down on them with upraised machete. The gunner fired into him point-blank and stitched a row of dark-red blossoms across the black man's chest.

He staggered back a few paces, shook his head as if

he was a bull with a fly between its horns, and then kept coming!

"*Jesus, por favor!*" gasped the gunner, firing again, and this time the big Negro went down and stayed there. But the belt man shouted, "Run!" and the gunner glanced to his right to see a large, heavy woman, bleeding from the mouth, almost on top of him with her own machete high and gleaming like the hinges of hell in the sunset.

It was the last thing the gunner ever saw. His belt man made it almost thirty paces before another machete, thrown end over end, caught him between the shoulder blades.

Most of the guard detail got away. They didn't stop running until they'd put a good three kilometers between themselves and the plantation they'd been ordered to guard. By then the sun was down, but the sky still glowed red to the west. The attackers were methodically burning yet another plantation of the Pantropic Sugar Trust. It would make it the third in as many weeks. This latest attack was obviously not going to be the last. And sugar prices were up, damn it. Pantropic had not invested in new guards and the latest technology only to go out of business during a sugar boom.

And so a phone rang before midnight and Sir Basil Hakim listened with a pained expression as his caller described him as a cheating scoundrel, an Armenian rug salesman, and a stupid dwarf. Then, the salutations out of the way, Sir Basil sighed and said, "I am a British subject of Turkish ancestry, and I fail to see how your rude remarks about my size has anything to do with the products I sold you. Are you suggesting those machine guns you ordered from us don't work?"

The small dapper arms merchant yawned and held the earphone away from his gray head while a steady stream of curses crackled over the wire. He lay nude, propped on pillows in his fourposter, and the blonde, with her head between his raised knees, offered a most enjoyable diversion. But business came before pleasure and he ordered her to stop sucking as the tirade over the phone ran down for lack of breath if not inspiration.

Hakim gingerly placed the earphone against his head and said, "If you are through swearing, I have a few suggestions to make. Since the guns fire, they are obviously not being fired *right*. I have a very good ordinance man on my payroll. I think we'd better have him take a look at the situation and find out what's wrong before we curse each other any further. I'll get back to you after I make a few calls."

He hung up and asked the blonde, "Would you be good enough to go over to that desk and fetch my address book, my dear? I'm sure I have Captain Gringo's last known whereabouts—under T for Trouble."

The call girl slid off the satin sheets and went over to the oak desk as Hakim gazed admiringly after her. Like many small men, Hakim liked his bedmates big, but as a man of taste he chose nothing but the best, and she rather resembled a goddess carved from pink marble. The blonde found the book and brought it to him, sitting beside him as she handed it over with a puzzled frown. As Hakim leafed through it, she asked, "Isn't Captain Gringo that big American soldier of fortune? The one you had so much trouble with in Panama that time?"

Hakim chuckled fondly and replied, "Yes, he really spoiled a deal we had. I've never met a young man so good at starting and stopping revolutions all by himself."

The blonde stroked her master's genitals, saw he really had his mind on other matters, and said, "Forgive me if I seem curious, but didn't you have a murder contract out on Captain Gringo a while ago?"

Hakim said, "Ah, here it is. He's in Costa Rica. I did try to have him killed a few months ago. But he got my assassins. I told you he was good."

Hakim picked up the phone and asked the operator to patch him through to Costa Rica. He knew it would take a few minutes, so he began to stroke the blonde's thigh. But now *her* curiosity was up, and she said, "I know business is business, but this is ridiculous, Basil!

Have you forgotten Captain Gringo has promised to shoot you on sight?"

Basil Hakim chuckled and said, "Crush me like a beetle, I believe, were the words he used. He's a rather bitter young man. More to the point, he's the best machine gunner in Latin America. That's why I intend to hire him to clean up this mess."

"Do you really think he'll work for you, dear?"

"Hell, he's a soldier of fortune. A soldier of fortune will fight for the devil, if the price is right. And as you above all people should know, I pay top dollar for services rendered."

Hakim's contact agent in Costa Rica was a statuesque brunette who called herself Lilo Holzendorf. The first name on her passport had been given her by a family who preferred to think she was dead. Her original last name had started with a 'Von,' but Lilo had preferred a life of adventure to the stuffy morality of the East Prussian aristocracy. She still looked like a lady, dressed and on her feet. She was looking forward to getting to know the American they'd told her so much about from a horizontal state of *déshabille*. Unlike many spies, Lilo enjoyed sexual intrigue. That was why she worked for Sir Basil Hakim. He'd bought her from Krupp, along with a formula for laminated steel armor plate and an improved patent regarding recoil cylinders. Hakim only dealt in deadly weapons.

Neither Captain Gringo nor his little old sidekick, Gaston Verrier, were to be found at the address Sir Basil had given her. So Lilo was a bit fatigued and not a little worried that afternoon as she made her way to the luxurious quarters of another female spy. Like Lilo, the other spy was one of the many Germans living in Costa Rica's large European colony. Unlike Lilo, she worked for British Intelligence, so the matter was a bit delicate. But Sir Basil had assured Lilo he'd been busy on that wonderful new invention, the telephone.

The other girl was blonde and expecting her. She

11

ushered Lilo into a rather exotic bedroom, tossed aside the kimono she'd worn to the door, and sprawled naked across her fourposter to say, *"Ich heis Hilda Rodenau. Und Dich?"*

Lilo perched primly on a hassock near the bed, and answered, "We'd best speak English. After all, our employers are British, *nicht wahr?"*

Hilda shrugged and said, "I noticed the Von in your accent, Toots. I'm a peasant girl and proud of it. But I'll pretend we're both nice little English girls if that's the way you want to play. What's the story? I understand the Jew you work for is looking for Captain Gringo. He must be crazy."

Lilo sniffed and said, "Sir Basil is a Turk, I believe. I *know* he belongs to the same club as His Highness, the Prince of Wales."

"Yeah, yeah, the prince has stock in Hakim's Woodbine Arms Limited, too, and since Hakim owns a slice of Krupp, we're all one big happy family."

"Exactly. I understand you know where Captain Gringo can be found these days. Or should I say nights?"

Hilda ran a wistful hand over her nude pubis as she sighed, *"Ach,* those were the good old days. We broke up when he found out I worked for the Crown."

"But you can locate him for me?"

"I have some people out looking for him. He's still in town. But we'd better talk about just how you'll approach him, Fraulein Von. Hakim must have told you he's a rather unusual man."

Lilo shrugged and said, "I read his dossier. He strikes me as the usual soldier of fortune, perhaps a bit better looking, and better able to hold his drinks. But I've never met a man I couldn't twist around my finger."

To Lilo's disgust, the blousy Hilda actually seemed to be masturbating now, as she sighed and said, "I used to say that, before I went to bed with him. *Gott,* if only he hadn't caught me lying to him. Would you take some advice from a girl who's been there?"

12

"I really don't think I need advice on how to handle a man, Hilda."

"You're wrong. Getting Dick into bed is no problem. He likes girls. If you want to spend *two* nights with him, forget what Hakim will have told you. If I can get you to him, don't play games. Tell him right away who you are and what you want."

"That's not the way it's usually done."

"I know. They make us play chess when the game is usually checkers. Dick is a very bitter man. He gets angry when people try to play tricks on him."

"That's the second time you've called him Dick. In my dossier his name seems to be Richard Walker. Do you know how he came to be called Captain Gringo?"

Hilda said, "Sure. Why don't you take off your clothes? It's hot in here. I'm hot, too, just thinking about that big American. Why don't we have some fun while I fill you in on his story?"

"*Zum Teuffel,* are you a lesbian, Hilda?"

Hilda shrugged and said, "No, I'm bisexual and jealous. You're a good-looking girl and I know what fun you'll have once I get you to Captain Gringo. Unless you let me in on it, I might not want to play."

Lilo got grandly to her feet, ready to read the other German girl the Riot Act. The stupid slut had *orders*.

As if she'd read Lilo's mind, Hilda said, "Look, I said I have some people out looking. There's no saying when or *if* they'll find the American. I mean, I can only do my best, and, meanwhile, I see no reason for us to *both* be frustrated."

As the brunette hesitated, knowing Hilda had a valid excuse to just send her on her way, the buxom peasant girl rolled over, opened a box on her bedstand, and took out an amazing device of pink India rubber. She leaned back with a roguish grin, opened her ample thighs, and inserted one end of the lifelike double dildo, saying, "Come on, I'll be the boy."

Lilo stared slack-jawed at the nude Hilda, who

looked as if she'd somehow sprouted a monstrous male shaft. Intrigued despite herself, Lilo said, "That's the most perverse suggestion I've ever heard! Even if I was interested in such a thing, it's too damned big."

"I thought you wanted to meet Dick Walker."

"I do, but surely you're not suggesting he's hung like *that*?"

Hilda sighed and said, "I had this made from memory. Why do you think I'm so upset about losing him?"

Lilo laughed and said, *"Ach, Du bist* wicked, Hilda!" And then they both laughed as she unpinned her hat and put it aside. It only took a moment for Lilo to undress, save for her stockings and high button shoes. Her heart was beating wildly as she gingerly got in bed with Hilda. She already regretted her impulse as the brawnier peasant girl took her in her arms, and as their breasts flattened together, Lilo murmured, "I don't know. I've never done this sort of thing before."

"I know," soothed Hilda, "isn't it fun to lose your virginity again?"

And then, as the bigger girl rolled atop her, Lilo decided she most definitely did not want to go through with it. The other woman's female flesh felt wrong, and the long hair brushing her naked shoulders sent an odd thrill of disgust through her. Then she felt the big rubber device questing between her trembling thighs and thought, "Oh well, it's in the line of duty."

So Hilda screwed her. And it mixed up Lilo's head. One part of her said the whole idea was more silly than perverse. Another part made her move her hips to meet the thrusts, and as she felt herself going with it, she kissed back and marveled, *"Zer gut!* But what are *you* getting out of it, *Liebling?"*

Hilda was sweating and panting with her own pleasure as she replied, "I've got the bigger shaft inside me. It teases delightfully. You'll see, when it's your turn on top."

Lilo started to say she'd do no such thing. But she was coming and even as she started to say she could never play the male part, she found herself wondering what it would feel like.

But the adventurous Lilo never got to find out. She was in the middle of a wild abandoned orgasm when a male voice said, "Oh, *excusez-moi*, Hilda. I did not know you were entertaining."

Lilo, on the bottom with her legs around Hilda's waist, turned beet-red as she opened her eyes to see a short, middle-aged man with Gallic features observing them clinically from the doorway. Hilda looked over her shoulder, laughed, and said, "*Ach*, Gaston. May I present Fraulein Lilo? I was hoping you'd bring Dick, when you heard we were looking for you."

Gaston Verrier sat down and started taking off his boots as he shook his head and said, "I warned you my young associate was idealistic, Hilda. He is still most annoyed about those reports on us you sent to British Intelligence."

Lilo saw, to her dismay, that the Frenchman seemed to be getting in bed with them. She said, "Enchanted, *m'sieu*, but am I to understand you are not annoyed with Hilda here, for spying on you?"

Gaston laughed and said, "*Mais non*, people are always spying on us, but, as you just learned, Hilda is a tigress in bed, and a good lay is harder to find, in this part of the world, than a spy."

As Gaston joined them, Hilda rolled off, withdrawing her strange toy to expose Lilo's wide open lap to the little Frenchman's gaze. She blushed again and started to cover herself with her hands, but Gaston gallantly slid into place atop her, and as she protested, "*M'sieu!*" he entered her with his smaller but much more live-feeling shaft. She gasped and said, "*Lieber-Gott!* I seem to be getting raped!"

Gaston moved judiciously, and as he felt her internal muscles contract, he said, "I was only trying to make friends with you. Do you wish for me to stop?"

Lilo moaned and sighed, "It's too late and you know it, you bastard." So Gaston screwed her, too, as Hilda

15

bounced beside them and kept chanting, "My turn, my turn, my turn."

Gaston, of course, was too polite to stop until Lilo had climaxed with a confused sob. But when she opened her eyes to smile up at him the Frenchman was finishing with Hilda, dog-style. Lilo said, "This is disgusting. I wasn't sent here for an orgy. I came to make a business deal, damn it!"

Gaston hissed, closed his eyes, and flattened Hilda face down across the mattress before he recovered himself and asked, dryly, "Forgive me, Madame. How much do you usually charge?"

"Are you insane? I'm not a whore, I'm a secret agent!"

"I am most relieved. I didn't think to bring much money with me when I heard Hilda here, was looking for us again."

Hilda wriggled her derriere under Gaston and said, "She works for Sir Basil Hakim, and apparently has a deal for you two boys. Could you move it some more, Gaston? You have me sort of hanging right on the edge."

Gaston began to move in and out of her with languid strokes as he turned to Lilo and asked, "What sort of a deal does Hakim have in mind, Madame?"

"For God's sake, are we having an afternoon orgy or a business meeting?"

"Both. We French are most *practique,* and Madame is already about to destroy our new relationship by fibbing to her elders."

Lilo sat up on one elbow to ask with a puzzled frown, "What on earth are you talking about?"

Hilda sobbed, "I'm coming!" as Gaston reached over to fondle Lilo and say, "You must know that my friend, Dick, has been told lies by your employer in the past. We shall get nowhere unless you level with us, as the Americans say."

Lilo started to push his hand away, decided she liked what he was doing with his old but practiced fingers,

16

and said, "Hilda just advised me to tell you boys the truth."

Gaston withdrew from Hilda, remounted Lilo, and said, *"Bien.* I happen to know Sir Basil likes to chat on the phone while making love to an employee, and you work for him. So let us have no more bullshit about combining business with pleasure. Ah, I feel you are finding this most pleasurable, so let us get down to business. Just what does Sir Basil have in mind this time?"

"This is the craziest conversation I've ever had in my life. Sir Basil sent me to seduce Captain Gringo, and I keep getting raped before I've even spoken to him!"

"I'm enjoying your visit, too. Before we come, suppose you tell me where you want Dick and me to go."

Lilo closed her eyes and moaned, "British Crown Colony, oh, that feels nice."

"Mais oui, we both have lovely bodies. Is there any particular reason for us to go to this colony of yours, or is Sir Basil just looking for more trouble?"

Lilo moaned, and raked Gaston's back with her nails as they shared a long shuddering climax. Hilda had been watching and pleaded, "My turn, Gaston."

Gaston sighed and said, "Wait, *mon petite.* We were discussing business before we were so rudely interrupted. What is so important about this British colony, Lilo?"

The brunette laughed and said, "Zombies. I didn't believe in them either, until I met you."

Gaston remained in place, moving gently, but frowning as he muttered, *"Merde alors,* I thought you were here on serious business. By zombies one assumes you mean those unfortunate walking corpses the benighted Voodoo priests claim they can raise from the grave?"

"That's exactly what I mean. I don't know who's behind it, or how they do it, but whatever they are, they keep burning plantations and even machine guns can't stop them."

Gaston moved more sensuously, but sounded interested as he asked, "Sir Basil, as usual, has supplied the machine guns for which these zombies refuse to lie down. I begin to see some method to Madame's madness after all."

"You call *me* mad, you sex maniac? I was sent to persuade you and Captain Gringo to work for us. We need an expert who can either tell us why the machine guns fail to stop the zombies or, better yet, stop them."

Gaston rolled off Lilo to mount the anxiously pleading Hilda, but he kept right on talking to Lilo and asked, "What sort of money did Sir Basil authorize you to offer?" As Hilda started going wild in his arms, he added, "We shall save time if you get right to the point and don't try to dicker. I suppose Sir Basil assumed you could beat Dick down on the price with your fair white body, *hein?*"

"Well . . ."

"You will only make him angry. One time a girl he was in love with tried to set him up for a firing squad. It has made him most cynical."

Hilda pleaded, "For God's sake, are we going to screw or talk?"

So Gaston excused himself to Lilo, and ravaged Hilda thoroughly before he snuggled between the two of them with a satisfied smile and sighed, "Now we have time for a quiet discussion. You were about to mention our fee, Lilo."

Lilo said, "Hakim will pay the two of you a hundred dollars a day each as ordinance consultants."

"*Merde,* you screw like a princess, but you talk about pennies like a milkmaid!"

"Wait. I'm not finished. Hakim is doing this as a service to a customer. The customer is the Pantropic Sugar Trust. Do you know of them, Gaston?"

"But, of course. Pantropic is a big Anglo-American company. Is it their plantations and machine guns we have under discussion?"

"Yes, and they have money they'd rather burn than see another season's crop go up in smoke. Hakim said to tell you it will be all right when they make you a better offer. He's sending you in as ordinance experts. After you show Pantropic how much you know about guns, they'll steal you from us at a higher salary, plus, of course, the usual battle bonus."

Gaston lay between the two German girls, feeling up both of them as he sighed, "Decisions, decisions. I wish Dick were here, right now."

Hilda sighed, "So do I." Lilo was more than a little intrigued, but she said, "All in all, I think I'd rather meet him under more dignified circumstances."

"She's a Von," explained Hilda, squirming against Gaston's left hip.

Gaston pulled Lilo against his right side and said, "You had better allow me to handle Dick, *cheri*. You are *trés* lovely and *formidable* between *les* thighs. But I don't think Sir Basil was very wise in sending you to deal with Captain Gringo. I'll do the job better."

"My God, is he bisexual too?"

"I hope not. The thought is rather frightening to a man my size. What I meant was that seducing Dick Walker is a waste of time. As Hilda here, found out, it can be a pleasant waste of time for all concerned, but if you think he's going to do what you want him to just because he's been to bed with you, you are *trés* wide of the mark. My young friend is inclined to become most quickly disenchanted with strangers, and I think an aristocratic nymphomaniac would only confuse him."

Lilo stiffened, and was about to ask Gaston how he dared to call her a nymphomaniac. But she had a better sense of humor than most Germans of her class and was as curious as most women. So she snuggled closer and said, "The two of you have me convinced that Captain Gringo is a moody borderline case. Can anyone tell me *why?*"

Gaston said, "Oh, Dick is one of the sanest men I have ever met. Nine out of ten men would have been driven completely insane by the raw treatment he received from his own countrymen. To his credit, it only made him

19

a survivor. You see, he once had everything. He was an officer in the U.S. Cavalry, stationed in the West to keep an eye upon *les* Apache."

Lilo said, "That's in his dossier. He's a renegade who deserted the U.S. Army to become a soldier of fortune, right?"

"Wrong. Dick Walker was an officer and a gentleman. The U.S. Army deserted him. Through a complicated misunderstanding he was court-martialed and about to be hanged, when he broke out of the guardhouse and escaped across the border."

"Is that where he met you?"

"*Oui*. I came to Mexico with the French Legion before either of you precious things were born. But let us not dwell on the misadventures of the Emperor Maxamillian, it was most banal even when he was in power. To get back to Dick Walker, we met in a Mexican jail and were slated to face a firing squad together. We agreed this sounded most fatiguing, so the rest is history."

"How did he get the name, Captain Gringo?"

"What else would Mexican rebels call a big blonde, blue-eyed moose? Besides, there is a reward on Dick in the States, dead or alive, and so he does not brute his real name about if it can be avoided."

Gaston drew the two girls closer, luxuriating in the sensual sandwich of which he found himself a part, and observed, "My friend is homesick and most bitter about the way he has been used by fate, and the scoundrels who keep hiring us down here. Sir Basil Hakim is hardly one of Dick's favorite people, but the more I think about his offer the more I like it. Sir Basil must be desperate to offer such an honest, uncomplicated deal. The attempted seduction and suggestions of a double cross are probably as close to honesty as he's capable of coming. I'll talk it over with Dick and let you know. Will you be staying here with Hilda?"

Lilo started to reply with indignation. Then she considered what it would look like if this sardonic little man were to appear at her luxury hotel. So she said, "I guess so, if Hilda doesn't mind."

Hilda said, "I don't mind. It's your turn to get on top."

"For God's sake, Hilda, haven't you had enough for one afternoon?"

"There's never enough for one afternoon. Are you coming back with Dick, Gaston?"

Gaston sighed and said, "I may not be coming back at all. There's only a fifty-fifty chance that Dick will go for the deal, and, if he does, you know he's strictly business."

Patting Lilo's rump for attention, he added, "You'd better write down all the details before I leave, and I'd better be going soon. I was to meet Dick right after La Siesta, and I'm already late."

Lilo sat up and reached for her purse on the carpet by the bed while Gaston admired the view. She said, "I have all the instructions here on paper." Gaston sat up and said, "Bien. I believe I left my socks somewhere around here."

He dressed with practiced speed and left with the written instructions before Lilo had time to adjust to his abrupt change of pace. Like most soldiers of fortune, Gaston was a shifty target.

As soon as they were alone again, Hilda said, "Well, I didn't think it would be so simple. Why don't we wash up before we try a little sixty-nine?"

Lilo sat up in bed and said, "This is all very confusing. I'm supposed to be a very high-class adventuress, and I was sent to seduce Captain Gringo."

"I know. But relax. Gaston is doing your job for you, and Sir Basil will be satisfied even if you never meet Captain Gringo."

Lilo looked wistful and said, "After hearing the two of you talk, I'll admit I was rather looking forward to meeting him. Since you obviously know both of them at first hand . . ."

"Gaston's good, but Dick is better." Hilda grinned, adding, "He won't come here, knowing we're both spies out to tempt him. I know I'm being spiteful, but in a way I'm glad. I'm one up on you, Fraulein Von. You just got to sample half the team. I've had them both in my box."

"That was a bitchy thing to say," sighed Lilo, wondering why she felt so unsatisfied all of a sudden. Her eyes swept over the rumpled bed sheets until they locked on the big pink dildo, peeking coyly out from under a pillow. She licked her lips and asked, "You say Captain Gringo is hung like that?"

"Better. You want to try taking the bigger shaft this time?"

"Well, as long as I have to wait here . . ."

Chapter Two

"No, nada, never, and negative!" Captain Gringo repeated as Gaston went over it a second time. They were seated at a metal table in front of a sidewalk cantina, and the tall blonde American was attracting curious stares from the passers-by. Even in quiet repose, Dick Walker stood out in a Latin American crowd. He stood well over six feet and his whipcord and whalebone body could have been sculpted by Rodin, who'd have doubtless substituted a fig leaf for the tight linen pants and thin cotton shirt.

Captain Gringo's .38 was less visible than the rest of his chest, tucked as it was in a shoulder holster under the open linen jacket he wore over the shirt. He usually tried to hide his blonde hair under a straw planter's sombrero, but nobody was looking for them at the moment. Costa Rica was one of the few countries in Latin America with a stable government, and hence a safe vacation spot for soldiers of fortune without a contract. Captain Gringo didn't want another contract at the moment. He still had some money from their last frantic job, and a date with a very nice-looking Senorita, if ever the fucking sun went down.

Gaston lounged across the table from him, eating peanuts and drinking cerveza as he observed, "It sounds like easy money, Dick. I checked it out with the grapevine this afternoon. The colony is an island just off the coast of British Honduras, and the Pantropic Sugar Trust owns it all. You might call it a company island. Any law out there will be working for our side."

The tall American growled, "That's a switch. But Sir Basil has his grubby little paws on the strings, and when he plays puppet master, people tend to get killed."

"True, they do not call him the merchant of death because he is a noted philanthropist. But we'll be working for Pantropic."

"Meaning a Goddamned bunch of Wall Street robber-barons."

"What are you, a Fabian Socialist? Only half the stockholders are American. The other stock, and most of the power, is in British hands. My sources tell me the Princes of Wales has a piece of the action and, while His Highness is perhaps a fat womanizer, he is said to be a gentleman, *non?*"

"Bullshit. He's a buddy of Sir Basil's and that makes him a shit in my book! He may talk a little fancier, but ruthless fat men scare me."

Gaston nodded at the papers on the table between them, and said, "You read the offer. It seems open and aboveboard to me. Pantropic is as ruthless as any other international trust. But they have a good credit rating. I just spoke to some associates who once cleaned out some natives for Pantropic. They say they got paid, and I can vouch for them still being alive."

Captain Gringo shook his head and said, "There has to be a catch. Nobody is about to pay that kind of money for a simple job. Any half-ass pro could whip up there and train the company guards like they want us to. Why us, and why does Hakim expect them to top his offer with even more money?"

24

Gaston said, "I told you they were in some kind of a flap about the native rebels. The Honduran guards keep running away from them. They seem to think the rebels have enlisted zombies and . . ."

"Jesus H. Christ, Gaston! There's no such thing as a zombi. And even if there was, what would a zombi be doing off the Mosquito Coast? I thought that zombi shit was a Haitian superstition?"

Gaston nodded and said, "It is. We French had certain dealings with Voodoo when we owned Haiti. It was all before my time, but I have heard strange tales from older legionaires. As to what zombies might or might not be doing off Honduras, the British imported some West Indian Blacks to Honduras a while back. It didn't work out too well. It is one thing to work a Negro where he can't avoid one's lash. Given a jungle to hide out in . . ."

"I know about the Maroons in the Blue Mountains of Jamaica, and those Dutch slaves who ran into the bush of Surinam. Are these rebels we're talking about Blacks?"

"Some would seem to be. Others are the usual mestizos of the Mosquito Coast. For some reason they resent the Pantropic Sugar Trust taking over their island. Blacks and mestizos have joined forces to resist progress."

Captain Gringo frowned thoughtfully and said, "Maybe we should join the other side then. The rebels sound like my kind of crowd."

Gaston shook his head and said, *"Mais non,* I checked that out, too. The rebels are not your usual idealists. Before the sugar trust took over the island and started to clear it, it had a most evil reputation among the mainland peones. The people squatting in the jungle out there were known as pirates, raiders— even cannibals."

The tall American snorted in disbelief and said, "Oh shit, first zombies and now cannibals! Don't tell me you buy any of that, Gaston."

Gaston shrugged and said, "Cannibals are not as unreasonable as zombies, when one considers the Black

25

Caribs have never been completely cleaned out along the Mosquito Coast. As to zombies, you read the reports. How would you account for those machine gun positions being overrun by natives with machetes, Dick?"

Professionally interested despite himself, Captain Gringo shrugged and replied, "Hell, there are easier answers than black magic. As a soldier you know the limitations of any weapon. Out in Arizona our army was confused as hell when the Apache lived through cannon fire a couple of times. It never occurred to headquarters that Indians might have sense enough to dig foxholes."

"These attacking natives walked right through machine gun-fire, Dick."

"So what? The gunners were probably poorly-trained and like most greenhorns, they thought a Maxim cuts a solid swathe through the air. A machine gun throws six hundred rounds a minute, right?"

"If you say so. A lot of lead, at any rate."

"Back up, and think again. If you sweep the muzzle rapidly from side to side the bullets fan out three or four feet apart. More, if you panic and start hozing wildly. A man is only about a foot wide. Do you want me to draw you a picture?"

Gaston mused, "Hmm, I can see how people could walk between the bullets, although I think it would make most men *trés* nervous. The reports say some of the zombies, or whatever, got up again after being shot."

"All right. A guy's hopped up and charging. A stray round pinks him and puts him on the ground with a flesh wound. He's in a battle frenzy, and since he's not really hurt, he recovers to press the attack. Big deal. These rebels sound like highly-motivated fighters, or fanatics. I guarantee that none of them kept moving with a solid round in the vitals. That zombi shit was the excuse the company guards gave for punking out, period. They ran into better fighters and don't want to admit it. People used to tell me stories about Apache being hard to kill. I found they died just like the rest of us when you shot them right."

He took a sip of his own cerveza before he added, "Officers and men who get whipped never admit they were whipped by ordinary men. That would make them less than ordinary and the truth hurts. Good fighters always get the reputation of being mad monsters ordinary weapons can't stop."

"A machine gun is an ordinary weapon, Dick?"

"It's just a gun that fires faster than usual. It's as deadly as the man using it. No more. No less. You can't stop a man with a Krupp siege gun—if you aim it at the wrong position."

Gaston brightened and said, *"Bien,* in that case this deal is found money. We simply have to run up there and show them how to aim a machine gun properly, *non?"*

"Forget it. The last time Sir Basil hired us to pull his chestnuts out of the fire he neglected to tell us they were bombs with the fuses burning."

Before Gaston could answer they were joined by a third man who sat down uninvited at their table. They both knew him. He wore the mushroom-colored uniform of the Costa Rican Guardia.

Gaston nodded and said, "Good afternoon, Sergeant. What are you drinking?"

The Costa Rican sighed and said, "Nothing, thank you. I am on duty and officially I am not here. They sent me to look for you two, but since I am not here, I haven't seen you yet."

Captain Gringo took out his wallet and flattened a bill on the table as he asked, "You wouldn't by any chance know what they want with us, I suppose?"

The money vanished as the sergeant shrugged and replied, "All I know, officially, is that you are both to report in with your passports."

The tall American placed another bill on the table and asked, "So what do you know unofficially?"

The Costa Rican glanced uneasily around and murmured, "Something to do with a request from the U.S. Consulate. Please don't tempt me with more money. I am poor but honest. I don't know any more than that."

Gaston asked, "Were your orders to arrest us?" The unhappy sergeant nodded, but said, "They said to see if you boys would come quietly, but to bring you one way or another. The Yanqui from the Consulate spoke to my superiors about a reward. I, of course, recalled how seldom we enlisted men are asked to share windfalls with our officers and, besides, we are friends, eh?"

Gaston looked across at Captain Gringo and asked, "Shall I trot back to our place and pack, Dick?"

Captain Gringo shook his head and said, "No. They may have sent less friendly people there. I'll see about the tickets and pick up some gear. You run over and see if you can shake some advance money out of Sir Basil's cunt. Meet me by the cathedral steps in an hour." He rose and strode away as Gaston and the sergeant remained seated for a moment. As Captain Gringo turned a corner the sergeant asked Gaston, "Did I do that right?"

Gaston reached for his own wallet as he grinned impishly and replied, "You are a born thespian, my old and rare friend. Your timing was perfection, and you remembered your lines. What more could any director want?"

The sergeant smiled, confused, and said, "Well, I did what you told me to do, but I still don't understand what that act was all about."

Gaston peeled off some bills and soothed, "The plot of my drama is too complicated to go into at the moment. Suffice to say, it worked."

"You are playing a little joke on your big friend, no?"

"*Oui.* Sometimes I must do such things for his own good. But let us keep our little secret, *hein?* He'll kill us both if he ever finds out."

Chapter Three

Captain Gringo leaned against the starboard rail, smoking a Perfecto as he stared morosely at the moonlit sea. The bow wave formed a ghostly pale-green stripe across the inky water, and from time to time a firefly's flicker betrayed a fish in the tepid phosphorescent water. It was cooler out on deck, but that wasn't saying much. The cabin they'd booked was an oven where someone had once baked dirty socks.

They were aboard the *S.S. Pomona,* a Clyde-built, three island freighter of British registry. They were steaming up the Mosquito Coast just a few miles offshore. Captain Gringo had mixed feelings about this. The poorly charted Mosquito Coast was notorious for hidden shoals and islands that weren't always where the map said they were. On the other hand, the *S.S. Pomona* was apparently held together with a little paint, and a lot of rust. Just so they wouldn't have too far to swim, when the tub fell apart like a house of cards, he thought.

The sea was gentle. Another break. The ship's screw

was off-center and every time they crossed a slight swell the blades came part way out of the water to wag the stern like a puppy's tail, and every once in a while another rivet popped.

As he finished his cigar and flicked it out across the water, a soft feminine voice recited,

> Dragon ships on moonlit water
> Oar tips dripping cold green fire
> Come to Erin, out for plunder
> Up the Shannon, bent on slaughter.

The tall American at the rail turned to see a dark, dim figure that came just to his shoulder wearing a big Paris hat draped with mosquito netting. He smiled and said, "I never heard that poem before, ma'am."

She answered with a trace of brogue, "I just made it up. I'm not sure the seas around Ireland are phosphorescent, but isn't it the grand image? If Viking raiders didn't drip cold green fire, they should have. Don't you agree?"

"I guess so," he chuckled. "But I never saw a dragon ship, and you're the expert on Irish waters if I'm right about that County Cork you'd be speaking after."

"Och, are you Irish? It's Mab O'Shay I'm called, and my people came from Kerry and not Cork, thank you very much."

"I'm Dick Walker, and I'm afraid our old sod might have been closer to London before they boarded the Mayflower or a sister ship."

"Well," Mab said dubiously, "as long as your people were Yankee in this century we'll say no more about it. It was in 1836 they took the vote and our Irish Home Rule away from us. What would yourself be doing on this dreadful English tub, Mr. Walker?"

He said, "I was about to ask you the same thing. It's a funny place to meet an Irish rebel."

"Och, bite your tongue. It's an American citizen, I am. I don't know whether the seas of Erin hold cold fire, for I've never seen them. As for Auld Queen Victoria, she's no better than she should be, but I've no dark Fenian plans to topple the auld bawd from her throne.

30

It's a registered nurse, I am. I've been working down in Panama against the Yellow jack. Now I'm bound for the Crown colony of Nuevo Verdugo to patch up the sugar cutters."

"You've been hired by Pantropic?"

"Didn't I just say so? I understand they own the whole island. Where are you bound for, Mr. Walker?"

He frowned and said, "Same place. I'm an ordinance consultant for Woodbine Arms Limited."

Mab's laughter seemed a little forced, but her voice was light as she said, *"Och,* won't that be grand? You'll shoot them and I'll patch them up. In a way one could almost say we are in the same business.

Captain Gringo shrugged and stared at the horizon. He didn't know what she looked like, and in any case, he was tired of defending his trade. He said, "The stars are either going out or there's a squall line over to the east."

Mab said, "It is getting darker, and the water's stopped glowing, too. Have you any idea why that should be?"

He said, "Sure, the wee beasties that make the water phosphorescent are dropping deeper. We're on the receiving end of a cold front and a lot of fresh rain water. We'd better get you inside."

A gob of rain the size of an egg splattered nearby on the deck and he added, "See what I mean? I'll see you to your cabin."

She said, "It's early. What about the ship's saloon?"

"Have you seen what they call a saloon on this tub?"

"You're right. At least my cabin has a window, and I've a fifth of the creature in my trunk. It's down this way."

He took Mab's elbow as they stepped away from the rail. She made no comment as the deck was suddenly canted by the rising seas from the east. By the time they made it to her cabin door more gouts of tropic rain were leaping like wet frogs across the deck, spit under the overhang by the gathering storm. As Mab unlocked the door, he hesitated, not sure of the form. Then she opened it and said, "Come in before you drown out there. There's supposed to be a light switch somewhere in here."

He joined her inside as a gust of wind slammed the jalousied door shut, plunging them in darkness while, at the same time, the ship's stern rose and the steel all around them vibrated alarmingly.

Mab found the switch and turned on the Edison bulbs as she gasped, "Jesus, Mary and Joseph! What was that?"

Captain Gringo stared down at what he now saw was a saucy little redhead with hellfire-green eyes he felt like swimming in. He smiled and said, "It's just a crazy screw."

"I *beg* your pardon, sir!"

He laughed and quickly added, "The ship's propeller. It's called a screw. It's bent or missing a blade or something, and every time it breaks water it shakes the whole ship like that."

Mab flushed and said, *"Och,* I thought . . . well, never mind what I was after thinking. Find yourself a seat and I'll be seeing if I can find the bottle."

The only seat the tiny cabin offered was the bottom bunk of the two that were built into the bulkhead. Even if climbing into the top bunk hadn't been a ridiculous idea, it would have been impossible. Mab had it piled with luggage. So Captain Gringo sat down with his knees a bit high for comfort and watched the redhead rummage in a steamer trunk in the far corner.

Her back was to him, so he noticed for the first time that her thin shantung dress was forest green, and that because of the heat and lack of need, she wasn't wearing the usual whalebone and obscenely vulcanized unmentionables women over fourteen seemed to find so necessary these days. Her skirts belled out below her trim waist, but, Praise Allah, the bustles and dolly vardens of the eighties were no longer the fashion, and a man could

32

get a better grasp on the size of a woman's behind. Mab's derriere looked just about right as she bent slightly to reach deeper into the trunk. The ship's stern rose, too, and as the crippled screw surfaced everything again went Voom-Voom-Voom. It jiggled Mab delightfully, but she straightened up as if she'd been goosed and gasped, "Oh my eyebrow! We're sinking sure!"

Captain Gringo said, "Relax, I didn't hear anything break loose that time. I think we've about shed all the rivets and and paint that figure to come off tonight."

He saw she had a bottle of white rum when she joined him on the lower bunk. She said, "I can't find my teacups. We'll have to share the bottle raw." Then she uncorked it, took a healthy swig, and handed it to him. He said, "For a lady, you're a two-fisted drinker. Most *men* need a little lemon juice to cut this white-lightning."

"*Och,* I was raised on poteen. No Dago rum can froosh an Irish lass."

Captain Gringo put the bottle to his own lips, noting that the glass still tingled from her own saucy rosebud lips, and managed not to gasp as the raw white rum ran over his tongue like hot lava. He lowered the bottle, exhaled an invisible dragon flame, and said, "Smooooth," and handed the bottle back to her. She was welcome to it. He was a big man who could hold his booze, but this was liquid dynamite and there didn't seem to be anything with which to chase it.

The bunk tingled under them as the stern rose again, and Mab spilled some rum in her lap when she was working on the second round. The vibration made them both aware that their hips were touching in the crowded quarters. But he figured it was up to her to move away if she aimed to. She didn't. If anything she pressed her softer flesh closer as she said, "Wheee! It feels like a roller coaster."

He said, "Yeah, the seas are really rising. I hope the man at the helm knows enough to quarter into them. Those ground swells feel like they're touching bottom."

"Oh dear. Do you think we'll be shipwrecked?"

"I hope not. If there was anything but mangrove jungle along this stretch of the Mosquito Coast we wouldn't be aboard this rust bucket much longer. Traveling by mule would be faster as well as more comfortable. But there don't seem to be any roads, so . . ."

"Jesus, I don't want to wind up in no jungle. I hear there're cannibal Indians as well as alligators and great man-eating snakes."

She took another heroic swig of rum and he viewed her alarming drinking with mixed emotions. Liquor certainly simplified relations between the sexes, but he wasn't a necrophiliac, and Mab just didn't have the body weight to absorb that much booze. He said, "You'd better take it easy, honey."

She grinned at him knowingly and asked, "Would you be the sort of rascal to take advantage of a maiden in her cups, sir?"

He doubted she was a maiden, but he said, "That's the least of your worries. We're standing off a lee shore in a full gale and we may have to do some serious swimming before sunrise."

Mab took another swallow, considered, and said, "You're right. We'd better take our clothes off before we wind up dead and drowned."

She handed him the bottle and started to unbutton her bodice. He saw no reason to object. She wasn't *that* drunk, but he'd played this scene before. He wondered if someday men and women could simply get together on some casual innocent sex without all these foolish games.

He knew she wanted it as badly as he did, but while Queen Victoria had managed to produce a full platoon of babies, she'd done it without admitting she enjoyed a good lay. Any white woman who wasn't an outright slut had to pretend she was being victimized by her brutish quarry. He wondered if Mab was going to put him through the usual tears and remorse in the cold gray light of dawn. She probably was, but what the hell, it went with the icing on life's bitter-sweet cake.

34

A pink nipple peeked out at him coyly when Mab suddenly had second thoughts and said, *"Och,* you'd better turn out the lights. I'm not one to be naked like a Carib in broad daylight, even to save us from drowning!"

He got up with a grin and flicked off the switch. Outside the rain was slobbering against the cabin door but a faint dim light came through the slits in the jalousy. The decking careened wildly under him as he groped his way back to the bunk. He put a hand out to steady himself and it landed right in Mab's naked lap. She gasped when he say beside her, leaving his hand in her moist thatch, and he said, "Sorry. I was reaching for the post."

"Sure and I'll bet you were, you awful thing." She giggled, and, since she didn't seem to be avoiding the fate she'd set up rather obviously, he pressed her back across the mattress with her feet still on the floor and kissed her as he started working her up with the fortunate hand.

It didn't take much to fire her boiler. Mab responded to his kisses and put her own hand on the back of his to move it faster. Then she came up for air and said, "Wait. I have to take precautions. Take off your own duds while I practice medicine."

She rolled away and moved somewhere in the darkness as Captain Gringo proceeded to peel. He heard the tingle of glass above the howling storm sounds and another series of alarming thuds from the ship's screw as they wallowed over the next swell.

Then Mab was back and all over him, sobbing with desire and smelling of rum and perfume. She groped for his shaft, found it, and gasped, *"Och,* Jesus, Mary and Joseph, you might have warned a girl!" She forked a thigh across him and sank down on it with a moan of mingled awe and pleasure. He reached up in the darkness and took her soft, rounded torso in his arms to pull her on like a boot as the bunk tingled under his nude rump and the ship muttered "Voom-Voom-Voom!"

Mab laughed and said, *"Och,* ain't this grand? The darling ship is doing half the work for us!"

35

Mab proceeded to do the other half. She moved up and down like a pro. But since money hadn't been mentioned, he assumed she was a free thinker with advanced views for her generation. Being a nurse gave women certain advantages. He knew she knew more about anatomy and birth control than the average, properly raised Victorian Miss, and her wandering ways suggested an adventurous streak, too. He wondered how often she'd done this and decided he didn't really want to know. It was stupid for a man to expect a long series of innocent virgins. But Victoria and John Calvin had messed up male thinking, too, and he was trying to learn to rise above it, or maybe sink below it.

They were both hot as two dollar pistols, but he tried to make it last. So Mab came first and collapsed against him, crooning in the Gaelic, *"Och, ma bhirmohr go brach!"* as the screw surfaced, bounced him up and down, and he fired his charge unexpectedly. She contracted on him with pleasure and purred, "Jesus, that was a lovely gusher! I hope there's more where that came from!"

So he rolled her over and got on top to do some serious loving. She was over her first awkwardness, too, and so now that they were friends she worked her legs up to hook a heel over each of his shoulders, and though he was surprised to notice she still had on her high-buttoned shoes and stockings to the knees, he had no complaints. The rest of her felt like velvet where it wasn't whipped cream. He was grateful for the storm. Without the damp cool draft from the jalousy they'd have been sweating like pigs by now. But it was cool enough for heavy pounding and he knew it was what she'd had in mind from the moment she'd approached him spouting poetry. The real thing was more poetic than any verse ever written.

They went at it hot and heavy until common sense and mutual exhaustion called for a break to get their second wind. As she snuggled against him on the narrow bunk, Mab moved her legs experimentally and murmured, "I thought I'd dislocated a hip, but I think I want you to try and cripple me some more. Can you reach the bottle? I forgot where I put it when you leaped on me like a maniac."

He rolled over and groped along the rolling floorboards until he found the fifth of rum, on its side but corked by a lady who obviously planned ahead. He handed it to her, but said, "I'll settle for a smoke. I can't handle you, a storm at sea, and white rum at the same time."

He fumbled again and found his jacket crumpled on the floor. He fished out a Perfecto and some matches, and while he was at it, retrieved his shoulder holster and hung it on a nail driven into the post at the head of the bunk. He struck a light and Mab glowed up at him with the matchlight reflected in her green, feline eyes. She said, "I think I'll stay sober, too, if you'll share that cigar with me."

He lit up and took a drag without comment. More than one lady he'd met shared the forbidden joys of the manly weed. He passed the smoke to her by kissing open-mouthed and he noticed she inhaled it deeply. Mab was a girl who lived life to the hilt.

She laughed when she exhaled and took the cigar for a more serious puff. Then she said, "I don't want you to leave until just before dawn, if we're still afloat. That little old man you're traveling with won't come looking for you, will he?"

Captain Gringo said, "He'd better not. Let him find his own girl."

"I don't think there were any others traveling alone on the passenger list, darling."

That was another slip, but he didn't comment as he took the cigar back, hoping he was wrong. Captain Gringo had an ear for accents and he knew her brogue was Ulster even though she claimed to be from the Black Irish southern counties. But what the hell, she was a great lay and he could be getting paranoid. There were plenty of

Catholic rebels even in loyal Ulster, and while it seemed odd that an innocent traveling nurse had been going over the passenger list with the purser, it wasn't proof of anything but advanced female curiosity. If Sir Basil did have another agent checking up on them he owed the old bastard a hearty thanks. Since she'd have nothing to report to her boss, if he was her boss, why not just enjoy it?

The ship rose on another swell and dropped alarmingly as Mab stiffened in the dark and clung to him. The bunk under them tingled as if a giant dentist's drill was boring through the hull, and she gasped, "Oh my eyebrow! What was that?"

He patted her soothingly and said, "We just scraped bottom, I think. Things are looking up. I don't think we could sink far enough to matter in this shoal water."

Privately, he was more worried than he let on. He knew the seas would pound this bucket of bolts to bits in no time if they really grounded. But there was no sense in both of them sweating it out.

His calm tone seemed to comfort her, and more to soothe her than because he really cared, he changed the subject by saying, "You must have come across some West Indians down in Panama, right?"

"I did. There's a mess of them working on the new canal. The poor creatures have been dying like flies, too. Some say Negroes are used to Yellow jack, but the ones I was caring for in the company infirmary died just as often as anyone else. It's a disgusting way to die, for anyone. Its Spanish name, *Vomito Negro,* fits it better than the graveyard whistle of Yellow jack."

"I know. I've had it."

"Have you now? Well, that's one thing you'll never have to worry about again. Now you'd be immune, but sixty percent of them that gets it never recover. I've had my bout with Yellow jack, and as you see I'm still here. They say there's no fever where we're going, if we can only get there without drowning."

He passed her the smoke and said, "Let's get back to those West Indians in Panama. Did any of them ever talk to you about zombies?"

"*Och,* of course. Dreadful superstitious they was. I remember them beating Voodoo drums every time we had one dying on us."

She inhaled, let it out, and added, "In God's truth, the medicine we had for Yellow jack wasn't much better. Nobody really knows what causes the damned fever."

"Did any of those Voodoo guys claim they could bring a dead man back to life, Mab?"

She thought before she said, "No. That zombi stuff is like the Hindu rope trick. Everybody knows somebody who's seen it, but they haven't seen it themselves."

"How do you feel about the notion, as a nurse?"

"*Och,* I think it would be marvelous, if it worked. God knows I've seen enough people die before their time. But believe me, Dick, when people die they stay that way, especially in the tropics. It's a terrible thing to see them starting to bloat before you can get them to the morgue."

"There's supposed to be some kind of zombi cult in Nuevo Verdugo, where we'll be landing in the morning. Did anyone mention it to you when you took this job?"

Again she thought before she replied, "No, I don't remember mention of such things. But I'd have signed on anyway. I've an open mind about banshees and wee people. But I've studied enough medicine to be sure of some things—the dead don't ever get up again."

He said, "I read a library book while we were waiting to board this tub. Did you know there are statutes on the books in Haiti forbidding people to practice Voodoo."

"*Och,* there used to be laws in our books forbidding witchcraft, too. You can pass all the laws you like. You can even grant people a license to do it, for all it matters. Leaving out the theology about immortal souls, anyone who knows simple biology knows that even a living vegetable has a chemistry that makes sense. Dead muscles stiffen like hard-boiled eggs before they start to fall apart. A fresh cadaver twitches a bit as it stiffens, but that's the end of it. You couldn't move a limb with a decomposing muscle, even if your brain was still alive."

He grimaced and said, "Glugh. It sounds pretty grim."

"It is. I've been there when they have amputated a dead limb from a living body. If a man with blood poisoning has no feeling or movement in his dead tissue, how could the whole dead thing get up and walk a-round?"

"Try it this way. One writer suggested that so-called zombies aren't really dead, but drugged some way. As a nurse, do you think a man hopped up on some jungle joy-juice might be able to keep going with a mess of bullets in him?"

She handed back the smoke and said, "Well, I've seen insane or hysterical patients do some wild things and that's a fact. But even drugs have limitations. Enough anesthesia to block out all feeling would have you sleeping soundly on your back."

"What about a combination of pain killing drugs, a stimulant, and a hard sell about one's cause?"

"Well, you'd wind up with a very sick lad in the end, whether someone shot him or not. But I suppose someone full of opium and strychnine would look and act pretty strange."

Then she bagan to fondle him as the ship mounted another wave and she said, "Speaking of stimulation, I'm well-rested and ready when you are."

He moved his hips and stubbed out the smoke as she teased him with her hand and then, to speed the process up, slid down the mattress to take him between her saucy rosebud lips. She apparently liked to inhale that way, too, and he liked it.

But as he rose to the occasion and was about to suggest doing it right, he heard his name above the rain and wind outside. He said, "That sounds like Gaston."

She stopped long enough to suggest, "I thought he was supposed to get his own girl?"

Captain Gringo sat up as once again he heard Gaston, in an oddly weak tone, call out, "Dick? *Merde alors,* where are you?"

Captain Gringo said, "He sounds like he's in trouble!" He swung his feet to the floor, went to the door, forced it open against the wind, and called back, "Here! What's up, Gaston?"

The small Frenchman tottered toward him in the dim light on the wildly swaying deck. He was limping and looked like he was about to fall. So the tall American stepped out into the rain and steadied him, repeating, "What's up? What's the matter with you?"

Gaston said, "I seem to have been bitten by a snake."

"Out here in the middle of the ocean?"

"I agree it is *trés* ridiculous, but I assure you I did not plan for such an event. I awoke to find it in bed with me. As we were discussing the matter it got me just above the knee."

The American hesitated, aware he was stark-naked clinging to a man in soaking wet pajamas. Mab had heard and said, "Bring your friend in here, Dick." She he did.

Mab flicked on the light, and to Captain Gringo's relief she'd slipped into a print kimono. It was hanging open, but Gaston was in no shape to ogle. Is the light he looked like death warmed over. The two of them got him on the mattress they'd just vacated, and Mab dropped to her knees to start ripping Gaston's pajama leg open along one seam while she asked in a professional tone, "What kind of a snake was it?"

Gaston stared at the part in her red hair with some confusion and said, "*Sacré!* How should I know? The creature is in the sea with a very flat head at the moment. One does not bite Gaston lightly."

Then he stared owlishly up at his naked friend and asked, "Are not introductions in order, my old and rare friend?"

41

Captain Gringo said, "Her name is Mab O'Shay and she's a nurse."

"Ah, I thought she was a maniac intent on my groin. I expected to find you with a beautiful woman, but a nurse was almost too much to hope for. Don't you ever make a false move, Dick?"

"Never mind all that. How does it look, Mab?"

"Like a snake bite. A big one. Can't you remember what it looked like, Gaston?"

The Frenchman tried to sit up, fell back weakly, and said, "It was as big a serpent as one could wish for in a nightmare. It looked something like a rattlesnake with a glandular problem, but it had no rattles."

Mab said, "Hold this, Dick," as she started to rise. Captain Gringo took the ends of the rag tourniquet she'd improvised around Gaston's thigh. The fang marks below it were dark open punctures surrounded by swollen white flesh. Mab hauled open a drawer of her steamer trunk and Captain Gringo asked her, "What difference does it make what kind of snake it was, Mab?"

She dropped to her knees beside Gaston, spread her kit open on the sheets and replied, "It sounds like he was bitten by a bushmaster. If he was, this antivenim is the one to use."

Gaston asked, "What if it was not a bushmaster?"

"You'll probably be dead in minutes," Mab said bleakly. Then, without further consultation, she drove her hypodermic needle into Gaston's thigh above the tourniquet, put a rubber suction cup to the wound, and started pumping.

Captain Gringo said, "It would bleed faster if you cut it open like the Indians do, wouldn't it?"

She said, "Yes, and then he'd have an even bigger entrance for infection in this climate. The Indians don't have antivenim. I do, if I used the right antidote. You see, a bushmaster is a viperoid snake. That shot should counteract viper venom. If that's a cobroid bite, well . . . "

"Don't you have both kinds of antivenim?"

"Of course I do."

42

"Then why not give him both?"

"It would be quicker to put a gun to his head. The two antivenims would fight each other, and your friend has enough of a problem as it is!"

"Is she always so cheerful, Dick?" Gaston asked with a sigh.

Captain Gringo pasted a smile across his own numb lips and said, "Yeah. It sounds like a bushmaster to me, too." He almost added that they'd know for sure in a minute, but he figured Gaston knew that.

Mab squirted her suction cup into a glass and reapplied it to Gaston's leg while she said, "Ease up on the pressure a moment, Dick. We have to allow some circulation."

Captain Gringo released the tension, and Gaston blanched and muttered, *"Merde!"*

"How are you feeling, Gaston?"

"Too angry to be dying. I was too excited to consider the matter when I woke up with a serpent in my bed. Now that I have had time to reconsider, you were right. Getting bitten by a jungle snake is an unusual sea adventure, *hein?"*

"It might have crawled up out of the cargo hold. Which bunk were you sleeping on?"

"Yours, of course. It seemed obvious you had other plans, so I saw no need to recline in the top bunk with the ship rolling like this. There is a ventilator over the top bunk. But as I was not up there, it seems obvious that the snake did not drop on me from there."

Mab had been listening. She shuddered and said, "If someone *put* the bushmaster there, Dick, it seems they were aiming for *you!"*

Captain Gringo wondered what else was new. He asked, "How do you know for sure it was a bushmaster?" But Mab said, "Easy. Gaston's swelling is going down."

"I am well?" Gaston said and smiled.

She said, "No. You're going to live. But you're going to be a very sick lad for a few days. As soon as we get to Nuevo Verdugo it's the infirmary for you, me bucko.

You'll be lucky if you're able to walk without a cane in two weeks at least."

Gaston tried again to sit up, fell back with an annoyed groan, and said, *"Merde!* I feel as weak as a kitten! But I must rise to strike back. When I find the *couchon* who threw that serpent at me, I intend to bite him back!"

Captain Gringo said, "Relax. There's an outside chance it was an accident, and if it wasn't, our snake charmer must still be somewhere aboard this ship."

Gaston made it up on one elbow this time, and gasped, *"Aux barricades!* Why are you just standing there in your ridiculous nudity? When do we search the ship for my attacker?"

Captain Gringo glanced at Mab and asked, "When do we take this tourniquet off, doll?"

She said, "Now. The antivenim seems to be taking."

She dug a tumbnail into Gaston's thigh and asked if he felt it. He said, *"Oui.* But you are feeling me up too low. I don't suppose you would consider massaging my. . . never mind. When are you going after them, Dick?"

Captain Gringo let go of the tourniquet, sat down and started getting dressed. He said, "Aside from the other passengers, there's a good-sized crew. The bridge hands are mostly Brits. The Black Gang's Chinese and probably doesn't speak English *or* Spanish. I don't speak Hindi, so it would be a waste of time to try and question the rest of the crew. Most of the deck watch is Lascar."

Gaston said, "So I noticed. But could there not be a snake charmer among those Lascars? India has a certain reputation for such nonsense."

Captain Gringo shrugged as he pulled his boots on and said, "I think East Indians play with cobras. That bushmaster was a West Indian critter." He turned to Mab, who was eyeing his fly wistfully as he stood up to button it, and said, "You're the expert on bushmasters, doll. Am I right in assuming it's a pit viper?"

44

She said, "I think so. I'm not sure what the difference between vipers is."

He said, "Snakes in the cobra family strike at prey they can see. Pit vipers strike at the warmth of a target in the dark. A Lascar crewman who might have handled cobras in India wouldn't know much more than us about handling a bushmaster. If that snake was tossed in here it must have been via a bucket or basket against the door slats. You sure don't carry one in a warm hand in the dark!"

Gaston stared morosely at the jalousie of the closed cabin door and said, "Bah. The creature I woke up with was too big to fit through there. It was as big around as my wrist and I felt like I was arm wrestling, when I got it down and stood on its head."

"Was the door locked?"

"But of course. Who sleeps in a strange place with his door unlocked?"

Captain Gringo nodded, reached for the gun rig on the post and strapped it on, saying, "I'll be right back."

He went out into the storm and made his way along the wet slanting deck to his and Gaston's cabin. The wind and rain were letting up, but the seas were still high and the deck was deserted. He didn't know what he'd say to anyone he met out there in any case.

He drew his .38, took a deep breath, and stepped inside, crabbing sideways to avoid being outlined in the doorway as he fumbled for the light swtich.

The cabin was empty, and despite Gaston's hurried departure and the unlocked door, nobody had been at their minimal luggage. He could see where Gaston had stamped the bushmaster to death on the floorboards with his bare but tough old heel. There was a little blood on the sheets, too. But that was about it. The vent above the top bunk was screened with a solid-looking grating. There were no large gaps in the wall paneling or baseboards.

He waited until the ship was in a trough and switched off the light, bracing himself with his free hand against a bunk post. A pale gray slit in the otherwise total

45

blackness gave the show away. One of the wooden slats near the top of the door had been pried away. A missing slat on a tub this old meant little. But no snake had slithered six feet up a wet door and dropped in unassisted as well as uninvited.

He locked the door as he let himself out, brows knitted in thought. He knew he hadn't done it, Mab hadn't done it, and it seemed pretty obvious Gaston hadn't done it. But there were well over thirty people aboard who could have.

He knew the watch officer would have a list of every crewman whose duty would eliminate him from the time slot involved. But that would mean long tedious explanations and wouldn't prove enough to matter. If one or more ship's officers was involved it would only add to the confusion. Almost anyone aboard could have slipped away for a lousy five minutes and nobody else would remember that he had, too.

He went back to Mab's cabin and told them, "The snake wasn't looking for us. It was pushed. If a crew member did it, we'll probably never find out why. If it was a passenger, they'll be getting off with us at Nuevo Verdugo."

Mab asked, "Aren't you going to tell the captain he has a murderer aboard?"

Captain Gringo shook his head and said, "That's his problem and the least of his worries. This tub figures to sink any minute. Right now, whoever did it is holed up in the dark, waiting to hear all the noise when someone's found dead in my bunk. It might be interesting to just watch and see who looks most surprised when the three of us walk down the gangplank alive."

Gaston nodded and said, "I see it as our best move, too."

But Mab said, "Don't you think they'll try again, once they know they've failed?"

Captain Gringo's eyes were grim as he replied, "I sure hope so."

Chapter Four

The Crown colony of Nuevo Verdugo was a slab of British Honduras that had broken off and floated out to sea. "Crown" status meant it was run "At Her Majesty's Pleasure" by an appointed governor general who didn't answer to Honduras or the House of Commons in London. It was considered a royal estate, like Buckingham or Windsor. Since Her Majesty had enough housekeeping to worry about back home, she sublet her Crown colonies, and the Angle-American Pantropic Sugar Trust could just about do anything they liked with it as long as they didn't sell it to Bulgaria, sink it like Atlantis, or, God forbid, give it back to the natives.

The only harbor and main town was the preciously named Utopiaton, a little bit of Olde England recreated out of corrugated iron with imported Australian pines and blue-gums standing in for the yew and hearty oaks of England around the manicured village green. The Union Jack hung listless on its white-washed staff above the sunset gun as Captain Gringo and his friends came down the gangplank of the ship tied at the quay. To his mild surprise, none of the other passengers appeared to be getting off there. He wondered if they knew something he didn't.

Gaston's leg was stiff and he still felt weak, but he was trying to act as if he'd never seen that snake. Whoever had tried to kill one of them was probably watching and wondering what had gone wrong. But since he or she wasn't coming ashore, that was that.

They were met at the foot of the gangplank by a pale, malarial young man who looked like he'd rather be playing tennis in England. He said his name was Webster and that he'd been appointed to escort them wherever during La Siesta. Nuevo Verdugo was ever so British, but there were limits in the tropics to what a sensible white man could get away with in the noonday sun. The ship had put in late because of the storm the previous night, and it was hotter than hell.

Mab said Gaston needed to be put in hospital at once, and asked where the company doctor was. Webster said, "The infirmary is that white-washed building just across the way, ma'am. We no longer have a doctor. What's our emergency of the moment, the usual tropic tummy?"

Before either of them could signal her, Mab said, "M'sieu Verrier was bitten by a bushmaster and needs bed rest. What do you mean, you don't have a doctor? I understood I was coming here to assist a Doctor Lloyd."

Webster said, "Snake bite, eh? How curious. That's what poor old Lloyd died of, too. Allow me to help you with your luggage, ma'am. I'll have the niggers deliver your trunk in a jiff. Your patient does look a bit wonky, what?"

Captain Gringo saw Gaston was having trouble standing and took his arm while he frowned down at Webster and asked, "When did all this happen? How long ago was Dr. Lloyd murdered?"

Webster picked up Mab's valise and said, "Oh, I'd

hardly call it anything as dramatic as that. Poor blighter was taken by a snake as he was stepping out of his shower. He gave himself a shot, of course, but it didn't seem to work. It happened about a week ago. Fortunately, it's a rather healthy isle and the rest of us have been trusting to gin and tonic."

Captain Gringo glanced westward beyond the moored steamer as he and the others followed Webster. The mainland was a dark line on the horizon, but there was a lot of shark infested water between here and there. He mused aloud, "Funny, I thought snakes were rare on offshore islands. I know there are none in Cuba. What kind of snake was it?"

Webster shrugged and said, "I'm sure I can't say. Nobody but poor Lloyd ever saw the blighter and *he* obviously used the wrong antivenim. But you're right about any sort of serpent being rare out here. We were all rather surprised about it at the time. As I said, it's a rather healthy spot, despite this beastly heat and the trade winds that blow the wrong way for the mosquitos over there on the mainland. We didn't know there were any snakes when we picked Nuevo Verdugo for our experiment."

"Experiment?"

"Sugar, and all that rot. You surely know how fast vegetation grows in this humid heat. Our crops mature weeks ahead of those in Jamaica. But most places along the Mosquito Coast are simply impossible for white men. Even the perishing natives tend to curl up and die along the east coast of Central America."

Mab said, "I know. I just came from Panama. Half the Canal workers seem to die before their first payday."

Webster nodded and said, "Saves on labor costs, no doubt. But even a nigger has some value, and we can't cut cane with corpses. So the company selected this relatively healthy island as its site to put Central American sugar on a paying basis."

By then they'd reached the infirmary and a black girl in a white uniform came shyly out on the veranda to curtsy to Mab. Webster said, "Willie May, this is your new memsahib, Sister O'Shay. Mind you, obey her or it's back to the skullary for you, my girl."

He turned to Mab and added, "I don't think she understands a word I say, but they respond like a dog to one's tone of voice."

Mab shot him an annoyed look and told the black girl, "We have a sick man here, lass. Is there a bed properly made up inside?"

Willie May said, "Yess'm. We was expecting y'all, and the place is spit an' polish fo' you' inspection."

The two women took charge of Gaston and their few bags, while Captain Gringo said he'd stay with Webster and meet the other company men. He waited until he was alone with Webster before he said, "That colored girl sounds American."

Webster shrugged and replied, "Dammed if I know. They're all alike to me. We can't get the perishing natives we found here to work for us, so the company has been recruiting from all over. What difference does it make? She doesn't even have a nice ass."

Captain Gringo waited until they were walking toward the headquarters building further up the green before he said, "You were a little rough on her with that remark about dogs. I used to command a troop of the colored Tenth Cav, back in the States. I found I got better results by treating my troopers like people."

"Oh dear, you should have warned me you were a nigger lover."

"I'm going to pretend you never said that. I fought Apache with some colored guys, but I don't remember us getting mushy about it. The point I was trying to make is that you catch more flies with honey than you do with vinegar. If all of you have been talking to your help like that, I can see why you need machine guns."

Webster smiled and said, "Oh, the niggers on our

payroll know their place. But you probably know about our problem with the Voodoo chaps."

"Yeah. What's this shit about zombies over-running your guards?"

"Shit expresses my opinion rather neatly. I think our superstitious help tends to excuse their own cowardice and poor marksmanship with fairies in the bottom of the garden. Have *you* ever seen a zombi, Captain?"

"Not yet. What was the medical report on the attackers your men *did* stop?"

"Medical report? Good Lord, poor old Lloyd never got a chance to perform the autopsies he kept talking about. You see, the enemy has this distressing habit of recovering its own dead."

He tittered and added inanely, "No doubt their Voodoo Queen repairs them and sends them back at us good as new, eh what?"

Captain Gringo frowned and said, "Voodoo Queen?"

Webster nodded and said, "Mamma Macumba. Wonky name, eh? The natives say she's a beautiful mulatto who's rather thick with some jungle god called Mumbo Jumbo, or some such rot. He's supposed to be a giant serpent as well as her lover. Sounds like some old nigger witch likes to stuff snakes up her twat. Disgusting, don't you agree?"

Captain Gringo didn't answer. Webster was a silly twit who was starting to get under his skin. Privately, the tall American knew Macumba was the South American version of what most Anglo-Saxons called Voodoo, and that it was Mambo Jumbo, not Mumbo Jumbo. It meant "Great Serpent" in some West African dialect. Conversations around a campfire with an old sergeant who'd been born a slave hadn't been a complete waste of time after all, though he now wished he'd paid more attention. He didn't remember Sergeant Brown discussing zombies, but he knew the Mambo Jumbo cult was older and more powerful than a lot of people thought. He had other

51

questions. But he decided to wait and see if Pantropic had hired anyone with more brains than Webster. It seemed impossible that they hadn't.

Webster led him up some steps and ignored the two mestizo guards who popped to attention and presented arms on either side of the doorway. Captain Gringo decided it was as good a time as any to start establishing himself. So he returned the salute, paused, and asked the more experienced-looking guard, "Soldier, what's your seventh general order?"

The guard looked surprised. Then he grinned and answered, "Sir! My seventh general order is to talk to no one except in the line of duty!"

Captain Gringo nodded and said, "Carry on," before joining the bemused Webster inside the open doorway. The Englishman asked, "What was that all about?" The Amrican said, "They presented arms U.S. Army style. I wanted to see if they were really trained or just going through the motions. Where did you recruit them?"

"Dashed if I know. All you soldiers of fortune have rather murky records. I believe the one you spoke to is a Mexican now that I think about it."

The American nodded. He knew the Mexican Army was U.S. trained, with a rather high desertion rate, thanks to the strange ways of the piss pot dictatorship Washington and Wall Street hailed as a "stable government." Things were looking up. Pantropic had hired men with at least some military experience. But if the company guards were not the usual rag-tag collection of adventurous peones, how come they couldn't stand up to untrained jungle raiders? He didn't know much about Voodoo or Macumba, but he tended to doubt many witch doctors gave close order drill.

Webster led him along a corridor and ushered him into a room where a fat pink man was sitting naked in a big galvanized tub of water while a rather pretty mestizo fanned him.

Webster introduced him as Colonel Gage, the Governor General and Company Supervisor, all rolled in one

52

florid package. Gage smiled up at Captain Gringo and said, "Forgive me for remaining seated and I'd offer my hand but it's wet. I suppose you're wondering why I'm soaking myself like this, eh what?"

Captain Gringo shook his head and said, "No sir, I just came in from the noonday sun."

Gage sighed and said, "Right. Nuevo Verdugo is no place for a sober white man. Webster there, survives on gin and tonic. But I find I tend to put things off if I'm three-quarters smashed."

Webster said, "The captain brought that nurse we were expecting and the French chap they cabled us about, Gaston Verrier. He's in the hospital at the moment with a snake bite problem. Rather wonky, what?"

Gage gasped and asked, "Snake bite, *again?* Dash it all, there aren't supposed to *be* any venomous snakes on this bloody island!"

Captain Gringo said, "It happened last night aboard ship, sir." Then he told the governor the story as the mestizo fanned him, and his fat face kept getting redder. When the American finished, Colonel Gage scowled down at the water he was soaking in and said, "That does it. I'm sending for the Royal Marines. I'm tired of mucking about with these bloody natives. It's time they received a good lesson."

It sounded like a good idea to Captain Gringo. He and Gaston were getting paid per dium no matter how it was settled. But Webster cleared his throat and said, "I'm not sure that would be wise, sir. You know what White-hall cabled back the last time you asked for direct military intervention."

"Bloody asses!" snorted Colonel Gage. Then he saw Captain Gringo wasn't following the conversation and explained, "It's your American Monroe Doctrine, no offense meant. London feels we have to slaughter natives delicately in these parts, since Washington can be so stuffy about a spot of gunboat diplomacy when it's not a U.S. gunboat. We're supposed to be able to handle things here without direct help from the Empire. But you know all about that, since Sir Basil sent you. How is the old pirate these days, by the way?"

Captain Gringo shrugged and said, "Still pirating, I guess. Woodbine Arms Limited sent us to find out just what the problem seems to be with those guns he sold you."

Gage nodded and said, "They don't work. Bloody natives walk right into them and still do all sorts of dreadful things to our plantations."

"I read the reports, sir. It's my understanding Woodbine's guns are a direct steal, or let's say, a copy, of the American Maxim patent. Are you suggesting they don't fire?"

"Oh, the bloody things make a dreadful racket and spit bullets all over Robin Hood's barn at thruppence a round."

"Anything wrong with the ammo? I understand they're chambered for .30-30 deer rounds."

"They are. I just said they cost too much. I'm ahead of you on the ammunition. We tested the guns on oil drums and made sieves out of them. The machine guns fire. The bullets hit hard enough to puncture mild steel, and the bloody raiders are half-bare. But I still say your guns don't work. They didn't *stop* the perishing natives like they were supposed to!"

Captain Gringo said he'd check the guns out and Webster offered to show him to his quarters. But the tall American asked the fat man still sitting in the tub, "How do you feel about this zombi notion, Colonel?"

Gage said, "I feel bloody awful. I don't believe in magic. I served in Inja and they told us the Thuggi were immune to bullets too. But when we shot the perishing Wogs they all fell down. I tell you, it's those bloody new guns!"

He stared wistfully into space and added, "Don't see any sense to so much racket anyway. In my day we did it with single shot Enfields with a spot of buttstock and bayonet at close quarters, eh what? Give me a platoon of

Highlanders from the old Indian Army and I'd clean those black buggers out in a month."

He suddenly looked older as he mumured, "As it is, we'll be out of business in a month if we don't start shipping sugar. The bloody stockholders are getting restless and, thanks to those damned natives, we haven't shipped enough to matter since we took this fucking steam bath island over!"

Chapter Five

All the other Anglo-Americans seemed to be holed up for La Siesta. The dithery Webster showed Captain Gringo to the quarters he was to share with Gaston, when and if the Frenchman got out of the bed in the infirmary.

The American threw his bag on the bed and asked Webster, "Who's in charge of the guard detail and when do I get to inspect the guns?"

Webster said, "I just told you Captain Burton was resting in his quarters. You'll meet him this aft' at tea time."

"Meanwhile it's only a few minutes past noon and I still want to know who's in charge. You do have *somebody* on guard, don't you?"

Webster blinked and said, "Oh, I suppose Sergeant Montalban and his dagoes are watching the bush for us. I thought you meant a white man."

"I don't care if he's purple if only I can get a handle on what's going on. Where do I find this Montalban guy?"

"Good Lord, in this heat? I suppose he's in the guardhouse. It's across the green; I'll show you how to get there. But you'll find it a waste of your time as well as sweat. The blighter doesn't speak English very well."

Webster led him out to the veranda and pointed out the smaller, white, brick building across the way. He didn't follow as Captain Gringo left the shade to leg it across the clipped bermuda grass of the green. The American was relieved.

Sergeant Montalban was a nice-looking mestizo sporting a neatly tailored cotton khaki uniform and a gold tooth. He seemed surprised that Captain Gringo wanted to talk to him, although they'd told him an ordinance expert was coming to inspect him and his men. He leaped up and saluted before he said, "I am at your service, señor. Most of my men are out on their posts, but I can manage a guard mount for you if you wish to see how well we keep our weapons."

Captain Gringo said, "I'm sure your men are spit and polish, Sergeant. I'm just trying to get the feel of things. How about a quick tour of your outposts? I may be wrong about the scale of the map they gave me, but you seem to have your sugar fields spread out all over the place. Is there any reason for this?"

Montalban nodded and said, "As you will see, Señor, the plantings are widely spaced through the brush because this island is mostly rock. Come, por favor, you will see that thanks to science we do not have far to walk."

He led the way out a backdoor to where a narrow gauge train sat steaming and dozing in the sun. There was a little Shay locomotive and a string of hopper cars with a canopied open caboose to the rear. A fat guard sat near the engine under the shade of a cabbage palm. He rose from his box when he saw them and presented arms with his Remington .12 gauge.

There was nobody else in sight. Montalban asked, "Gordo, where is the engine crew?" The fat boy said, "It is siesta time, my Sergeant."

57

"Nombre de Dios, I didn't ask what time it was! I asked where the triple-titted bastards *were!* We wish to ride the train around the plantings."

Gordo said he'd see if he could find the crew, but Captain Gringo said, "I know how to run a Shay, Sergeant. I'm in a hurry too."

So Montalban shrugged and with the fat guard they climbed aboard. There was a full head of steam on the gauge and the tender was filled with bagasse, the bamboo-like residue of crushed sugar cane. The firebox smelled like a burning candy shop when Gordo opened it to shove in more fuel.

Captain Gringo cracked the throttle and with him driving they lurched forward, while Gordo acted as fireman and Montalban lounged out the far window of the small cab. The narrow tracks had been surface laid with no ballast between the hardwood tiles, so Captain Gringo drove slowly. When he commented on the casual construction of the roadbed, Montalban explained, "Termites, Señor. We must keep replacing the ties and they last longer when exposed to the sun."

Captain Gringo drove past a sugar mill, shut down for La Siesta, and as they passed the last ramshackle cabanas of the town he got a better look at the local terrain.

Nuevo Verdugo was built like Florida or Yucatan, far to the north. Limestone, the color of dirty plaster, cropped up between stretches of terra rossa, the rich red soil of limestone country. You have to melt a ton of limestone to get a pound of terra rossa, so the soil lay in shallow beds above and surrounded by bedrock. He nodded and said, "Now I see why your fields are scattered. Pantropic picked a funny place to set up a massive sugar operation."

Montalban said, *"Si,* only a fourth of the land is good for growing anything, but it is a big island and they own it all, so there will be enough land once it's all cleared."

Something wet splashed on Captain Gringo's elbow,

58

resting on the sill. He glanced up and saw they were in for more rain. It promised a break in the heat and a pleasant evening after all. But he hadn't come to talk about the weather.

He said, "Big island or not, I can see why the natives could get sort of truculent about such fertile soil as there might be on this slab of rock. How many natives are there, Sergeant?"

"In God's truth, Señor, nobody knows. There were only a few Cristanos holding land here when the company came. They have, of course not, been deprived of their holdings, since they have legal title from Spanish times. They are most contented. They have done well selling produce to us. There are also some charcoal burners. What you call beach combers? They too, have been getting rich since the island began to be civilized."

"Then who in the hell are the rebels you're having trouble with?"

"Like their numbers, Señor, that is a mystery."

Gordo said, "They are Black Caribs. Slaves who ran away to join the Indians many years ago. They are pagans and cannibals. Have you heard about the zombies?"

Sergeant Montalban looked pained and said, "The open mouth catches flies. I told you I wanted to hear no more nonsense about zombies, Gordo."

Gordo shrugged and said, "I was there when they raided milpa three. They looked like zombies to me."

"I spit on your zombies, you idiot! You and the others ran away from men who knew how to fight."

"You were not there, my Sergeant. They were not all men. Some were women. They all looked like they'd just climbed out of their graves. I shot this one fat woman at least three times, and I am a good shot."

"And then you ran, eh?"

"You were not there," said Gordo stubbornly.

The rain was coming down harder, hissing on the boiler-plates ahead like spit on a hot stove. The track was winding through a thick cover of Crown Of Thorns and

Manacheel. Captain Gringo said, "I'd have that brush cleared away if I was running this railroad, Sergeant."

Montalban said, "I suggested as much to Captain Burton. He said as long as they don't seem to have sense enough to attack the work trains, the labor is better spent on the crops. They only clear where the soil is rich."

Captain Gringo nodded, wondering what he'd gotten into this time. He knew the perils of fighting with the underdog's lost cause all too well by now, and the underdogs on this island didn't sound too nice. But it still seemed sort of shitty to grab the little fertile soil and leave the natives shifting for themselves on the leftovers.

He knew little about the so-called Black Carib culture, if they had any. But he'd spent some time with jungle Indians and knew it wasn't as easy to live off the country down here as romantic whites assumed. Most hunting and food gathering tribes grew at least some roots and manioc or bananas, and even the sparse game depended on the wild plants growing on the richer patches of soil.

They passed a clump of beheaded palmetto and he knew someone back in town had enjoyed a small salad at the cost of a dead tree more than once. He didn't say anything. He knew how his own kind had gutted a continent in the name of progress and he knew it probably couldn't be helped. If it was a choice between having wheat fields or buffalo and Sioux, the smart money didn't bet on the buffalo and Sioux. The natives here, had the same rights everyone else had. If they could drive the whites off the island they'd keep it. If they couldn't, they wouldn't. It was that kind of a world and only a fool tried to change it. Gaston had told him that more than once and this time he was going to try and pay attention.

They chugged into a forty-acre clearing and he shut off the steam. The irregular sugar field was immature cane and some workers were weeding between the rows under the watchful eyes of a three-man guard detail near the tracks.

As he and Montalban climbed down, Captain Gringo saw he was going to get wet. The gun crew and their copy of a maxim were already wet. But the gun was well-covered with oil and the water beaded and ran off. Montalban introduced him to the crew and as they stood respectfully aside he opened the breech and checked the weapon out. It was clean and in perfect firing condition. He said as much to Montalban, but added, "You only have one gun. Who positioned it like this?"

Montalban looked puzzled and said, "Captain Burton did, Señor. What is the matter? From here we have a full sweep across the milpa, no?"

"That's not how you set up machine guns, Sergeant. There should be at least two to each field. Three would be better."

He picked up a sliver of old cane and drew lines in the damp dust as he added, "You set up a killing zone like so. Two guns fixed on their tripods to fire a steady V or L at a common crossfire point. You hose the third gun back and forth to drive people into the steady fire."

"You mean this machine gun your company sold us is no good?"

"I mean, it's set up wrong. It's a perfectly good gun. But it's not a magic wand. Were the overrun guard units set up like this?"

"Of course, Señor. That is why they sent for you. The machine guns didn't stop the . . . the attackers."

One of the gunners frowned down at the hasty diagram and said, "I see it! If a gun was shooting a steady stream in one place nobody could pass through it. But when you are hosing to the right, people can get at you from the left!"

Captain Gringo said, "Exactly. I'll talk to Burton and see if we can't work things out. We sold you people a warehouse full of these things. Where the hell are they?"

Montalban looked abashed and said, "In the warehouse, Señor. Captain Burton said one to a milpa was enough, and we have not cleared all the land they intend to plant yet."

Captain Gringo nodded, but waited until they were

back aboard the train and moving on before he asked the sergeant, "Do you know where they got this captain of yours?"

Montalban shrugged and replied, "I am not certain, but I think he is related to Colonel Gage by marriage, Señor."

It figured. He'd thought Webster was the idiot of the bunch. He owed poor Webster a silent apology. At least Webster tried to think with the few brains they'd issued him. Things were looking up. The problem here was simply incompetent leadership versus some determined native guerrilla fighters.

It was really starting to rain now and he'd seen enough, but he decided as long as they'd come this far he might as well complete his tour and get the layout fixed in his mind. Montalban said there were about thirty-odd fields scattered along the track in various stages of growth, not counting the ones that had been burned out.

They passed a freshly ploughed field with nobody guarding it. Then they rode through a mile of thick brush and came to a field of charred stubble. He knew before Montalban told him what had happened there.

As they rolled through more dripping greenery, the sergeant explained, "We are trying to get a steady state of production with each milpa coming to maturity in turn. But every time a crop seems ripe for harvest . . ."

"Gotcha. Somebody on the other side is a wise ass. Instead of hitting wild here and there, they concentrate their attacks where they'll hurt the company the most."

Montalban nodded and said, "The next milpa up the line is almost ready to cut. As you shall see, I posted extra guards there to protect the workers."

"Are they cutting cane right now?"

"No, Señor. They start Monday, but I thought it best to guard the sugar over the approaching weekend."

Captain Gringo didn't ask if he'd cleared the idea with his officer. He knew good noncoms seldom did, when the officer was an obvious idiot.

They rounded a bend in the rain and heard the sudden woodpecker sound of a machine gun up ahead! Captain Gringo opened the throttle wider and drew his gun while Montalban did the same and shouted, *"Madre de Dios!* It's happening again!"

The Shay swayed dangerously around another curve and then Captain Gringo hit the brakes when he saw a big rosewood tree down across the tracks ahead. They slid to a stop with the cowcatcher buried in the green leaves of the felled timber. Captain Gringo shouted, "Watch out, guys! That tree was cut down to stop us. Follow me!"

He jumped out the wrong side and started legging it back along the track as a bullet spanged off the steel sill where his elbow had just been resting!

He led the other two about fifty yards before he cut to his right and plunged into the brush to circle back toward the sound of the fire-fight. Montalban said, "Ah, I see what we are doing. For a moment I thought I had misjudged you, Señor."

The tall American said, "Keep it down to a roar. Gordo, you drop back a bit and stay covered as we work in behind the gun crew. If things go sour, run like hell and tell my friend, Gaston, what I did wrong."

Up ahead, the machine gun hammered again and fell silent. Captain Gringo cursed and said, "Montalban, take the lead. You know where the fuck we are, which is more than I can say. Can do?"

"Si, Señor. I know where the gun and my men are."

The smaller but tough noncom bulled ahead through the wet shrubbery with Captain Gringo behind him and the nervous Gordo bringing up the rear. The machine gun failed to repeat its position and Captain Gringo said, "Careful. It looks like they've broken. The next guy we meet could be one of ours."

Above them the sky was ripped open by a flash of lightning and it began to rain cats and dogs. This covered the sounds of their own progress, but it meant they couldn't hear the other side either.

Montalban moved around the bole of a big balsa and as the lightning flashed again, Captain Gringo shouted his warning a split second too late. A bear-like black man stepped in Montalban's path with upraised machete and brought it down, splitting the sergeant like a banana from the top of his head to the belt buckle!

Captain Gringo fired into the gory red V of the sergeant's falling mangled body and the machete wielder grunted as the bullet took him in the chest. Then, as the American fired again, he raised the machete and kept coming!

Captain Gringo muttered, "Aw shit," and emptied his revolver into the looming Negro at point-blank range. He started to *really* worry when the hammer clicked on an empty chamber and the big black figure stepped over Montalban's body, machete still raised and dark face twisted in a ghastly grin!

Behind him, Captain Grongo heard Gordo shout, "For God's sake, *run!*" The sound of crashing branches told him he faced the zombi, or whatever, alone. Captain Gringo moved backwards, fumbling for the ammo in a side pocket and found himself saying inanely, "Take it easy, fella."

His attacker didn't act like he'd heard. He was naked save for a cotton breech clout and his eyes, above the ghastly grin, were glazed and devoid of expression, but he seemed to know what he was doing. As the American turned, walking backwards, the zombi followed. A root snagged Captain Gringo's heel and he swore as he fell backwards into a tree trunk. The zombi bored in and swung the machete while the American ducked by sliding down the wet bark. The blade thunked into the tree as Captain Gringo braced himself and kicked hard, driving his heel into his attacker's groin. Captain Gringo was a big man and he had a tree bracing his back, so a kick like that should have been more than enough to stop a grizzly. But while the zombi staggered back a few paces, he remained on his feet and, recovering his balance, came back for more—empty-handed!

Captain Gringo grabbed the hilt of the machete stuck in the bark above him, slid upright, and swung with all his might. There was a ghastly twang, and the sound and feel of cutting through a head of cabbage, and that did it. The zombi, or whatever, stood there, headless, for what seemed a long undecided moment. Then it collapsed at Captain Gringo's feet.

Swiftly, sobbing for breath, the American reloaded. Then he heard someone coming, tensed, and saw it was two uniformed guards running like hell. It seemed like a very sensible move even before one of them passed, yelling, "Save yourself, Señor! There's no stopping them now!"

As they vanished he nodded, holstered the gun, and bent down to pick up the headless black corpse. The man, or thing, he'd beheaded was heavy, but there had to be some answers to this nightmare. Captain Gringo staggered out of the jungle with the body on one shoulder and the gun in his free hand. He just made it. The train was spinning its wheels in reverse on the wet tracks but starting to move, and he heaved the body aboard a sugar hopper then hauled himself aboard.

Leaving his victim with a silent prayer it would stay put, Captain Gringo made his way across the cars to the engine, where a very pale and frightened Gordo introduced him to the other survivors. They were scared shitless too. Gordo crossed himself and said, "I lost my gun, but this time an Anglo saw it! Will you tell them we were not cowards, Señor? No mortal man should be expected to stand up to the forces of hell!"

The guard at the throttle said, "They walked right over the man on the gun. I did not run until they had our machine gun. After that it would have been pointless to stay, no?"

Captain Gringo said, "Take it easy, *muchachos*. I ran, too."

Gordo asked, "Do you believe in zombies now, Señor?"

Captain Gringo said, "I don't know what the fuck

that thing I'm taking back with us is, but I sure aim to find out!"

Utopiaton was quiet in the rain as they chugged backwards into the siding behind the guardhouse. But it didn't stay that way long, when Gordo and the others fanned out, shouting like Hispanic Paul Reveres in the tropic rain.

Webster and another Northern European met Captain Gringo on the wet grass of the green and Webster introduced his companion as Captain Burton, Commandant of the Guard. Burton was a good-looking but rather flabby guy, who had an unexpected American accent. He asked what the hell all the noise was about.

Captain Gringo said, "I was out in the bush with Montalban. He's dead. They overran another of your guard units. I think you just lost some sugar, too."

Webster gasped, "Oh God! Did you get a look at any of the blighters, Captain?"

"Better than that. I cut off his fucking head. I've got him over on the train. I was about to suggest an autopsy."

Webster looked puzzled and asked, "Whatever for? You just said *you* killed him by chopping his ruddy head off, what?"

Burton, despite his bush-league ideas on military tactics, had more brains than Webster after all, which only seemed reasonable once you thought about it. He said, "Right. I'll get some of my men to carry it over to the infirmary." He suited actions to his words by heading off a running guard to shout, "You there, what's your name, get a four-man litter detail together and meet me behind the guardhouse, chop-chop."

Webster stared after him, bemused, and offered, "I still don't understand. Even if the blighter's cause of death eludes you, who in blazes do we have that can perform an autopsy? Doctor Lloyd is dead and we're still waiting for his replacement, eh what?"

Captain Gringo said, "Let's get out of this rain before we're all dead and drowned. Nurse O'Shay can give us some educated guesses about the son of a bitch."

They legged it through the rain toward the infirmary and Captain Gringo explained how hard his attacker had been to stop. He said, "I could have missed hulling his vitals with five rounds, but the shock alone should have made him lose at least a little interest in what he was doing. He didn't mind a good kick in the balls either. I want Nurse O'Shay to tell me why."

"Oh, do you think he was on drugs or something?"

"He sure wasn't *born* that tough."

"Well, at least we know they can be stopped by cutting their heads off, eh what?"

"Oh, for Chrissake, there's got to be an easier way. I'm not up to stakes through the heart either."

They'd been spotted crossing the green and Mab O'Shay met them at the door. Captain Gringo asked how Gaston was, and Mab said, "He's going to be all right, Dick. But what's wrong with you? You look like you've seen a ghost."

He said, "I might have. Are you up to performing an autopsy, Mab?"

The Irish girl looked surprised. Then she shrugged and said, "Well, I know my basic surgery."

She led them inside and down a corridor to the one small operating theater. He filled her in and asked, "Do you know how to test for drugs and such in a cadaver, Mab?"

"I think so, if it's not something too unusual. I mean, there are standard tests for the standard drugs and poisons, but I'm no expert. I'll have to consult the books in poor Doctor Lloyd's office."

Burton called down the corridor, "Hello, all. Where do you want this big buck?"

Captain Gringo called back and saw Burton leading a litter party. There was a bit of confusion but soon they had the headless black corpse on the operating table.

Mab looked sort of green around the gills as she stared down on the wet, muscular mess, and Burton said, "Built like a damned bull. What did his face look like, Walker?"

Captain Gringo said, "Like a dead man's. I mean, before I killed him. What's the procedure, Mab? I'm sort of in a hurry for some answers."

The redhead rolled up the sleeves of her white uniform and licked her lips before she said, "Well, I can see he's been shot and beheaded. I suppose we start with blood samples."

They all found themselves looking at the pink circle of wet raw meat where the corpse had once had a head. It was curiously clean, probably from the rain. The machete had been razor sharp and there'd been little tearing of the flesh. It looked sort of like someone had sliced salami instead of a man's neck.

Mab went over to a cabinet and got a lancet and some test tubes. She took a deep breath and cut into a vein on one arm. Nothing much happened. She frowned and asked, "How long has he been dead, Dick?"

"Not more than an hour or so, why?"

"He doesn't seem to want to bleed. Wait a minute."

She got a hypodermic and tried that. She looked relieved when she drew dark-red fluid and began to squirt it into her test tubes, saying, "I've never seen anyone with their head off before. I guess they bleed pretty dry. How did you manage without getting blood all over *yourself*, Dick?"

He held a wet sleeve out to the light and said, "Beats me. I guess the rain washed us both off when I lugged him through sopping wet leaves. Not that I'm complaining. What have you to say about those bullet holes in his chest?"

"They're all close to the heart. You must have been aiming for it. Let me check these samples out for drugs and stimulants before we get your dear bullets back."

She left the room and Burton said, "I noticed. Nice

68

shooting. I could cover all five holes with my palm, but I'm not about to."

Webster said, "I'd say they were mucking up his heart a bit, too, but I shot a lion one time in the ruddy heart. Blighter ran a good hundred yards before he dropped. Gave me a bit of a turn too. You see, he was running toward me."

Captain Gringo shrugged. He could have pointed out that a man is not a lion, but he didn't want to hear any Great White Hunter tales, even if they were true.

They heard the sound of broken glass from the other room. Captain Gringo stepped over to the door to peer in. Mab was leaning against a counter, staring down at the test tube she'd dropped as if it was about to bite her. Her face was chalk white and he knew she was about to faint. So he moved swiftly to her side to steady her and asked, "What is it, doll? You've got plenty of those test tubes."

Mab shuddered herself back from the black pit she'd been staring into and literally whispered, "Dick, that man in there is dead!"

"Hell, of course he's dead. What did you find in his blood?"

She licked her lips and said, "There *isn't* any blood in him. I thought at first I'd made a mistake. I think I'm going to be sick."

"Just hold on a second, Mab. What do you mean there's no blood in him? I just watched you draw a needle full of blood from his vein."

"It's red because they put dye in it."

"Somebody put red dye in that guy's blood?"

"Damn it, you're not listening!" Mab sobbed. Then she threw herself against his chest and added, in the voice of a small frightened child, "His veins are filled with embalming fluid. That corpse in there has been dead for God only knows how long!"

69

Chapter Six

Gaston waited until the two of them were alone in his infirmary room down the hall, before he put a finger alongside his nose and said, "The Irish girl is in on it."

"Mab? How do you figure that, Gaston?"

"Cherche la femme, my old and rare friend. She picked you up aboard the ship before we got here. Who is to say she did not slip that snake in our cabin before she encountered you on deck, discovered you were not in your bunk where you were supposed to be and . . ."

"Oh, for God's sake, she didn't try to *kill* me in her cabin."

Gaston made a lewd gesture and insisted, "How do you know she didn't intend to slit your throat in your sleep, *hein?"*

"We weren't sleeping. We were . . . never mind. Anyway, when you were bitten by that bushmaster she saved your ass. Have you forgotten that?"

"Mais non. She might have wanted to build charac-

70

ter with the man they *sent* her to get. I will admit all this just came to me while you were bringing me up to date. I don't intend to stay here tonight in her power."

Captain Gringo said, "That's stupid. She'd have given you the wrong antivenim if she wanted to harm a hair on your lopsided head. What's gotten into you all of a sudden?"

Gaston frowned up at his younger friend and said flatly, "Embalming fluid. *Merde alors,* you are the one who needs to have his head examined, Dick! I am willing to believe you chopped a man's head off as he was trying to kill you. I am willing to believe a well-embalmed corpse might last a month or so in this heat. I am not about to believe both stories, and since I know *you* don't lie very often . . ."

"Back up. Are you suggesting Mab made funny-funny with her test tubes?"

Gaston looked disgusted and replied, "Suggesting? *J'accuse!* I agree she is nice-looking. I agree she is a nurse. But her trick was childishly simple. She just drew some blood from a freshly killed corpse, got rid of it, and *voila!*"

Captain Gringo shook his head and said, "Credit me with common sense. That's one of the first things I thought of. So *I* took the hypo and drew my *own* sample from the guy on the table. Then I ran my own test. He was still embalmed. The blood's been replaced by a tropic mixture, strong as hell. It's got arsenic and camphor in it, and the book says a stiff can last a couple of months or longer before it starts to go bad."

"The book, Dick?"

"The chemistry book from the doctor's desk. Do I look like an undertaker? I had to read how to test for all the goodies Mab insisted were in the son of a bitch. I followed directions and got the same results."

Gaston frowned and asked, "Do you believe everything you read?"

"Oh sure, Doctor Lloyd had a special private print-

71

ing of a textbook, knowing he was going to die and that a couple of suckers were coming along to read his private library. That's pretty wild, Gaston."

"So is an embalmed corpse coming at one with a machete. Given a weird plot by a mad doctor or something, that is simply not possible. *One* must go with one's *possible* fantasy, *hein?*" Gaston thought before he added, "I like that better than Mab being in on it. How do we know Doctor Lloyd is really dead? Have any of us seen his corpse?"

"Oh shit, we wouldn't recognise him if we met him alive. The whole damned colony says he's dead. That's how we know he's dead. Are you suggesting everyone we've met so far is in on some crazy plot?"

"Well, at least that is *possible*. Once she calmed down, did Mab finish the autopsy?"

"No, I did. I only had one question. I cut open the chest and found five bullets, right where they were supposed to be. One smack in the heart and the others close enough to stop it through hydrostatic shock. That idiotic Webster kept telling me about some lion he'd seen charging on after being shot through the heart. It got pretty tedious."

Gaston pursed his lips and mused, "I have seen men stay on their feet for an astonishing length of time after being fatally shot, Dick. A man too excited to give a damn can last up to four minutes with a stopped heart, and four minutes is a long time in a fight."

Captain Gringo nodded as he relived those awful moments in the jungle. He said, "I've considered that. I figured that had to be the answer. I expected Mab to tell me he'd been hopped up. She really threw me when she said he was dead before I ever met him."

Gaston shrugged and said, "Very well, if we accept that, what does it mean, Dick?"

"That modern science is full of shit and we're in big trouble, or that Mab and I were tricked."

"I like that better. How do you think it was done?"

"If I knew that we wouldn't be tricked, damn it! The

stiff was only out of my sight for a few minutes, and Burton and his guys got to it before anybody could have possibly drained it and embalmed it."

"How do you know *they* didn't do it?"

Captain Gringo stopped and thought before he shook his head and said, "No. Even if Burton was some sort of maniac there wasn't time. I asked Mab how long it takes. She's worked around hospital morgues. She said it takes close to an hour to do it right, and she said they did it right. She pointed out the sewn up incisions where they'd drained and flushed his veins. The hell of it was, even I could see it had to be a while ago. The real blood on the stitching was dry and hard as plaster. I'm no doctor, but I believe her when she says that guy has been dead a while. How long is hard to say, but over two hours means I somehow tangled with a corpse. I don't think I'll get much sleep tonight."

Gaston sighed and said, "Lucky girl, whoever she turns out to be. Have you checked out the local talent?"

"No, the siesta is just about over and I'm invited to tea at the governor's. So I guess I'll get to meet everyone important. I'd take you along, but Mab says you need more rest. It looks like you'll have the novelty of sleeping alone again tonight."

Gaston chuckled and said, "Speak for yourself, Dick. I know your plans for the head nurse here. But now that I have had time to reconsider my suspicions, there is one a bit darker with a *trés formidable* derriere and . . ."

"Jesus Christ, Gaston. You're asking for a heart attack."

"I don't think so. She looks like she can take it. If she starts to expire I just have to pull this bell cord here, to get medical assistance for her."

Captain Gringo laughed and said, "You'll be gentle with her, I'm sure. Who is it, that American girl, Willie May?"

"*Mais non.* Even I can do better than that. If you wish, I can ring for her. Perhaps she has a friend."

"If she has, and if I know you, you won't need me.

73

But for Chrissake, take it easy, Gaston. Mab says you could have a relapse."

"Bah, she says dead people run through the jungle waving machetes, too. I shall go with my own medical theories, and if you return to find me dead, it shall be with a beautiful smile on my face, *hein?*"

Captain Gringo left, shaking his head fondly. He had to admit Gaston had a point. Mab was only a nurse and he knew even less about medicine. Either of them might have missed something a doctor wouldn't have. It was sort of convenient to have the only doctor on the island dead when stiffs got up to walk around.

He'd stolen a book from the late Doctor Lloyd since there'd been no way to ask him for it, and he hadn't wanted to rattle Mab any further. He patted his hip pocket. The small, spooky book was still there. It was an English translation from the original French, published years ago in Haiti. It was pretty obvious why Lloyd had been reading up on Voodoo. Captain Gringo intended to bone up on the subject, too, as soon as he had the time to read it. Voodoo sounded silly, and zombies even sillier, until they started ganging up on you. He'd never meet Lloyd, and it was odd to grieve for a man he'd never met. But he sure wished he could have had a chat with the medical man before he died, or before somebody murdered him.

He'd wanted to check that out too, while he and Mab rummaged through the dead man's office. But Mab had said the only way to test the label on Lloyd's antivenim vials was to let a snake bite you and see if the stuff worked.

He wasn't that curious.

So it had to stay an educated suspicion. If someone had switched labels before leaving a snake where the doctor could be bitten, it had been neat but simple. He could see a dozen ways they could have done it. But who were *they?* The natives? That seemed neat and simple too. But there was something wrong here. Something he'd worked out for himself as a kid when he first read about witchcraft.

Witchcraft had to be the bunk. Not just because science said so, but because it made no sense to be the classic witch or witchdoctor.

He got to expound on that idea a bit at tea, once he'd cleaned up and presented himself at the governor's.

Tea was late that afternoon, thanks to the rain as well as all the excitement. But it was *veddy veddy* British and Captain Gringo found himself the only man there not wearing a tie and madras jacket.

Tea was served under an awning behind the governor's tin mansion by colored servants who looked a bit silly as well as uncomfortable in startched white linen uniforms. He already knew most of the men that mattered, and didn't worry about the other three or four whites introduced as junior executives of Pantropic Limited.

The women had been allowed to dress more sensibly in low-cut taffeta or prints. Governor Gage's wife looked something like a horse when she smiled. But the honey-blonde across from him was a knockout. He was surprised and disappointed to learn she was Captain Burton's wife, Alice. The fat old colonel and the horsey old dame were her parents. So, Burton, the son of a bitch, was their son-in-law, as well as the guy who got to sleep with Alice tonight.

It hardly seemed fair. Burton was maybe a little smarter than silly Webster and Captain Gringo supposed he was all right, but Alice had a body that set her cameo face off like she'd been designed by Louis Tiffany, for finer tastes than her flabby husband seemed to have. He tried not to picture her in Burton's embrace. But while he could get her husband out of his picture of her going to bed, it still left *her* there, and it was giving him a most uncomfortable erection.

Despite not showing up with a tie, Captain Gringo

had better manners than to bring up forensic medicine over tea and crumpets. But Burton, the only other American at the table, embarrassed him by asking if he'd figured out how the Voodoo Queen the natives talked about had sent that dead man at him.

Captain Gringo said, "Voodoo and witchcraft is self-contradictory, Captain Burton. But since you brought it up, has anything been done about poor Montalban and the others?"

Burton said, "Oh sure, I sent a burial detail out just before we came over to join the folks."

Mrs. Gage looked like she was about to throw up, but she went on pouring tea. The poor thing probably didn't know what else to do.

Her daughter, Alice, shot her husband a warning look and probably to change the subject to less grisly matters, asked, "Why do you say witchcraft is self-contradictory, Captain Walker?"

He smiled across at her, an easy task, and said, "Simple. If you were a witch, I mean a real witch with real powers, would you live in a shack in some swamp, muttering to your bats and toads? Or would you prefer Buckingham Palace?"

Her mother looked up from her pouring to say, "Perhaps witches are eccentric, dear boy. I mean, they're said to be old crones who cackle a bit overmuch."

Webster chimed in, "Quite so, boil and bubble and all that rot. A person would have to be rather senile to begin with, what?"

But Alice smiled and said, "I think I see what you're getting at, Captain Walker. A person who had magic powers, real magic powers, wouldn't have to *be* old and ugly. If I had magic powers the first thing I'd do would be to take off twenty pounds and give myself lavender eyes."

Captain Gringo said, "I don't think you have much room for improvement, ma'am. But that's the general idea. Who'd live the way witches or witchdoctors live if they didn't *have* to?"

Webster nudged Burton and said, "I say, spot of gallantry and all that, what?"

But Burton was probably used to the idea that other men found his ravishing wife attractive. He ignored Webster and said, "I can see your objections to *civilized* witches and warlocks, but what about the native kind? I mean, a jungle bunny might stumble over a few spells and incantations and not know enough to improve himself."

Captain Gringo shook his head and said, "Nobody's too dumb to want simple luxuries. Maybe a native witch-doctor wouldn't want to move to London or Paris, but at the least he or she would have a decent hut and all the food they could eat for themselves and their friends. We had these Apache Devil Dancers back home when I was with the Tenth Cav. They were pretty good at ventriloquism and sleight of hand. They gave us a lot of trouble and nobody ever figured out how some of their tricks worked. But they started losing their hold over the Apache when some smart young Christian Indians asked how come they could evoke a hundred and one Apache gods but couldn't produce a bushel of corn or enough tobacco to go around."

There was a polite chuckle around the tea table and Alice Burton said, "I quite agree. If this mysterious Mamma Macumba they talk about had real magic powers, she wouldn't muck about with raids and arson. She'd simply produce a few million pounds and *buy* all the land she wanted!"

Captain Gringo asked, "Is Nuevo Verdugo up for sale?"

Colonel Gage said, "Good Lord, of course! Pantropic Limited would sell it gladly for enough to cover its losses to date. I mean, we're in business to make money, eh what?"

Captain Gringo nodded and said, "I can see making a profit here might be harder than you folks planned. But if you're aiming to sell out, I don't see what all the excitement is about."

Gage replied, "I said we'd gladly sell off these holdings for the chance to break even. I didn't say anyone has made us an offer! Who's about to buy a perishing tract of semi-jungle infested with hostile natives, with or without this Voodoo business thrown in?"

Webster said, "News of these zombi chaps has reached the marketplace. It's a bit like trying to offer a house with rats in the walls. We can't sell before we've disinfected the premises. But, of course, if we could get the rats out of the walls, we wouldn't want to sell out."

Mrs. Gage had a biscuit halfway to her mouth. She grimaced and put it back on her plate as she murmured to her husband, "Must we, at *tea?*"

Gage said, "Quite right, old girl. We were talking business, Webster. I was about to ask Captain Walker here, if he was satisfied working for Woodbine Arms Limited. I shan't ask what Sir Basil is paying this season, but if I know him, it can't be as much as we're in a position to offer. How do you feel about joining us, Walker?"

Captain Gringo glanced at Burton. The other American at the table nodded and said, "It's okay. You wouldn't be breaking my rice bowl. I'm really an engineer. I wound up commanding the guard because of a misspent youth at a military school. I'm not really cut out to run a jungle war."

Captain Gringo tended to agree, but he was too polite to say so. He turned back to Gage and said, "I'm flattered, Colonel. But you sure make snap judgements. We haven't been on the island a full day."

Gage said, "Nonsense. Sir Basil cabled your qualifications before you and Verrier got here."

Gage turned to the others and explained, "They call him Captain Gringo in Mexico. Seems he and his friend took on the whole Diaz dictatorship one time and almost won. He tamed a tribe of wild Indians in Panama, too. Need one say more?"

Alice Burton dimpled at Captain Gringo and said, "How thrilling. You must be very brave, Captain."

He read the smoke signals in her eyes and answered, "I've learned to be a little cautious about charging into disputed territory, ma'am."

What was the matter with the silly dame? Her fucking husband was sitting right there! He'd heard the British colonial set liked to screw around, but Burton was a Yank.

To change the subject and give himself time to think, he turned back to Gage and said, "I'd have to talk it over with my associate, Gaston, sir. Frankly, I don't know whether you need a professional exterminator or not. Has anybody tried *talking* to the natives?"

Burton said, "You just met up with them this afternoon, Walker. How conversational did you find the one who killed Montalban?"

"He was sort of unfriendly, come to think of it. But I was thinking about a powwow with the tribal leaders. Even Apache seem willing to chat once in a while if they think you're making them an offer."

Gage said, "Black Caribs aren't Apache. Not even the Christian natives on this island have ever managed a word with them. We're not utter savages, you know. When we first took over here, we left gifts for them at the tree line. We've tried repeatedly to contact them for a discussion of our differences. A local priest even offered to walk into the jungle alone with a cross in one hand and a white flag in the other."

"What happened?"

"He never came back."

Captain Gringo frowned and said, "Hmm, I would have assumed that they'd at least made the usual demands and speeches about the spirits giving them these lands as long as the grass shall grow and so forth. Do you mean it's a pure no quarters race war, shoot on sight?"

Burton said, "Exactly, and as you just found out, the so-and-sos are hard to shoot. The one you got was the first time we've even managed to verify a kill."

He glanced at his mother-in-law and chose his words as he added, "Let's not go into just when he died. The point is that you got him, and we've yet to see you in action with your machine guns. Gordo told me you'd said something about our setting them up wrong. I'm perfectly willing to step aside and let you take over."

Captain Gringo said, "We'll talk about it later then."

Alice Burton said, "Oh, why don't you sup with us this evening, Captain? We'll be dining at eight and you boys can discuss military strategy in private as long as you like."

Burton for the first time looked a little uncomfortable. Captain Gringo wondered how often his wife had put him through this, and what he did about it. Being married to the boss's daughter beat getting one's own job, but on the other hand, you couldn't beat your wife, so it evened out.

Captain Gringo said he might drop by but that he wanted to look around some more and see how his friend, Gaston, was. That gave him a good reason to excuse himself from the tea party, so he did.

Webster tagged along as he left the governor's garden to head into the native quarter. The town was wrapped around the big central green like a squared-off horseshoe, open to the waterfront. The company buildings fronted on the green with other streets onion-peeling in an ever growing horseshoe until they ended in less formal clusters of housing, cleared lots, and gumbo limbo thickets. The Anglo-American and executive Hispanic housing lay to the upwind side of town, with the sugar mill, engine, and machine shops contesting with native shacks for the space downwind.

That was where he was heading. Webster, at his side, said, "I thought we were on our way to see your chum at the infirmary."

Captain Gringo said, "I was being polite."

"Oh quite. Bloody bores, those tea parties, eh what?"

"Yeah. I noticed there was only a handful of people there. I thought there were more Anglo-Americans here than that."

"Oh, there are. But the colonel's lady is a bit of a snob, for one thing, and prefers intimate teas for another. You won't be invited tomorrow. She rotates the honor among her victims. We don't have to attend her court again until everyone has had some of her dreadful tiffen. Takes her nearly a week to poison us all."

The taller American did some mental guestimation and said, "So there are a couple of dozen off-islanders here in Utopiaton?"

"About seventeen white men and their womenfolk, not counting you and Verrier. Of course, they have to entertain the local gentry from time to time. Just the leading families and, of course, the Papist priest."

"They're colored people?"

"Not exactly. Exotic Spanish types. I've never quite figured out what a Dago is. I mean, they're not really niggers, but, dash it all, they could hardly be called white."

Captain Gringo didn't want to go into it with the twit. He said, "There's usually a plaza and marketplace in the towns down here. I haven't seen anything like that."

Webster said, "You're headed the right way. The Dagoes use the street across the tracks as their Bond Street or Piccadilly. The town was laid out by a leading architectural firm in London, but the damned Dagoes have no idea of form."

They followed an alley off the green and crossed the tracks Captain Gringo remembered. He saw the puffing billy train and sugar mill to his left and the loading docks framing a patch of sea to his right. They walked through a block of shabby tin houses apparantly inhabited mostly by kids and chickens. Then they were on the real main drag of a real town, no matter how they'd laid it out on paper.

People were like that. Utopian planners never seemed to know-how real people liked to live. He remembered all the action back in Washington had been off to one side of the sterile mall and marble tombs, too.

The narrow crowded side street was lined with *can-*

tinas, farmacias, and *bodegas*. Native peddlers squatted along the few blank walls to make a post siesta sale before the sun went down, which wouldn't be long now. Captain Gringo spotted a corner *cantina* and was about to cross over to it as soon as that carriage coming passed by. It was an open coach and four, driven by an elderly Negro in a high silk hat. Two women were in the back, wrapped in black Spanish lace.

Suddenly, as the carriage drew abreast of the two men, a ragged, cotton-clad figure materialized from the other side, waving a machete.

Webster gasped, "I say!" as Captain Gringo moved forward, grabbing for his shoulder holster. The attacking native leaped aboard the carriage on the far side while the women cowered down in their leather cushioning. The man with the machete wasn't after their money. He obviously wanted their heads. So as he raised the machete to swing, Captain Gringo fired across the women's knees and jackknifed the assassin off the far running board with a .38 slug where his belly button used to be.

After that it got sort of noisy. One of the women was wailing like a banshee, the confused coachman was cursing as he fought his rearing horses, and people charged in from every direction, yelling fit to bust. He recognised the fat guard, Gordo, in the crowd, and since Gordo was shouting, *"Viva* Captain Gringo!" he assumed they weren't mad at him. But they were stomping the man he'd shot pretty good.

Captain Gringo went up and over the coach, saying, "Excuse me, ladies." On the far side he fired in the air for attention and shouted in Spanish, "Enough! I want to question him! Sergeant Gordo, move these people back!"

Gordo yelled, "You heard Captain Gringo, you idiots! This is our prisoner you are kicking as if you owned him. Back, I say, before we show you real slaughter!"

Abashed, the peones formed a circle around the mess they'd made of the gut-shot man in the roadway. Someone had already stolen his machete. Captain Gringo dropped to one knee and felt the side of his throat. Then he muttered, "Shit." The man was dead.

Behind him, a soft sultry voice said, "We are in your debt, Señor."

Captain Gringo stood up and turned around, wishing he had a hat to take off. The face he saw framed in old Spanish lace belonged in a portrait frame. She was obviously pure Castilian with aquamarine eyes, ivory skin, and a ringlet of burnished copper hair curled right in the middle of her forehead. Gordo joined him, to doff his cap and murmur, "I kiss your foot with respect, Dama Luisa. May I present Captain Gringo, as he is called?"

The girl had spoken to him in English, so Captain Gringo said, "I'm Dick Walker, and I'm honored, ma'am."

"My poor dueña is too upset to thank you properly, Mr. Walker. But we are both in your debt, nevertheless. Dear Gordo will direct you to our home when it is convenient for you to call and receive the honors due you."

He didn't know how to handle that, so Captain Gringo said, "*Por nada,* my Dama. Have you any idea why that man just attacked you ladies?"

Dama Luisa glanced rather disdainfully down at the battered corpse in the roadway and said, "I never saw him before. Have *you* any idea who he might have been, Gordo?"

Gordo shook his head and said, "No, Dama Luisa. He is not from this part of the island, I am certain."

Captain Gringo turned and took another look. The shabby man had Hispanic features and mestizo coloring. Dama Luisa said, "He does not look like a Carib, Black or Red. But who else *is* there on Nuevo Verdugo? Are you certain he is not one of the off-island workers that your company imported, Gordo?"

"It is possible, Dama Luisa. But we shall soon know, in that case. What are your orders on this matter, Captain Gringo?"

83

"I think you'd better take the body to the infirmary and have Sister O'Shay look at it. She'll know the tests I have in mind as soon as you tell her where you found him. Then see if you can get each foreman of a work crew to take a look at him. With luck, someone may know him and we can start from there."

Gordo looked uneasy and said, "Forgive me, my Captain, but though you called me Sergeant I have yet to make Lance Corporal."

"You're wrong. Colonel Gage just offered me Commandant of the Guard, and I just made you Sergeant."

"Por favor, I don't know how to read or write!"

"I've seen you twice in action, Gordo. You've got some rough edges, but you do what you're told, and that's enough for me. So carry on, Sergeant Gordo. We have to get this street cleared and see these ladies on their way."

Gordo grinned boyishly and began to bluster the crowd back as Dama Luisa murmured, "You are a kind as well as quick-thinking man, Mr. Walker. I have known Gordo all my life. You have made a devoted friend from common clay indeed."

He smiled back at her and said, "I do mean to drop by your place some time, but not because you owe me a sandwich. I need to talk to people who know the island. I don't think Colonel Gage knows much about common clay. When would it be convenient for you and your husband, ma'am?"

She laughed and said, "That's usually *our* ploy. I never realised how obvious it must sound to you men. To answer your question, I'm not married. Gordo would have told you I was a widow in any case, but I admire a man who makes direct moves, as long as he's not *too* clumsy."

The older woman at her side, who'd been taking it all in as she decided whether to faint or not, sat up to nudge Dama Luisa and mutter something. Luisa laughed and said, "Tia Consuela thinks we are flirting. Will you tell her we're not flirting, Mr. Walker?"

"I never lie to a lady, ma'am."

This time the dueña laughed, too. Dama Luisa said, "I am otherwise engaged this evening, but we'll expect you just before La Siesta tomorrow. Until then, you know you have our heartfelt thanks. Drive on, Bruno."

The Negro cracked his whip and the coach and four moved on. Captain Gringo saw that Gordo had enlisted a couple of boys and a burro to carry the body away. He remembered Webster and noticed for the first time that the twittery Englishman was gone. It didn't surprise him.

Since everything seemed to be getting back to normal, he walked over to the cantina, went in, and sat down at a blue-washed table. The cantina girl said anything he ordered was on the house, and he got the idea somehow, that this included her. But she had a moustache and was sort of shapeless, so he ordered cerveza.

Captain Burton and a quartet of guards found him there, working on his second beer and chatting with the other customers, when they burst in, looking sort of excited.

Burton asked, "What's up? Webster came in panting about you getting into a brawl over here in the native quarter."

Captain Gringo said, "I figured he might. Sit down and have a drink. It's all over. Some clown tried to hack a couple of women with a machete and I sent the body over to the infirmary. By the way, I just promoted Gordo, if you really don't mind my taking over."

Burton said, "God no. We both know I'm lousy at the job." Then he turned to the guards he'd brought and added, "This is your new C.O. Savvy?"

The four guards presented arms and one of them said, "We await your orders, Captain Gringo!"

"Okay, my first order is that we all cool off with cerveza. Stack arms and sit down while I figure our next move."

Chapter Seven

The dead man wasn't a zombi. Mab said there was enough alcohol in his blood to get a vampire stinking drunk, and she thought he'd been on opium, too. But he only died once. Captain Gringo's bullet had given him a good start, but the cause of death was brain damage from the stomping he'd received and no doubt deserved.

They were alone in Doctor Lloyd's office when she told him all this. The sun was going down and it would soon be night. It seemed incredible that so much had happened since they'd arrived that noon.

Mab was leaning her buttocks on the doctor's desk while they spoke. He stepped closer and put a hand on each of her hip bones and said, "Well, I'm writing it off as a crazy drunk with no connection to the other troubles. Gaston's okay, and there's nothing to do on a moonless night but wait for more light on the subject. So, where's your bedroom, doll?"

Mab turned her face as he leaned in to kiss her, and he frowned and asked, "What's wrong?"

She said, "We have to be careful. I've already been snubbed by that jumped-up *auld* Gage woman."

"Hell, nobody snubbed you, Mab. Webster says they rotate the tea shit. You'll probably get invited tomorrow or the next day."

"That's easy for yourself to say, Dick. You was invited *today!* I'm a single woman in a tiny nest of gossipy *auld* bawds. It's my head I have to be holding up in this little town. You know what they'll be saying if you spend the night here."

He parted her thighs under her white linen skirt with his knee and moved closer as he soothed, "Hell, who's going to tell them? The colored girls working for you won't talk. And if they do, you've got Gaston on them. I know he's got at least two of them lined up."

"That's disgusting. Miscegenation is against the law."

"Maybe back in the States. Down here folks don't worry about each other's complexions as much. Makes for some interesting-looking gals."

He tried to kiss her again, and again she resisted, saying, "Please don't, Dick. You're just teasing us both."

"What the hell's going on? Are you a nurse or a nun?"

"You know I want to, Dick. It's just that I've my reputation to consider."

"Okay, they gave us private quarters in a wing of the headquarters building up the green. It's getting dark. Why don't we just go out the back way and . . ."

"Don't be silly! We'd get caught for sure, that way!"

He was about to suggest locking the door of the room they were in, but he couldn't see tearing off a quicky on a desktop when there were beds all over the place. She was beginning to piss him off. He saw she hadn't thought ahead when she started her shipboard romance. That eliminated one of Gaston's suspicions, but it wasn't doing a thing for his erection.

He was expected at the Burtons' in an hour or so. He'd wanted to tear off some ass and get his nerves under control before he faced that honey-blonde Alice again.

But, damn it, Mab was making him work too hard for it, considering she'd already been down on him the night before.

Mab shoved him away and said, "Come back later, when everyone has gone to bed, and maybe we can sneak in a little loving if the coast is clear."

He said, "I think I'll just read that book about zombies. There sure are a lot of frozen bodies around here."

She didn't get it. She said, "I know. They buried that . . . that thing we looked at this afternoon. The natives wanted to do something silly with a hardwood stake, but I told them not to."

"I missed that. Where did you plant our zombi?"

"Over by the town dump. They say they bury suicides there too."

Then she shuddered and leaned against him, now that he'd stopped trying. Women were like that. She said, "Dick, I'm frightened. I still see that thing, every time I close my eyes."

"Well, that's one of the problems we have to face if we sleep alone."

"*Och,* you know I want to doze off naked in your arms, darling. But people talk so ugly."

"If you say so. Is that why you move around so much, Mab?"

"Dick, what are you after intimating that I'm a loose woman?"

"I'd hardly call you loose. But I think you worry too much. I get the impression there's a lot of hanky-panky on this island, but everybody is ever so proper at tea. I don't think anybody gives a damn who's screwing whom, as long as it's not in the middle of the green at high noon. Come on, doll. Let's get out of this ridiculous vertical position."

"Maybe later," she insisted, adding, "come to me at midnight."

He gave up and chuckled wryly, "I'll come to thee at

midnight, though Hell should bar the way, huh? Okay, Bess the landlord's daughter, I'll see if I can stay awake that long, but don't bet on it. I've had a rough day."

She followed him out and as they said good-bye at the door to the infirmary Mab took his hand, placed it on her starched breast, and said, "I'll leave a light if the coast is clear."

He kissed her, but muttered, "Aw shit," and walked back to his own quarters. He still wanted Mab, but he didn't understand this new act, and no mortal woman was worth jumping through hoops over. They usually waited a month at least before they started playing games. That was probably why everyone called it the honeymoon. She'd somehow gotten on a faster track. She dragged him into bed minutes after picking him up, so now she was having the vapors about it ahead of time, too.

He went to his quarters, caught a servant in the hall, and ordered a hot bath. While he was waiting, he peeled off his jacket and shirt, sat under a ceiling fan with a handy Edison bulb mounted in its hub, and cracked open Lloyd's little Voodoo book.

It read pretty silly, even to a man who'd *met* a zombi.

The French doctor who'd written it thought the priests of Mambo Jumbo used some unknown tropic plants to induce a deathlike trance in their victims. Breathing and vital signs faded to where even an M.D. might be fooled into signing a death certificate. So the semi-dead victims were buried, the Voodoo guys dug 'em up, and revived them.

So far, so good. But then the Frenchman suggested that the revived victims were kept in a trance with other drugs and made to slave for their Voodoo masters. They worked at night partly to keep their living relatives from spotting them, and partly because the drugs sensitized their eyes to sunlight. Zombies had just enough muscular control to carry out orders, not enough for reflexes like squinting in bright sunlight, etc. The good doctor said the

89

Voodoo priests got a year or so of unpaid hard labor out of them before they died again for keeps, of malnutrition and the effects of the dangerous drugs.

Captain Gringo muttered, "Bullshit," and ran that information through what the locals had told him. He didn't see how a poor guy too doped up to squint at sunlight could charge and overwhelm a machine-gun crew, even badly positioned. Besides, the attack that afternoon had taken place in broad daylight and . . . wait a minute. It had been raining and the sky was overcast. Hmm.

The hall porter knocked on the door and announced that his bath was ready. Captain Gringo decided he'd better read some more in the tub. Maybe, just maybe, the French doctor who said he knew about zombies might have something after all.

A small shy mestizo let him in, when Captain Gringo knocked on the Burtons' door an hour later.

She led him down a hall and past the dining room he spotted through an archway. The dining room was dark and the table hadn't been set. They had said tonight, hadn't they?

The serving girl led him into a back room opening onto the patio. Alice Burton was lounging on a couch by a small table piled with fruit, cold cuts, and a magnum of madiera. She was wearing a kimono of maroon silk. *Thin* maroon silk. As the serving girl left them, closing the door after her, Alice waved her guest to a seat on a hassock near the couch and said, "It's cooler and less stuffy in here. Would you prefer to fuck or eat first?"

He sat down and answered gravely, "That's the dumbest question I've heard in a long time, doll. But what about your husband?"

"What about him indeed? As you see, he's not here. I thought we'd be more comfortable together if we got the sexual tension out of the way right off."

He slid off the hassock to kneel over her and she calmly smiled up at him. He slid a hand inside the kimono as he bent to kiss her. She responded hungrily, and her tongue entered his mouth at the same time his fingers parted the thatch between her thighs. He felt her clit was already turgid, and her vagina was almost gushing. So he asked, with his lips against hers, "Shall I douse the lights?"

She sighed, "No. Just do it. I don't like these long seduction scenes."

He laughed and said, "I noticed," and started ripping off his clothes. She unfastened her kimono and opened it in welcome as he mounted her. She looked better in the nude than he'd imagined and he was already frustrated, so his performance delighted her. She moved her perfect body expertly and suggested, "Prop yourself up a bit. I want to look down between us and watch you going in and out."

He did as she asked and found it exciting, too. They both stared down at their pounding genitals and she said, "Oh, isn't that beautiful? You have a lovely prick, Dick."

He went as wild and came as fast as any man would at a time like that. Then he settled in for some serious screwing.

She licked her lips and said, "Oooh, I like what you're doing. Don't ever stop."

He said, "I don't aim to, but while we're on the subject, that patio door is wide open, the lights are on, and you're a married woman!"

She bumped teasingly and said, "A *neglected* married woman, thank you very much. You must have guessed by now that this is more than simple lust."

"Oh? Are we talking about revenge?"

"I'm past caring that much. Charles only married me for my father's money. We haven't done this sort of thing for months."

"Old Charlie must be crazy. You don't mean he's cheating on *you?*"

"Don't slow down. I love it when you hit bottom. I don't know what's wrong with Charles, but I know my own needs. The servants say he's been mucking about in the native quarter with some Dago wench. But he was rather disappointing on our honeymoon. I've always suspected he might be queer, if not impotent."

"I like that better than cheating. It's impossible for him to be getting anything better than this away from home."

As he'd expected, she responded to the flattery by wrapping her legs around him and getting wilder. He'd said it to be polite, even though he knew Burton would have to go some to get better loving. Alice was a little unromantic in her approach to sex, but she was beautiful and a fantastic partner. He supposed it was like that old joke about the guy who'd been having filet mignon every night and wanted beans for a change. The cheating was cutting Alice up, despite her cool comments on it. Nobody liked to be used, and a beautiful woman needed even more reassurance when she felt rejected. She was less used to it than the rest of the human race.

So he made love passionately as well as skillfully, though it hardly took much effort with anyone so lovely in his arms. She sensed his sincere desire for her and responded harder. She screamed aloud in mingled pleasure and surprise and gasped, "Oh my God, I'm actually coming!"

He didn't ask dumb questions and just pounded against her sobbing flesh. He knew she'd done this before, with God only knew who, and that up to now it hadn't worked for her.

She sighed and said, "Jesus, you're going to have a hard time getting away from me, Mr. Walker." Then she throbbed her way down from heaven in time with his slow gentle thrusts.

He chuckled at her mock formality and said, "I wasn't planning to leave you on somebody's doorstep, Alice."

"Do you love me? Would you do anything I say?"

He was too polite to laugh. He said, "It's a little early to know, honey. At a time like this it would be very easy to *say* I loved you. I have too much respect for you as a person to say things I'm not damned sure about."

"Pooh. I'll bet you've said *that* before to someone else."

It was true. She was too smart to be talking so dumb. He kissed her to shut her up and started moving faster.

She responded, but pleaded, "Let's change positions. We're getting sweaty rubbing tummies. I want to try it deep and dirty, doggie-style." He said, "Okay, but let me turn out the damned lights."

"Are you afraid you'll blush to see my arse winking up at you?"

"Hell, I'll shove it in there if you want. But the damned door is open and the whole fucking world can see us!"

"Nonsense, there's a wall around the patio and Charles will come in the front way, if he comes at all."

Captain Gringo got to his feet and Alice rolled over with a roguish laugh and peeled off the kimono. She braced her knees under her center of gravity and thrust her lovely rump up at him, saying, "As a matter of fact, Charles always comes in the front, when he can manage to come at all."

He thought, "Boy, she's really pissed off at her old man!" But that wasn't his misfortune, so he placed a hand on each of her hip bones, and, standing upright, pulled her on like a tight wet sock. Her passion-flushed buttocks slammed against his own hip bones and she gasped with pleasure and moaned, "Oh yes, that's the way I like it. That's the way I need it. Slam it in as far as it will go and never stop."

So he did. And it was fantastic, but that open doorway made him uneasy. He hadn't played this *exact* scene before, but he'd met ladies trying to pay back a cheating husband before. Pounding away and enjoying it, he glanced down at his clothes scattered across the rug. The shoulder holster was neatly placed on the hassock. He'd shown that much common sense even without thinking. So he kept his eye on the door into the darkness as he went on enjoying himself. He could make it to his gun in one smooth duck if he had to, so what the hell.

His distraction put Alice ahead of him and he wasn't expecting it when she gasped and straightened her legs to fall forward. As they lost contact she sobbed, "Help! I'm coming, damn it!" So he followed her down, spread her cheeks with his hands, and got it in again as she gasped, "Oooh!"

He realized where he was too. But as he started to withdraw for a better aim she clamped down hard and moaned, "Leave it there! I'm . . . Oh Jesus!"

He came too. Neither moved for a few moments as her rectum throbbed around his shaft. Then she suddenly twisted out from under him and ran out of the room.

Careful not to soil the upholstery, he rolled over, and got to his feet. He bent down, got a kerchief from his crumpled pants and wiped himself reasonably clean. That open door was a pain, so while Alice was away he stepped over to do something about it.

But he had second thoughts as he stood naked in the doorway, staring out onto the patio. Alice had been right. There were three solid walls facing him with the usual glass shards imbedded in the stucco atop the walls. They were safer with the door open than if it suddenly burst open by surprise. There was another room opening onto the patio, but the small window was barred. Anyone aiming to surprise them in the act first would have to come over the wall and then drop down.

He moved back to the couch and Alice returned, totally unabashed by her nudity, and carrying a damp towel. She said, "That would be a nice way to fuck if it didn't act as an enema. Sit down and let me clean you too."

He did so and when she sank to her knees to wash him off, she smiled fondly at his erection. She said, "It's still nice and hard," and she squeezed him teasingly. He ran a hand through her golden hair and said, "Ladies built like you have that effect on me."

So they made love again and Alice made him show her every position he knew, and he even thought up, or remembered, a couple of new ones. But all things must end, so they finally wound up sitting on the floor with their backs to the couch, sharing the cold cuts and wine.

Alice said, "As soon as we get our wind back I want to try it out on the patio under the stars."

He said, "There are no stars. It looks like it's going to rain some more."

"All right. Let's rut in the rain."

He took a swallow of madiera and said, "Listen, this may be safe, but it's making me nervous. Why don't we go over to my quarters and, for Chrissake, lock some doors?"

Alice answered, "Heavens, my parents live right next door to the headquarters building and my mother tends to prowl at night. I'd die if she found out."

"You don't seem worried about your husband, doll."

"Pooh, he's not my mother. You see, my silly parents *approve* of Charles. I was more or less forced to marry the dumpy old thing."

"You're over twenty-one, Alice. Why do you stay with him if it's as bad as you say?"

She popped a pickle in his mouth and sighed, "What chioce have I? My parents are High Church and they'd disown me if I got a divorce. I'm really not cut out to be 'play the typewriter or take in washing,' and despite what you might think, I can't give myself to just anyone, so *that* source of income is out."

As he chewed and swallowed she fondled him and asked archly, "If I wasn't so prim, do you think I'd make a good whore?"

"You'd make a fortune. But you're right. You like it too much to peddle it. How the hell did old Charlie get in so thick with your folks? He's a Yank, like me, and I didn't think he was all that smart *before* I learned he was neglecting something like you."

Alice shrugged and said, "Oh, he's a jack-of-all-trades-and-a-master-of-none. So he's useful to the company, in his own plodding way, and besides that, his family owns some shares in Pantropic."

"Charlie's rich?"

"His family is. They do something odd to pigs in Chicago, I think. They had a little trouble with Charles as a boy. He kept getting thrown out of schools for some reason. Anyway, when they invested in sugar they sent their black sheep to reform him, and my silly old father likes him for some reason. I seem to have been a bit of a worry to my family, too, though I can't see why. Anyway, they more or less forced the two of us into this ridiculous marriage."

"You mean he was drafted, too?"

"I don't know what I mean. I suppose he thought it would advance his career. But I hardly remember if he proposed or if it was my father."

Then she suddenly rolled over and sat in his lap, facing him with a thigh on either side of his hip and said, "The hell with the past. Let's make tonight count!"

It was raining again when Captain Gringo walked through the dark of midnight. Alice had begged him to stay longer, but sleeping over would have been pushing it past common sense. He knew the servants would talk if he wasn't in his own quarters when they came to waken him at dawn.

As he passed the infirmary, he saw a light in Mab's window. He chuckled fondly and was about to walk on. Enough was enough and she'd had her chance. He didn't think he could get it up right now with a block and tackle.

So why did the idea give him a tingle?

"You're getting to be a dirty old man before your time," he chided himself. But on the other hand, Mab was going to be sore as hell, and like the joke said, after filet mignon a bowl of beans tasted fine. He might need an alibi, too.

He went to Mab's French window and tapped. The curtains parted and Mab peered out, nodded, and let him in. She was wearing a black lace nightgown and had let her red hair down. He noticed she was shorter and built rounder and softer than he remembered from their boat ride.

She said, "Oh my eyebrow, you're soaked. Where have you been? I was beginnning to think you'd never come."

He grinned and said, "Coming was what I had in mind."

She lowered her lashes and said, "I don't know, Dick. If anyone found out . . ."

"Look, if it's that upsetting to you, let's forget it."

"Well, I wouldn't want to disappoint you after making you wait half the night, dear."

So he couldn't get out of it, and once he got into it, it was better than he'd expected. He naturally took a long time coming and it drove Mab wild. But once the first excitement was over, she started dithering about her reputation again, while he held her in the dark in her old-fashioned bed. She said, "I'm trying to respond properly, darling. But I feel so low to be carrying on like this in front of the help."

"Oh? I thought we were *alone* in here."

"You know the servants always know what's going on. By this time tomorrow night the whole town will know about us."

"Look, Mab, the whole town is busy getting laid or trying too, if I'm any judge. Can't you get it through your pretty head that nobody that matters gives a damn about us?"

"There are always gossips."

"Sure there are. They gossip whether they know anything or not. Who listens?"

"That's easy for a *man* to say! I remember this girl back home, when I was little. The things my mother and maiden aunt used to say . . ."

"Okay. I'll nip back to my own trundle bed and make sure the hall porter spots me there in the cold gray light of dawn."

"You won't be angry, dear? We could do it again before you leave, but . . ."

"Maybe it's better this way. Quit while we're ahead and all that rot. Jesus, I'm starting to talk like these *veddy veddy* colonials. It must be catching."

He sat up and started to get dressed, so naturally, she suddenly wanted more. But he was tired as well as a little pissed, so he kissed her good-night and ducked out into the rain before she could fuck up their heads further.

He was really dragging by the time he at last got into his own bed. He'd intended going over the charts of the company holdings on the island before he turned in, but that had been a million years and two women ago. He'd worry about setting up better defenses in the morning. Nobody was going to burn anything in all this rain. So the natives didn't figure to attack until things dried off for a spell. If they did, it was still Burton's problem. So far he hadn't agreed to do anything but check the guns. There was nothing wrong with the fucking guns.

He slipped naked between the cool linen sheets and was asleep in minutes. He might have stayed that way indefinitely. But as he was just getting into an interesting dream he suddenly became aware that he was no longer alone in bed.

Captain Gringo opened his eyes in the dark as a hand gently fondled his shaft. He was surprised about that, as he was at the erection it was producing. He lay still until he got his bearings. The door and window had been locked when he turned in. But there seemed to be a naked lady in bed with him. She snuggled closer and he asked quietly, "Are you sure you're in the right room, honey?"

His invisible bedmate tittered and replied in a whisper, "Don't raise your voice, dear boy. It's almost morning and the servants may be stirring."

She rolled atop him and as he automatically embraced her he felt that whoever in hell she was, she had a nice body. But he couldn't place her. She didn't feel or sound like Mab or Alice. He'd heard of musical cunts, but this was getting ridiculous!

The unseen woman settled onto him and sighed, "Oh, nice. I was so afraid I was sacrificing myself to the usual banalities. But you really are quite nice in bed."

He started thrusting up to meet her. But he frowned and asked, "Did you say *sacrifice,* doll? What are you, some kind of a religious nut?"

The mystery woman leaned forward, planted a pair of heroic breasts against his chest, bounced faster while she explained, "I'm doing this to save my daughter." As she kissed him, Captain Gringo knew who she was. Nobody else had teeth as big as the horse-faced Mrs. Gage, Alice's mother!

He laughed with his lips pressed to hers, and her tongue tried to swab his tonsils. It was too crazy to be happening. The old dame was ugly as sin with her clothes on. But apparently screwing like a mink ran in the family and, ugly or not, the horsey old dame was *good*. So he rolled her over and did it right. She had a big ass that didn't require a pillow under it to meet him at a fantastic angle, and she had amazing muscular control between her thighs. He'd gotten enough rest before she crawled in with him to keep going, and he *had* to keep going quite a while, thanks to her daughter and Mab's earlier hospitality. So Mrs. Gage beat him there, twice. The first climax seemed to surprise her. The second, as he went on pounding, seemed to drive her out of her mind. They popped a bedspring and wound up halfway on the floor before he had managed to satisfy himself.

As he helped her back on the mattress Alice's mother sighed, "Heavens, I didn't expect that. It was wonderful."

He left it in to soak, and kissed her again before he said, "Life's full of surprises. Didn't you expect to like it, uh, ma'am?"

She moved her hips teasingly and said, "Under the circumstances you can call me Cynthia, Dickie-bird. I'm so glad we got together like this before you made the usual play for my daughter. You *are* going to leave her alone like a good boy, aren't you?"

"Wait a minute. Are you saying you seduced me to keep me from flirting with your daughter, for God's sake?"

"Not for God's sake, for the sake of her marriage. Alice has been a bit of a problem to us, you see. We thought marriage would settle her down, but for some reason she just won't behave."

"It must be hereditary. How long has she been such a cross for you to bear?"

"Oh dear, I caught her with the gardener in the potting shed when she was eleven. She may indeed have gotten her warm nature from my side of the family, but *I,* at least, have always been sensible about my passions."

"You call this sensible?"

"Of course. It's not as if I'm mucking about with the *servants!*"

"Thank you, I think. I'm getting the picture, weird as it is. You came in here to screw me silly so that I wouldn't make a pass at your daughter, right?"

Mrs. Gage wrapped her legs around his waist, tightened alarmingly, and began sliding up and down on his semi-erection while she said, "Of course. I always try to nip it in the bud. I saw the way she was looking at you this afternoon at tea. I thought it was a mother's duty to, well, make myself available."

He found himself responding. The grotesque situation was piquant, and she was so ugly she was exotic. As their passions rose once more she said huskily, "Will you promise to come to mother when you get these urges, Dickie-bird? I know my daughter is attractive and that you young men have needs, but . . ."

"Shut up and just do it, mamma," he growled, not wanting to lie, even to an ugly lady. His mock brutality excited her and she started going wild again. This time they really wrecked the springs and he pulled her off to keep from crashing through to the floor. He got her against the wall and they finished standing as she gasped, "Oh, the wall's so rough and you're so rough and I never want to stop!"

They had to, eventually. He half-carried her to a chair he remembered in a corner, and sat down with her in his naked lap. She kissed him and said, "Damn, it's almost light outside. I'm going to have to nip back to my room, but we'll get an earlier start tonight, eh what?"

He said, "I may be out in the jungle. Uh, how does the colonel feel about your sleepwalking, Cynthia?"

"Heavens, he never wakes up before ten. As you must have guessed, he's not a very active man."

"I figured your sacrifice was overdo. Do you sacrifice yourself a lot for Alice?"

"Not as much as I'd like to. That silly Webster made an awful fool of me when he first arrived. I mean, how was I to know he didn't like girls?"

Captain Gringo laughed and said, "You mean he's queer? It must have been an interesting night for both of you if you woke him up the way you did me. How the hell did you get in here, by the way? I thought I'd locked the door."

"You did. I have a passkey."

She got up and added, "I really must be going. Mind that you ignore my daughter's invitations. If I know Alice, she'll attempt to seduce you the first chance she gets."

He didn't answer.

He was trying too hard not to laugh.

It wasn't easy, but Captain Gringo also managed to keep a straight face when he met with Colonel Gage and Captain Burton after breakfast. He had the survey charts spread on the guardhouse table and was using a pencil for

101

a pointer while he said, "I've been going over the layout of your holdings. With the sugar fields scattered and spread out like this, surrounded by thick growth, your defenses are impossibly complicated. I could set up secure perimeters around each plantation, but the cost in men and materials would be more than the crops would pay for, and your rail network is impossibly vulnerable. I'm surprised they haven't torn up your unguarded tracks by now. It's all one narrow gauge ambush, even if we clear the brush back."

Burton said, "We've thought about clearing the jungle away, but the labor would be astronomical, Walker."

"I'm not finished. I agree with you there. The geology of this rock pile dictates spread-out plantings in scattered soil pockets. The distance between sugar fields dictates long communication lines. It would take more men and time than we have to secure it all. But there's an easier way."

He drew a line across the map and said, "Look. Nuevo Verdugo is shaped something like a flattened-out peanut. Set this narrow waistline about the center of the island? This town and all the civilized stuff is here at the north end. This slightly bigger half is pure jungle, and obviously where the natives hang out when they're not raising hell."

Colonel Gage nodded and said, "Quite so, dear boy. But the whole island is ours, if you're talking about a frontier."

"Let's not be piggy, Colonel. You can worry about the other half once you secure *this* half and get some crops to market. My plan is to set up a string of strongholds, each within machine gun range of the other, right across the island where it narrows. If we clear a six hundred yard swatch from coast to coast, with a machine gun nest every three hundred yards, we can forget about guarding the workers and sugar fields. Nobody can get near them."

Burton said, "Three hundred yards is the effective range, eh?"

"Yeah. They'll shoot further, but I wouldn't bet on hitting anything. Each machine gun nest will have four guns. They can lay a field of fire covering each other as well as the cleared killing zone."

Burton nodded, but the colonel asked, "Why six hundred yards, if the guns only fire three?"

Captain Gringo sighed and said, "The nests will be in the *middle* of the strip, Colonel. I don't know why those so-called zombies haven't seen it, but the guns set up at tree line are vulnerable to an attack from the rear. Put the crews out in the open, well dug in, and nobody can get near them. I noticed some rolls of glidden wire in the warehouse when I was checking the spare guns and ammo. I figure barbed wire around each nest and down the center of the strip would just about complete the picture."

Gage frowned down at the map and said, "Barbed wire? We never used barbed wire on the Northwest Frontier."

"I know. You did it the hard way. The German Army has been experimenting with the idea and the French have been getting good results in North Africa with it. Charging through barbed wire and machine gunfire seems to be rough on one's hide."

Gage sighed and said, "Well, I suppose you younger chaps know what you're doing. But I don't know what the world is coming to. War is getting to be just another mucking *trade*."

Burton nodded and said, "I read about the French and the Riff raiders in the papers. I hate to admit it, but I never even considered that we had rolls of the stuff on hand. If they ever have that big war everyone keeps talking about, it certainly figures to be a bloody mess."

Captain Gringo said, "I know. These days we've learned to mass produce everything but human bodies. But let's hope the new young Kaiser is just kidding.

Getting back to our own modest war, if I have your agreement, Colonel, I'd like to get started before this wet spell ends."

"Wet spell, dear boy?"

"Rain. Splash-splash sloppy in the cane fields. The guerrilas will hit again as soon as the trade winds dry things enough to burn."

Burton said, "I'm not sure they're that well led, Captain. You just pointed out that they've passed up some advantages. They seem to be mere savages who'd be no problem if only they didn't have that weird trick that has our men so rattled."

Captain Gringo said, "I don't know how they work that zombi shit, either. But I know that whatever they are, they can be stopped if you hit 'em hard enough. I've talked to some of the guards who've fought them. They do go down and stay there, after they've been hit a few times more often than usual. Let me set up a real killing zone and we'll worry after the sons of bitches walk through *that!*"

Burton asked, "What if they can?" Captain Gringo replied, "We pack up, go home, and wait for Mamma Macumba to take over the world."

Colonel Gage laughed nervously and said, "Right. A real army of real zombies would be able to do that, wouldn't it? I mean, dash it all, why settle for a jungle island when one has the secret of life and death?"

Captain Gringo nodded grimly and said, "Haiti never has been able to take over San Domingo, even though they share the same island. The Spanish in San Domingo don't claim to raise soldiers from the grave, either. See how silly it all gets in the cold gray light?"

Burton shrugged and said, "We still have to explain that creature you beheaded, Captain." But Captain Gringo said, "No, we don't. Not after he went down and *stayed* there. We're *supposed* to waste time on Mamma Macumba's parlor magic. I'd rather fence the old bitch off on her own half of the island and let *her* worry about *us!*"

Colonel Gage said, "I like that part. But, dash it all, that still leaves the bloody Caribs in control of more than half the island."

"The half nobody's using at the moment, Colonel. Even the native Christians and Creoles are on our side of the line I've drawn. Are you up to a short war story?"

"If there's a point to it."

"There is. Once upon a time there was a man named Geronimo. An American officer named Miles was sent to do something about that. Geronimo never had a hundred men under him at any given time and Miles had the U.S. Army. He had field pieces and Gatling guns. For a couple of years Geronimo made him look like an asshole. I know because I was there."

"Oh yes, we read about this Geronimo chap. He would seem to have been a native general with an instinctive grasp of warfare, right?"

"Wrong. Geronimo was just mean and knew the country. He made a fool of Miles because Miles went about it all wrong. He'd been a good officer in the Civil War, fighting for real estate, and moving his troops into standard positions. But Geronimo had never been to West Point like most Confederate officers, so he didn't know how the game was supposed to be played and nothing went right for poor old Miles."

"But you chaps did get Geronimo in the end, didn't you?"

"Sure. A couple of months after Miles went back east to explain why his assignment was impossible. The officer left in charge had no idea how you fought Indians. More important, he *knew* he didn't know. So he called in his junior officers and a smart chief scout named Tom Horn and asked them what he should do. We had Geronimo on his way to Fort Sill in a couple of months."

"Ah-ah! Foxy fighting using Apache tactics and all that, eh?"

"No. We stopped trying to figure out where the sly old bastard was aiming to go next. He had thousands of square miles in which to play tag. We moved troops in to

105

secure the waterholes, the passes, the camp sites, and pasture for his horses. We set up so that it didn't *matter* what the Apache plans were. Then we just waited until Geronimo gave up."

Burton said, "I thought you guys trapped Geronimo."

We did. He was trapped in miles and miles of barren wasteland. It was surrender or slowly die of hunger and thirst. So that was that. The last I heard, Geronimo was selling picture postcards of himself at Fort Sill. He looks silly as hell in a horseless carriage, but they say that one's selling well."

They both chuckled. But then Gage said, "Very well. We secure all the important parts of the island and leave the perishing natives the bush. But eventually we're going to have to clean them out. And they'll be able to survive indefinitely down in those southern jungles."

"Sure they will, Colonel. But eventually isn't this month or even this year. I'm not offering a final solution. Just a breathing spell. Once you get your colony on a paying basis there'll be plenty of time to screw the natives out of the rest of their island."

Colonel Gage looked pained and said, "I wish you wouldn't put things so brutally, dear boy. Her Majesty is not in the habit of screwing people out of things."

"I'm sure the folks who used to own India and most of Africa agree with you, Colonel. I wasn't sent here to choose nice words for raw conquest. I'm a soldier of fortune, not a missionary."

"Quite so, and, by the way, have you considered my offer to join Pantropic Limited?"

Captain Gringo said, "Yeah. I think we'll stick with Sir Basil and Woodbine Arms. I'll bail you out and see that the guns you paid for make you and yours all safe and snug. But just consider it part of our services."

"Well, if you and your friend prefer working for Sir Basil, that's your business. But once you secure things for us, who's to conquer the rest of the bloody island?"

"That's *your* business, Colonel. Gaston and I are professional soldiers, not butchers."

"Good God, you're not taking Mama Macumba's part, are you?"

"Nope. I'm not trying to save the passenger pigeon either. I just don't want to have to watch when the last pigeon and the last free native goes down."

Chapter Eight

Had it been up to him, Captain Gringo would have gotten started that morning. But another steamer came in and Burton had to do something about unloading more equipment. So he went to see how Gaston was feeling.

Gaston said he felt great and that the nurses had been treating him *trés* formidable. But he was still a little weak, either from the snake bite or from screwing himself silly, and Mab had insisted on another day in bed. Gaston said he could use some sleep.

Captain Gringo told him of his plans and the Frenchman agreed they made sense. He said, "I feel so useless, Dick. It seems a shame to take even Hakim's money for the little I've done so far."

The American said, "So far you've been bitten by a bushmaster on Sir Basil's time, so the bastard owes you. I've got to get going. Where's Mab? She wasn't in her room just now."

"Ah-ha, I might have known you'd go there first. I feel betrayed. I saw her just a little while ago. She said something about going to meet the ship. Perhaps she expects medical supplies."

Captain Gringo shrugged it off. He didn't want to see any more of Burton or Gage for a while. It had been bad enough holding a conference with the two men right after screwing both their wives. He was afraid he'd bust out laughing, now that he knew Webster was up to even wilder sex. He still choked every time he thought of prissy Webster waking up with old lady Gage clutching his pecker.

He remembered Dama Luisa had said she'd be expecting him and the meeting offered information as well as what he hoped would be some harmless flirting with a beautiful woman. It *had* to be harmless. He was still walking a little funny from the weird night he'd just spent.

A grave-colored servant let him in and he found Dama Luisa waiting for him at a table by the fountain in her patio. She was completely dressed in brown taffeta and a black lace mantilla. Her old dueña was seated discreetly under a distant archway, fanning herself out of earshot, but obviously keeping an eye on them.

He sat down with a nod of thanks to the Negro holding the chair for him at Dama Luisa's table. He went away but Dama Luisa said, "I've ordered coffee and pasteles, Captain Walker. I hope you don't prefer tea. I really detest it, but it's all they serve at Mrs. Gage's interminable afternoon affairs."

He said, "I like coffee fine, and I know what you mean. I was there yesterday."

"Oh dear, that means I probably won't meet you there this afternoon. It's my day for tiffen, I fear. She's a dear old thing, but a bit stuffy, don't you agree?"

He grinned like an idiot and said, trying not to laugh, "I guess she looks like that to most people. But aside from that, how do you and your Hispanic friends feel about being a British colony, Dama Luisa?"

"Please call me Luisa, Dick. I'm not touchy about being a Creole, either. Spain really messed things up when

109

they had their chance at an empire. We Creoles were only too happy to see these parts taken over by the British. The Spanish always looked down on us so."

He knew that as she meant the term, "Creole" meant anyone born on this side of the water, even obvious pure whites like Luisa and her proud family. But he said, "You do have a nationalist group on the island though. Is it safe to assume none of them are Blancas, like yourself?"

She laughed, and as the Negro returned to place a tray of coffee and pastry between them, she didn't wait until he was out of earshot before she said, with no hint of defensiveness, "I'm part Indian and, for all I know, part African. We were not always rich landholders. My late husband was an obvious mestizo. Does this bother you?"

"Not if it doesn't bother you. I know some of us Anglos say dumb things, but I've been down here a while."

She smiled archly as she poured and said, "Your little French friend prefers even less cream in *his* coffee, from what my servants tell me."

"Oh? I've heard they have a grapevine. I suppose you got a full report on *my* wild and wicked ways, too?"

She dimpled and said, "You seem to be more discreet. Your friend tends to be noisy for a man who's unshaded window fronts on the green. But everyone to his own taste. Sugar and cream?"

"I like my coffee any way it comes, as long as it's hot."

Luisa lowered her lashes and flushed a becoming shade that went well with her dress and copper hair. She murmured, "We were talking about the Carib rebels, Dick."

"We were? Okay, what do you know about this Mamma Macumba and her zombies, or whatever?"

Luisa said, "Not much, even though I was raised here on Nuevo Verdugo, save for my finishing school in

England. We Christian Creoles hardly ever see the bush natives and, of course, when we do, somebody usually gets hurt."

He frowned and said, "That reminds me. One of the foremen says he thinks that man who tried to hack you up yesterday came in with a recent shipment of laborers from Costa Rica. Have you any idea now why he might have attacked you?"

She shrugged and said, "No, but he was obviously too drunk to know what he was doing. He might have just run amuck and we were simply lucky."

"You call that luck, Luisa?"

She batted her eyelashes and said, "Well, we might not have met for days and days if that *pobrecito* hadn't introduced us so dramatically."

She was really coming on. But Hispanic girls flirted the way other girls did needlework. Having a chaperone in view gave a dame certain advantages, he supposed. She was probably only half aware of it and, of course, she wasn't wearing his tight pants.

He shifted in the chair as he sipped black coffee. That came on stronger and hotter than he'd expected, too. He told her what he planned to do across the middle of the island and she said, "How clever of you. I'm surprised nobody ever thought of that before, Dick."

He said, "So am I. I've been going over the maps. I noticed you and some other Creole families have bigger haciendas than I expected. Do you mind if I get personal?"

"About my land? Of course not. My holdings are a matter of public record. Between my dowry lands and my late husband's, I own about five square kilometers, or is it miles? Being a Crown Colony is so confusing."

"It's a big spread, either way. What I wanted to ask about was whether you Creoles have been approached to sell your old claims."

She shook her head and said, "We haven't. Our original coastal *fincas*, or plantations, compliment the planned economy London had in mind. We grow beef

111

and other food for the workers imported by the company. So there's no rivalry. As a matter of fact, to put it in a vulgar way, we never had it so good."

"Try it another way. Could any Creole *expand* his holdings if the big sugar company was driven out, Luisa?"

She thought before she answered, "Why would anyone want to do that? With the British gone, we'd have nobody to *sell* to. We'd go back to subsistence agriculture on a forgotten island. We can't grow crops for the world market with the small native population. Our only export is sugar, and very little of that, thanks to those silly natives."

"Then there's no reason anyone wearing pants might have for driving Pantropic Limited out, right?"

"I can't think of anyone, Dick. Even the jungle natives will lose in the end if Pantropic pulls out. Though of course *they* can't see that."

He sipped some more coffee before he asked, "How do you figure the natives stand to lose, Luisa?"

"Oh, no doubt they're happy making babies in the jungle at the moment. But we're on an *island*. If we all just went away and left them to their own devices for a few more generations . . ."

"They'd wind up eating each other, like the natives on other small overcrowded islands. But maybe they're not worried about the distant future. Pantropic Limited is clearing all the fertile land right *now!*"

She nodded and said, "Of course. But civilization only speeds up what's bound to happen sooner or later, and it can save a lot of pain and trouble. My Spanish ancestors have a lot to answer for, but they did stop a lot of cannibalism and human sacrifice, and who's to say an Indian is not happier wearing pants and going to Church every Sunday?"

He might have said some Indians he'd met didn't agree. But he'd had this discussion before, and didn't think beating a dead horse made much sense. So he said, "Meanwhile, nobody can tell me how many of those

Black Caribs there are, or just what their Mamma Macumba wants."

"Does it make any difference, Dick?"

"Hell, yes. Making a deal beats fighting any day. We'd still be fighting Indians back in the States if Washington hadn't got most of them to sign treaties in the end."

"Our Mosquito Coast Indians are a bit more primitive, Dick. As you know, the Black Caribs add African superstitions and somewhat advanced tactics to the original Carib culture, which was wild indeed to begin with. They say Mamma Macumba is part Ibo. The African Ibos were noted in the slave days for being clever and more treacherous than other tribes."

"All the more reason she'd be smart enough to see the advantages of a peace treaty. How did you Creoles handle them before the Anglo-Americans came?"

"We didn't, really. The Caribs gave their name to this sea in their day by ranging like red Vikings in their dugouts. But white men, starting with Columbus, have tended to fire cannons at them out on the open water. So they'd become landlubbers by the time slaves started running off to join them. The Negroes feared the sea from the beginning, associating it as they did with slave ships. So for many years the Black Caribs have stayed well back in the jungle, out of slave-raiding range of the coast. My people, on the other hand, preferred the coastline with its cool breezes and opportunities for trade. So until very recently the island was reasonably peaceful, with civilization hugging the coastline and the cannibals happily beating their drums in the interior."

"Sounds homey. Do you know for a fact that the Black Caribs are cannibals, or did that story start because they wouldn't go to Sunday School?"

"Your Spanish must be rusty, Dick. Carib *means* cannibal in my mother tongue. It's not just Papist propaganda. Columbus actually found them eating Arawak Indians when he discovered and named the Caribs. He said the Arawak were gentle and harmless by the way, so

113

we can assume he was being reasonably objective about non-Christian naked people. I know you think the early Spaniards were narrow fanatics, but Dutch and English explorers reported cannibalism among the Caribs, and more than one wound up in the pot."

She took a sip of coffee and added, "To be fair, the Blacks who ran away to join them in the bush were less savage. Few West African tribes went in for that sort of diet. So I suppose a Black Carib would be less likely to eat you than a Red Carib, but they are all pretty truculent."

"So I hear. But there must be some way to talk to them. The runaway slaves managed to find friends in the jungle."

"Not all of them, Dick. It's estimated that nine out of ten slaves who ran off to the bush were killed and eaten by man or beast. Here and there an Indian tribe took in a fugitive. But it was the exception rather than the rule. I've heard runaway slaves were put through brutal initiation rites, so that only the tougher ones survived to intermarry and blend into the tribes."

He nodded as he remembered how Creeks and Seminoles back home had adopted runaways, while Cherokee and most other American Indian tribes had sold them back to the slave catchers for trade goods.

He said, "They've been telling me how tough the Black Caribs are since I drifted down here from Mexico. How come, if the Blacks had better manners than the home-grown variety, that it's the Black Caribs everyone's afraid of?"

Luisa said, "It's probably partly racist. Black Caribs are bigger and, of course, darker. But it's mostly because other Caribs have slowly been tamed by intermarriage and salt."

"Salt?"

"Yes. Wild Indians are mad for salt because of their bland jungle diet. The missionaries have made more friends distributing salt than with all the glass beads and calico combined. But, of course, tribes along the Mosquito Coast can *get* salt from the sea and salt marshes so they see less advantage in being tamed."

He pursed his lips and thought about that before he nodded and said, "Okay, Mamma Macumba's people can't blend in because they look like a white colonist's picture of a born cane cutter and they don't need salt . . . but why? You said they don't come out of the bush to the sea coast, Luisa."

She said, "Well, I've never been deep in the jungle obviously, but they say there are salt springs near the center of the island."

"Which end?"

"South, I believe. Does it make a difference?"

"It sure does. I want to fence the guerrillas off. I don't want to drive them even crazier. If we pen them down in the south end with plenty to eat and salt with which to season it, they may just stay there."

"I thought you said they couldn't get through your machine guns and barbed wire in any case?"

"They can't, but I don't want to have desperate men trying. I hope to pen them down there with minimal bloodshed. They may not even try to cross the cordon, once we clear it."

She smiled at him and mused, "You're an oddly gentle man, for a soldier of fortune, Dick. I thought men like you delighted in battle?"

He shrugged and said, "Nobody but a sadist or a fool delights in battle. I'm in this line because I was pushed into it in the first place, and I'm pretty good at it in the second. But I'm a live-and-let-live guy, if people are willing to stay off my toes."

He drained his cup and added, "I'd better get going. You don't want to hear the story of my life."

Her eyes were glowing as she smiled up at him and said, "Oh, but I do, Dick. Will you come back some time and tell it to me?"

Captain Gringo stood with Burton in the bow of the steam launch as it puffed along the leeward coast of

Nuevo Verdugo. The tubby craft was a forty-footer with boiler amidship and no awning to catch the sometimes treacherous wind. So it was hot as hell, even in the bow. He was explaining to Burton how he intended to tow in barges with jungle clearing equipment once he'd surveyed the narrow waist of the island, but the other American didn't seem to be listening.

Burton glanced back to see that the guards they'd brought were chatting with the launch crew before he cleared his throat awkwardly and said, "Captain, my wife tells me you came over to fuck her last night."

Captain Gringo's face went wooden Indian as he met Burton's gaze, unwinkingly, and said, "Oh?"

Burton laughed nervously, and said, "Yeah, she said you have a bigger prick than me and that you made her come. Ain't that a bitch?"

"Bitch was the exact word I was looking for."

Burton said, "I know. She over-did it with the part about coming. That had to be a lie even if you didn't have an alibi."

"I've got an alibi as well as a big prick?"

Burton winked and said, "Don't be coy. I happen to know who you were in bed with last night."

Captain Gringo didn't answer. Couldn't *any* woman on this fucking island keep her mouth shut? He wondered what the colonel was going to say about all this.

Burton winked again and said, "Yeah, Willie May spotted you leaving that Irish girl's room at the infirmary about the time Alice says you were humping her. I don't know why Alice plays these stupid games."

"She may be trying to get somebody killed. That's the usual reason. How come you and Willie May share so many cozy secrets? Uh, never mind, I don't think it's any of my business. I'll just tell Mab to be a bit more discreet in the future."

Burton said, "Look, we're not back home and Black stuff's not that bad."

Captain Gringo didn't answer. Alice was barking up the wrong tree, but he didn't owe her any favors now. Let

116

her think her old man was fooling with some mestizo if she wanted. It was kind of funny in a pathetic way. Willie May wasn't just darker than what would be approved of by Anglo-American Society. She had a pickle ass and her face would stop a clock.

As if he'd read the taller Yank's mind, Burton said, "The nigger wench is ugly, but she likes to screw, which is more than I can say for Alice. I knew she was shitting me even before Willie May told me about you and the nurse."

"You and Miss Willie May must have had a busy night."

"Oh, she wasn't spying on you and the nurse. We have a little love nest in the quarter, and she was on her way home across the green when she spotted you slipping out of the infirmary. She told me this morning on the docks about it. Alice, of course, was bragging about seducing you at breakfast."

Captain Gringo stared at the wall of jungle along the shore for a time before he shrugged and asked, "Why are you telling me all this, Burton?"

"Because I don't want to get beaten up or killed, of course. If I know Alice, her next move will be to tell you I know everything and that I'm in a towering rage. I don't want a guy your size worried about me coming after you and doing something foolish."

Captain Gringo frowned and said, "I'd be foolish indeed if I got excited about a husband with nothing to be jealous about."

"Oh shit, she isn't going to tell you she told me you'd fucked her. She'll probably say I accused her and blah blah blah. Knowing you're innocent, she'll expect you to get indignant and come gunning for me. How do you think we should work it out?"

Captain Gringo said, "Well, we'll be landing soon. I'll take my men and bull through a survey line. Meanwhile, you'll circle the island in this launch to pick us up on the far side. We ought to meet there at about the same time if I've judged the distances right."

"Damn it, I was talking about my wife."

"Yeah, *your* wife, not mine, thank God. I don't know why she's trying to sic us on each other either, but it's not my problem. My problem is to see how feasible my idea of a fortified cordon is. I'm in charge of security. You'll have to take charge of your wife."

So they dropped it for the time being, and in a little while the launch put into a preselected cove down the coast.

As Captain Gringo, Gordo, and three guards leaped ashore, Burton asked, "Are you sure you don't want me to tag along?"

Captain Gringo said, "We're not playing tag. I'm depending on you to meet us on the far side. It's a hell of a way to walk if you screw up."

"I'll be waiting for you there. I expected you to take at least one of the machine guns."

Captain Gringo hefted the Browning pump in his right hand and said, "Scatter guns are best in thick brush and a Maxim is too heavy to lug through this mess. We won't need the machine guns until we hack out a clear field of fire for them."

He hadn't come all this way to give a lecture on basic tactics, so he nodded to his men and said, "Let's go. See you later, Burton."

The shoreline was marshy. It didn't improve when they moved into the trees. Gordo ordered a man named José to go ahead with his machete, but the underbrush wasn't much of a problem once they left the sunny shore growth. The mud underfoot was sticky marl the color and consistency of half-congealed blood. Captain Gringo said, "José, bear to your left. This low ground's no good. We'll have to see if we can run a contour line to the far shore."

José didn't know what he was talking about, but he hacked through a vine and headed that way. Gordo asked what they were doing, and the American explained, "Nuevo Verdugo seems to be two anticlines, or let's say

118

gentle bulges, connected by this neck that can't make up it's mind if it's land or sea. If we clear our cordon along the slight slope to the north, they'll have to come at us wading through this shit. So while it means a little longer defense line than I had planned, it makes for a better one. We'll knock the trees down in this swamp while we're at it."

Gordo stared up at the sunlit forest canopy high above, and said, "Forgive me, my Captain, but I have cleared much land in my time. These trees are monstrous. It would take an army a year to cut through here as you wish."

Captain Gringo noticed the ground was getting firmer and he explained, "We're not going to do it with machetes, Gordo. You know those big steam tractors they use to plough the cane fields?"

"*Si*, they look like locomotives that have wandered from the tracks."

"They're almost as powerful, and God knows there's plenty of fuel standing all around here. I figure we'll attach a long length of anchor chain between them, build up a good head of steam in each, and let 'em rip. The chain should cut a good swathe as we drag it through here."

"You mean you intend to pull down all these trees by combing the jungle flat?"

"Sure. None of these trees have very deep roots and the ground is soft. We'll snake the logs to the shore with another tractor and let the current have what we can't use for firewood or lumber. A lot of logs will be used to fortify the machine gun nests, of course."

Gordo thought. Then he nodded with a grin and said, "I see how we can do it. I remember the company used tractors to pull stumps when we first started clearing. I wonder why they did not think of your idea with the chains?"

"Colonel Gage is all right. He just hasn't gotten used to the idea that the world no longer runs on muscle power the way it did when he was growing up. They were still screwing around with picks and shovels when I left Panama. They're going to need those new steam shovels before the Canal down there ever gets dug. But the world is run by old men, and old men cling to the ways they learned years ago. This has been a fast-moving century, Gordo. I'm only in my thirties and most of what they taught me at West Point is already out of date."

"Ah, but you obviously keep up with the times, no?"

"I try to. But I sure hope the coming twentieth century will move a little slower. I've just about got steam engines straight in my head, and some crazy German just invented something he calls an internal combustion engine."

"What on earth does it do, my Captain?"

"Beats the shit out of me. What's that funny smell?"

Gordo sniffed and called ahead to the machete man, "José, watch out for *las breas.*" Then Gordo told Captain Gringo, "There are tar pits here and there on the island, my Captain."

"You mean like that asphalt lake on Trinidad?"

"*Sí*, but not as big and useful. The tar pits of Trinidad furnish asphalt for to ship for money. We, alas, are not so fortunate. There are only scattered pools of the treacherous stuff. Sometimes livestock becomes mired and even lost. I stepped in one near the town once. It cost me a sandal and I couldn't get the tar off for a week."

José hacked through some brush and stopped to say, *"Mirar!* That is what has been making such a stink, my Captain."

Captain Gringo joined José and followed the direction of his pointing machete with his own eyes. A puddle of ink black, evil-smelling liquid nestled in a bigger patch of red mud. As he watched, a big black bubble farted more rotten egg and road tar fumes. The tar pool was small enough to jump across, but it made more sense to walk around it. So they did.

As they left it behind, Captain Gringo asked Gordo,

"Does the company know about these natural asphalt pools, Gordo?"

"Of course, my Captain. When Colonel Gage first learned of them he became excited about the possibilities of shipping tar as well as sugar. But, as I said, we are not as supplied with the muck as Trinidad. There is only enough to smell bad here and there. The British sent some geologists to look at the tar pits. They said there wasn't enough to be worth developing. The islanders sometimes use some for to patch a boat or fix a leak."

Captain Gringo nodded and put the idea aside for now. If there was enough natural asphalt to waterproof the earthworks he planned around each machine gun nest he'd use it. If there wasn't, he wouldn't. Once this red gumbo really dried it stayed pretty solid, even in the rain. That was another future problem for Pantropic Limited that he sure was glad he didn't have to worry about. This red-clay soil turned to solid brick and stayed that way if you farmed it wrong. But he'd been hired as an ordinance consultant, not an agricultural expert.

The jungle was getting darker and thicker now. José was working up a real sweat with his machete when Captain Gringo stopped him and said, "Hold it. I hear something."

The little survey party stopped and listened as the shadows on all sides throbbed softly to a primitive pulsation. Gordo said, "I hear them. They are Voodoo drums, my Captain."

The American tested the wind with a wet finger, saw there wasn't any, and said, "Yeah. I make 'em miles from here to the south. Let's move it out, José."

Gordo asked, "Don't you mean *back,* my Captain?"

"If I'd meant back I'd have said back. Burton and the others will be waiting for us up ahead. Those tom-toms only mean somebody's down that way making noise. We already knew the Black Caribs were all over the south end of the island, and I guess they can make noise if they want to. They have no way of knowing what we're doing here."

José pressed on, but Gordo said, "We can't be sure of that, my Captain. What if they have posted scouts? What if they are watching for us?"

"That's why we brought these pump guns. You point 'em, pull the trigger, and bang-bang, the number nine buck goes out the other end."

He saw the others were as uneasy as Gordo and added, "Look, guys, you're not supposed to wear those soldier suits if you're afraid of meeting strangers. Mamma Macamba's kiddies can't be watching the whole fucking jungle. So the odds of running into anyone who could take us is pretty slim. If any of you *do* spot an Indian scouting us, for God's sake, don't fire before I say to."

Gordo asked, "What if he spots us and is running away to tell the others, my Captain?"

"You let him go. A man only moves through this tanglewood at a slow trot. The sound of gunshots travel seven hundred miles an hour."

Gordo said, "Ah-ha! I see, my Captain. Before a scout could reach anyone we would have many minutes to be somewhere else in the meantime. But roving parties would head directly for the sound of gunshots without waiting for an invitation."

Gordo was learning. It was pretty basic I & R tactics, but at least he didn't have to be led by the hand. Captain Gringo wondered why none of the guards had been given any training in jungle warfare at all. All they knew how to do was salute, for God's sake. Burton admitted he wasn't a pro, but the colonel kept bullshitting about the Northwest Frontier and the Indian Army. Didn't he know you don't make soldiers on the parade ground? If these guys were a sample of British military thinking, the British Empire was in trouble.

The Romans had screwed up the same way, he remembered from his history lessons. Civilized troops tended to walk over less advanced people on first contact. But then everyone rested on their laurels and as the first Romans, or Redcoats, got old and dropped out, they were replaced by men like the colonel. Men who *talked* of a good fight.

Meanwhile the Gauls, Hindus, or whatever, raised *their* kids on bitterness and stories of the mistakes they'd made the first round. In the end the dismissed natives came back for another try, armed with better weapons and a lot of tactical homework. And then some guy like Webster or the colonel wound up with a spear up his ass, wondering what had gotten into the ruddy wogs.

He'd met officers like the colonel in his own army. The last fighting Apache had started reloading their own shells and digging trenches, when he left. But some jerk-offs at the Officer's Club still talked about Indians as if they were retarded children and worried more about brass buttons and dismounted drill.

He told José to blaze a tree from time to time as they moved on. The going was rough, but not impossible for the big spiked wheels of the steam tractors.

He was behind José, thinking about how to fasten the ends of the anchor chain to the hitch hooks of the tractors, when José made a funny little sound and dropped his machete.

Captain Gringo glanced up, saw José was going down in two pieces, and swung his Browning up to fire into the blank face of the naked black man coming at him!

The shotgun blast blew the attacker's face off and he fell slowly back across José's mangled body, with his legs still churning like an off-balance wind-up toy. Captain Gringo didn't wait to see if he landed that way. Another nude figure was charging from his right! He swung the Browning's muzzle and fired while Gordo yelled, "My God, the zombies!"

Captain Gringo saw the second one was still on his feet and still coming, with his midsection blown to hash, so he fired again. The zombi dropped his machete, turned around, and walked away, blood, or something as red, running from his shot-out eyes. As long as he was going somewhere else, Captain Gringo concentrated on two more zombies boring in out of nowhere, staring blankly at him while they came with upraised weapons. One had a machete. The other had a tree branch spiked with nails. He fired at the machete wielder first, swung the gun as he pumped, and blasted the one with the club. They both looked like they had been hit in the chest with raspberry pies, and neither one went down!

He pumped his weapon again and it clicked just like any other empty gun. There'd only been five rounds in the tube and he'd used them all!

He wondered why nobody else had fired, as he backed away from the oddly walking but determined-looking men he'd shot. He glanced around and saw he was alone. His men had simply cut and run.

It didn't seem like such a bad idea. There were others coming, all walking quietly, blank-faced, in no hurry, but obviously unstoppable with an empty gun!

So Captain Gringo headed north through the trees on the double, fumbling with his free hand for extra shotgun shells. He called out to Gordo. Gordo didn't answer, but a funny bird call did, and he cut to the side when he realized there were others ahead of him in the jungle.

He was over his first shock and thinking on his feet again. He didn't believe what he'd just seen, but he'd worry about it later. If the things chasing him weren't zombies, they sure *acted* like zombies. The only thing he seemed to have going for him was their odd, slow pace. They didn't run. They didn't dodge. So he decided to do as much running and dodging as he was capable of to put more distance between them.

A fallen forest giant lay across his chosen path to elsewhere. He vaulted lightly over it, landed, and sighed, "Aw shit!" He was stuck to his knees in warm black tar. He'd landed in another asphalt pit!

He felt himself sinking when he moved his feet to withdraw from the natural trap. He leaned back against the log he'd jumped to keep from sinking deeper and reloaded his Browning.

He pumped a round in the chamber and looked up. They were in a circle all around him now. He estimated there were about thirty of them. He had five 12 gauge and five .38 rounds to stop them and they took a hell of a lot of stopping. They closed in slowly. Not one of them looked like he had sense enough to tie his own shoes, if he'd worn shoes, but they probably weren't expecting him to be leaving in a hurry.

He cursed and tugged at the tar around his calves as he watched them coming. That odd detached part of the mind that notices details when the rest of us is going crazy wondered why they didn't look like his preconception of Black Caribs. They didn't look like jungle natives of any race. They were both Black and mestizo and seemed to be peones or common farm workers. *Dead* common farm workers. There was no trace of emotion in their slack-jawed faces as he raised the shotgun and shouted, "All right, that's far enough!"

They kept coming. Slowly, like people strolling through a market plaza and not sure what they'd come to buy. He raised his weapon and aimed at the nearest one's face to fire into the eyes. The gun kicked, the zombi's face dissolved in crimson horror, but he didn't fall. He just stood there, swaying, as if confused by the lights going out.

Captain Gringo muttered, "Jesus," and shot another one. He, or it, sank to his or its knees and stayed that way, staring, or rather, trying to, with part of the skull gleaming like wet ivory through red ribbons of shredded face and oozing gore.

It was like shooting ducks in a gallery and Captain Gringo had one boot almost free when he fired for a third time. His charge failed to stop that one and he had to fire again to put the zombi on the ground.

He had one shotgun round left, so he had to make it count before he switched to his pistol. He chose his target and aimed. But then something smashed into the back of Captain Gringo's skull and when he fired, he fired into pinwheeling stars. The blow drove his half-free foot deeper into the tar and it seemed as if the tar was spreading and spreading and, when he dropped the shotgun, he followed it down and down into a spreading sea of tar black darkness.

Chapter Nine

It was hard to sleep with all that noise going on. Captain Gringo tried to turn over in bed and block it out. But he couldn't turn and he realized he wasn't in bed or even laying down. So he opened his eyes.

That seemed like a terrible mistake, but as his aching head cleared he kept his eyes open anyway. He was tied upright to a post in a firelit clearing. The sky above was pitch black, so he knew he'd been out for hours. The noise was coming from a nearby drum and the naked people squatting in a circle around him looked more like his idea of Black Caribs. They had nothing on but strings of seashells and mahogany skin oiled with butter or something. Their features were more Indian than Negroid but one guy had kinky hair, with what looked like a human femur through his top knot. Whoever was whamming the drum was behind Captain Gringo, out of his line of vision. He was facing what seemed to be the mouth of a cave in a low cliff of coral rock. The natives seemed to be expecting something to come out of the cave. They apparantly hadn't invited the zombies to the show, whatever it was to be. Captain Gringo glanced down. He still had on his pants and tarred boots. They hadn't piled brush around the post, so they weren't going to burn him at the stake at least. They'd ripped off his jacket, shirt, and shoulder rig. A damned mosquito was taking advantage of his bare chest and he saw other bites. They itched like hell, but he was in no position to scratch. His hands were bound tightly to his sides. He bent his knees to see if the stake had any give. It didn't. He was stuck here until somebody cut him loose. None of his captors looked like they planned to.

Somebody must have signaled that he was conscious. The drum beat changed and the natives stared expectantly into the dark opening in the pale gray rock. Captain Gringo did, too. There was a teasing delay, then a figure moved out into the ruddy firelight and the natives gasped in awe. Captain Gringo gasped, too. He hadn't expected a naked lady wrapped in the biggest fucking snake in the world.

She was a tall, shapely, jet black Negress with her head and everything else smooth shaven. Her ebony body had been oiled to gleam like patent leather and it contrasted starkly with the big boa constrictor coiled around her. She had the snake gripped just below its head, and it was hissing at her and darting its tongue as she blew in its face teasingly. He noticed she missed a beat while she half-pranced in place to the beat of the drum. She dug her nails into the snake with her free hand and adjusted the snake's coil lower, over a hip bone. The monster was trying to squeeze the breath out of its tormenting mistress, but she knew how to handle it. It couldn't crush her ribs if she didn't let it get purchase. The boa's tail thrashed in the dust around her dancing feet as it tried to find something to wrap around for leverage. The dance was more than show business. She was avoiding a coil around an ankle.

A male voice from someone he couldn't see started chanting in a language he couldn't understand. The tall black priestess swayed closer and their eyes met when she held the boa's ugly head up to him as if for his approval. He said, "It's swell. Now why don't you put the fucking thing away?"

The chanting and drumming got wilder. So did the colored lady with the snake. She spread her feet and writhed sensually as she ran the snake's head over her oiled naked flesh. One of the squatting Caribs was masturbating unself-consciously while he watched her, sweat beading his brow. Captain Gringo didn't find her act as sexy. It was too perverse. The priestess teased her own nipples with the boa's darting tongue. The crowd seemed to be eating it up.

The woman was actually fighting with the creature now, and she was obviously as strong as most men. The tormented snake was mad as hell and trying to crush her, but she moved too cleverly and her skin was too greasy for the boa to really get a grip on her. She slid the head down her belly, thrust her pelvis forward, and slid the boa's head between her greased thighs as the crowd gasped. It was too quick to be sure whether she'd really shoved it in her or not, but as she repeated the motion it looked like she was screwing herself with a fourteen foot boa constrictor, and enjoying it!

The snake didn't like it at all. It was hissing and snapping its jaws, and since Captain Gringo knew the thing had *some* teeth, even if it wasn't venomous, her act had to be a fake. That big boa *really* wanted to eat pussy, and the rest of her too!

The male chanter he couldn't see suggested something new, and the big black priestess moved closer to him. The drum beats stopped and she sank to her knees in front of Captain Gringo, the boa coiled around her hips, and she held the head out in an attitude of prayer. Then he grasped what the next act was and said, "Hey, I liked it better the other way. Now you're *really* getting dirty!"

The boa sensed freedom as it slid forward through her oiled palms. It darted its tongue out to touch Captain

Gringo's knee. Then it slid around and around, and as it unwound from the black girl's hips, it started climbing him and his post like a stripe going up a barber pole!

He struggled to free at least a hand, for God's sake. He could see a strong adult could wrestle a boa, with hands free to shift the coils. But he was helpless. The snake and everyone else knew that. The naked woman rose to her feet to step back, hands on hips, to watch. She was a beautiful animal, but Captain Gringo couldn't remember anyone he'd ever hated as much as he did her right now.

The boa slithered up him and he tried not to flinch as its oddly cool beaded skin caressed his naked torso and bound arms. Maybe if he held very still the fucker would mistake him for a tree?

It didn't. They'd starved as well as teased this stand-in for Mambo Jumbo and he knew now how it was supposed to go. The symbolism was all too obvious. First Mamma Macamba shows everyone the snake god is her lover and then she feeds somebody to him! The coils were tightening and it was hard to breathe as Mambo Jumbo rose ever higher for a better look at his meal to be. Captain Gringo tried to gain a little breathing space by moving his elbows out against the constricting coils. The boa tightened its grip painfully, but he could just barely inhale until his arms gave, and that didn't figure to be long. The night was young and nobody was in a hurry. The naked slut watching from a safe distance probably enjoyed a long last act. He wondered how often they'd done this to others. How often did you have to feed a snake, and where the hell was Mambo Jumbo going to put him? The boa was as big around as a man's thigh, but could it open its mouth that wide?

Apparently the snake wondered too. It raised its ugly head to his and started exploring his face with its darting tongue. The desperate and enraged American knew he was done for, but, damn it, if they wanted him dead they'd have to do it right. He wasn't about to be swallowed whole by a fucking animated sausage!

He pulled his head back against the pole behind him. The snake moved in to close the gap. Captain Gringo's head shot forward, teeth red in the firelight, and snapped like a trapped wolf. It even surprised him when he bit down hard on the snake's head, and found himself chewing!

The boa contracted like a vise as it tried to pull its head out of Captain Gringo's mouth. He felt his mouth fill with salty God-awful and sawed his jaw back and forth until things started to give. The Black priestess moved forward but froze as the headless end of the boa whipped away from Captain Gringo's face to hose her with spurting blood. The natives were on their feet and shouting as the big snake settled in twitching coils around his ankles. Then Captain Gringo spit the head out, bouncing it off one of the woman's proud black breasts as he snarled, "You dropped something, bitch!"

Naturally, they were going to kill him nasty now. But they'd already been killing him nasty, so what the hell.

But the big black woman held up her hand and started yelling in her native lingo. Some of the others didn't like it much, but she seemed to be the boss. So a Carib cut the thongs binding him to the pole while the priestess said, in perfect English, "If you value your life don't make a move. Are you listening?"

"Gotcha. What's the play?"

"Just follow me. Don't look right. Don't look left. Let's go."

She turned and headed for the cave entrance. He stepped away and staggered after her, stiff as hell. A Carib spit at him, but he just kept going until the two of them were in the cave mouth, and he noticed none of the natives followed. He wondered if they knew something he didn't.

The bald black girl parted some hanging curtains and he found himself alone with her in a chamber furnished with woven matting on the sand floor and some cotton pillows on a ledge. A big basket stood in one niche

131

and the place smelled like snake. He grabbed the girl, threw her on the floor and sat on her, growling, "Answers. Fast. Or I'll kick the shit out of you!"

"I *had* to do it!" She pleaded. "For God's sake, I just saved you!"

"After you wrapped a fucking snake around me? Who do you think you're kidding? Who the hell are you? Where did you learn to speak English?"

"You're hurting me. My name used to be Prudence Lee and I'm an American like you."

"You're the weirdest American I've ever met, and I'm not talking about your complexion! You're Mamma Macamba, right?"

"Yes. I just told them that your magic was even stronger than Mambo Jumbo's. With luck I may be able to convince them I need you as my bodyguard."

"Bodyguard, huh?" He mused, suddenly aware that he was sitting on a naked woman and keyed up almost to the point of hysteria. He started to unbuckle his belt and said, "Okay, let's start by seeing how good a body you want me to guard."

"For God's sake, I'm a virgin!"

That was the wrong thing to say. Captain Gringo was pissed, but he'd never raped anyone before and almost anything else she could have said would have stopped him. But this was too much. Whoever she was and whatever her story, she was still shitting him.

Mamma Macamba struggled, and she was strong. So he slapped her face and said, "I mean it. I'll punch your teeth out. I don't know what your game is, but I'm going to have one last lay before I die."

"I don't want to, damn it!"

"I know you don't. That's why I'm going to enjoy it."

The gummed-up boots were a problem, so he simply got his pants down around his knees, pinned her wrist when she tried to shove him off, and forced her to open her thighs as she closed her eyes and started crying. He said, "Shit, shy tears from a bitch who just jerked-off with a fourteen foot snake?"

"I used to be a missionary," she sobbed as he entered her. He growled back, "Don't worry, we're starting with the missionary position."

She gasped as he entered her to the hilt. He was sort of surprised too. She was as tight as a frightened teen-ager despite her muscular, almost man-sized torso. He settled his naked heaving chest against her eggplant breasts and moved a little more gently as he frowned and said, "This is crazy. You really do feel like cherry."

"Hurry and satisfy yourself if you must," she sighed in resignation, as she added, "they'll kill us both if anyone sees me like this. Can't you see the only hold I have over them is awe?"

He knew he'd made a mistake. But he was halfway there with a beautiful woman and she was unconsciously moving her hips to help him. He pounded harder and exploded in her before he said, "Okay, you're not a bitch, but this is still weird as hell. I'll stop if you want."

But she murmured, "Wait. Don't. The damage is done and something is happening and . . . oh, do it some more."

So he did. But he beat her again to a climax and she said, "I don't think I can respond. Those cannibals outside make me so nervous and it really is my first time."

He laughed and said, "They make *you* nervous? I thought you were queen of the whole shabang, Mamma."

"I wish you'd call me Prue. Before you threw me down and leaped on me, I was about to explain this mess to you. Do you have a name, by the way?"

"Call me Dick. I'll be good."

As he rolled off, Prue sat up with a Mona Lisa expression on her dark face, and said, "We'll see about being good together after we get out of here."

"There's a way out?"

"Yes and no, Dick. I can get us out of this chamber. This cave runs back under the hills for miles. But I've been afraid to make a break for it alone. Now that you're here ... come on, pull those silly pants up and I'll show you."

He did what she asked but he frowned at her thoughtfully and asked, "Are you really going to help me escape, Prue?"

She said, "Of course, if you'll help *me*. Did you really think I was here of my own free will?"

The fact that the Afro-American girl hadn't tried to escape on her own made more sense as Prue led him through the dank maze behind her living quarters. They both had torches, though she hadn't risked trying to get his guns back. So he could see the mouse-sized cockroaches and the moldy bat shit all over everything. The bats tended to flutter ahead of their approaching lights, but they sounded big as eagles. He asked Prue if there were snakes living in the caverns and she said she didn't think so. He didn't see why any snake in its right mind would want to either.

Running water had riddled the limestone like swiss cheese but Prue seemed to know where she was going as she guided him around corners and over fallen slabs of slimy rock. She said she'd explored a bit, trying to get up her nerve to escape, and he noticed the smoke smudges on the roof.

The cave system was a big one and as they wound through it Prue had time to tell him her story, weird as it was.

Miss Prudence Lee had been sent down to the Mosquito Coast by a Black Baptist congregation in Baltimore on a mission to the less frantic West Indians working on the Panama Canal. One gathered they were living in Papist error, and Prue had intended to convert them to well-scrubbed, sober Protestants. Her ship had run into a hurricane before breaking its back on the reefs off Nuevo Verdugo. The strong athletic missionary had been the only one to make it ashore.

The Black Caribs pulled her half-drowned body

134

from the breakers, and she'd thought at first they meant to eat her. They may have thought so too. But Mamma Macamba had had other ideas.

Captain Gringo said, "Wait a minute. I thought you were Mamma Macamba, Prue."

She sat on a rock to rest as she explained, "I am now. Or I was until a few minutes ago. You see, Dick, Mamma Macamba is immortal."

"Honey, I don't see shit."

"Let me finish. I was shipwrecked nearly five years ago. The woman who *was* then Mamma Macamba knew she was dying. Cancer, I think. Jungle medicine isn't as exact as people assume. Anyway, she took a fancy to me because I fit her picture of what a proud priestess should look like. I was her captive and she let me know it, painfully, the first time I tried to run away."

He nodded and said, "I get it, now. She taught you the lingo and trained you as her replacement."

"Yes. You know the rest, Dick."

"The hell I do. When did this other Mamma Macamba die and leave you her business?"

"A year or so ago, I think. It's so hard to keep track of the time with no calendar or watch."

"Never mind exact dates then. The Pantropic Sugar Trust has been having a war with you during your time at bat. How do you explain a nice little missionary gal leading all those attacks? We'll get to the spooky parts later."

She said, "Don't you see I'm just a figurehead, Dick? I don't *run* the tribe. I'm their, well, good luck piece or juju. I don't even know half of what's been going on. I understand there are civilized people living somewhere on the island, but I've been afraid, until now, to try and reach them."

He saw she was about to start crying again. So he wedged their two torches in a cleft and sat beside her to comfort her. He said, "I'll buy that, honey. But if Mamma Macamba is just a figurehead, who in blazes *runs* the outfit?"

"Brujos, witch doctors call themselves brujos down here."

"I know that. Are you saying there's a sort of witch doctor clique directing things? Okay, who's the head spook? Does he have a name?"

She shuddered in his arms and said, "Yes. They call him Pappa Blanco. I've never seen him; he doesn't attend ceremonies. He's said to live alone somewhere in the jungle and the others go to consult with him. He's the one who makes zombies out of our enemies. Or I should say, the Caribs' enemies now. Jesus, Dick, what if they catch us and turn us into zombies?"

"We'll be very upset. Get back to Pappa Blanco. Blanco means White. What's a white man doing playing witch doctor, and why is everyone talking baby talk? Caribs have their own native language, don't they?"

"Of course. But these have been converted to Macamba, and Macamba uses Spanish, French, English, and African words, just like the Catholics use Latin. I don't think Pappa Blanco is a white man. I've never heard of a white Macamba priest. He paints his face white. They say he looks like a grinning skull, and even the other witch doctors are afraid of Pappa Blanco."

"He's making *me* a little nervous, too. What can you tell me about his zombies?"

She shuddered again and said, "They're horrible. They say Pappa Blanco gets them from the graveyards of the Christians. He says it's better to let them lead the skirmish lines so that real warriors won't face bullets until the other side is confused and backing off."

Captain Gringo grimaced and said, "Great idea. But how the hell do you suppose he *does* it?"

"I don't know, Dick. I was only taught a few simple tricks. I know you think I was horrid with that snake, but I didn't know what else I could do and . . ."

"Forget it. It was me or you, and you thought fast when you saw a chance to bail me out. Pappa Blanco's not a snake charmer or a simple stage magician. He's on to something really evil."

She said, "I know. It's wrong to disturb the dead."

"Wrong? Hell, it's impossible. They've somehow shanghaid a bunch of derelicts and I'm starting to feel lousy about how I smoked the poor guys up, but, like you, I didn't have much choice."

"You mean they are not from the graveyard in town, Dick?"

"I doubt it like hell. But I'm sure going to check that out when we get back to town."

The mention of town reminded Prue of something. She said, "Oh Lord. I've gotten used to going stark naked since I washed up among folks who do it all the time. But what are folks going to say when they see a white man walking out of the bush with a naked nigger gal?"

"We'll find a fig leaf or something. The more important gossip is liable to be among the neighbors we just left. How long do you figure we have before they miss us, Prue?"

She shrugged and said, "I don't know. Nobody is supposed to come in the cave of Mamma Macamba and Mambo Jumbo. But you sure made a mess of that snake. None of the common Caribs will dare to peek, but . . ."

"Yeah, the witch doctors will wonder how you're getting along with Mambo Jumbo's unexpected replacement. Who was thumping that drum and, which way was he headed the last time you noticed? I couldn't see the bastard."

Prue said, "Oh, him. He was just a second class bad nigger. The others lit out someplace just before you woke up. You understand that sacrifice wasn't my notion, don't you, honey?"

"We've settled that. Keep going."

"Well, when they brought you in, knocked out and trussed like a pig on a pole, the priesthood started to get ready to fix you good, and told me to get cracking. But then a runner came in and they said to start without them. I think Pappa Blanco wanted them for a more important gathering."

"That makes sense. My friends are probably looking

for me and he's planning a reception for them. We'd better get moving, Prue. Even if we haven't been missed yet, I've got to reach my guys before they walk into something nasty."

He helped her to her feet, got the torches, and took the lead now that he had the smoke trail figured out. He asked her what the odds were that others knew of the far exit, and she said there were dozens of entrances and exits to the cavern complex. Apparently a big, pie wedge of coral had been shoved up out of the sea and eroded into a real puzzle under its cap rocks. He figured if they could get well away before daylight they had a chance. A pretty slim chance, but what the hell. Trying to shake off born jungle trackers on their own ground, unarmed and saddled with a frightened girl, beat the odds he'd faced just a few minutes ago with that fucking snake.

Chapter Ten

Daybreak found them on the marshy neck in the middle
of the peanut-shaped island. Prue said she felt silly being
stark naked now that they were almost home free. Captain Gringo said they were far from home free and the
nearest spur of the rail system was a good six or eight
miles ahead. But the erstwhile missionary picked some
plantana leaves and began to shred them for a skirt as
they walked on. Captain Gringo said he was hungry as a
bitch wolf and suggested she keep an eye peeled for
something to eat as well as wear. He'd shared some sour
sops they'd spotted at dawn with Prue, and while they'd
eased his thirst they hadn't stuck to his ribs. She said
there were avocado growing wild in the jungle and he said
it would be her job to find some. He had to watch the
ground. He didn't want to step in any more tar pits.

He'd shed the gummed-up boots and rolled the tarred bottoms of his pants up to his knees. So while he
could walk better, he was getting his shins cut up by the
underbrush. They had no machete and he had to bull

through in the lead, sparing Prue's long naked legs the wear and tear. She asked him why he didn't look for a trail and he said, "Trails are where you meet folks, honey. Do you want to meet anyone without so much as a club in your hand?"

She shuddered and replied, "Pappa Blanco will be awfully angry when he finds us gone."

"Yeah. So far I don't hear any drums. Let's hope he's a late sleeper."

Oddly, the light was better in the jungle at such an early hour. The low sun lanced through the tree trunks instead of trying to penetrate the dense overhead canopy. But it was still pretty murky.

They were near the area where he'd been jumped the day before. Captain Gringo told Prue to watch her step, and when he heard the loud buzzing of blue bottles he headed that way. Behind him Prue sniffed and said, "Something sure smells dead around here."

They were both right. He found what was left of his machete man, José, half under a bush and completely covered with flies. The zombies had been carried off, if they hadn't walked, but José had been left to rot.

Prue grimaced and said, "Oh, he's all icky. Don't touch him." But Captain Gringo said, "Move back and weave your skirt or something. I'm hoping *they* thought he was icky, too."

José had been hacked up some more since Captain Gringo had last seen him and the blue bottles swarming on the shredded flesh and bloody rags didn't do a thing to make José more appetizing. Captain Gringo took a deep breath, bent down, and rolled the mess over. Then he grinned and said, "Jesus, even better!"

He rose, holding José's shotgun and said, "I was hoping they'd overlooked his machete. He fell on his Browning and that puts us back in business. Hold this. I have to see if he has any spare ammo in his pockets."

The girl grimaced but took the shotgun while Captain Gringo knelt again, muttering, "Sorry, José," and started going through the dead man's clothes. He found a

140

couple of 12 gauge shells and a small gold cross. He sighed and said, "I'll see this gets to your family, kid. I'd bury you if I had a shovel and the time, but I don't have either, and what the hell, you wanted to be a soldier."

He got to his feet putting the shells and cross in his own pocket, and Prue said, "This gun's all icky, too."

He took it from her and said, "Only on the outside, where it doesn't count. I'll wipe it off with leaves or something. For a girl who plays with snakes you sure are getting delicate all of a sudden."

He led them on, Prue resuming work on her grass skirt while she walked, saying, "It's not the same. Besides, I'm already starting to feel like it was all a nightmare. I can't believe I spent all that time with a mess of bad bush niggers. Do you suppose they had me drugged or something?"

"You were acting pretty wild last night. They might have been spiking your food, but I think it was just propinquity. We all tend to act like the folks around us. Sometimes I catch myself acting more like a Latin American bandito than a West Point graduate. In a couple of months you'll be wearing new hair and a dress and feeling like a missionary again."

She said, "That doesn't seem possible either. But things are coming back to me. We're both American and once we get out of this mess we'll remember that you're white and I'm black and that . . . Jesus, you *touched* me, Dick! What kind of missionary gal fools around with white meat?"

"White missionary gals? Relax, honey. We're a long way from Baltimore, even when we reach Utopiaton."

"I know, but are you sure you want to have a black gal as your own there?"

He didn't answer. She wouldn't understand if he said he didn't want to be saddled with any *gal* on a regular basis. Aside from limiting his freedom, it would be rough on any woman to be tied in with a drifting renegade with a price on his head. Prue didn't press him. She was thinking of the snubs she'd been raised on back in the

141

States. She was wondering, too, if she really wanted to be known as a white man's pretty plaything. Her mamma had said dreadful things about that yellow gal everyone knew a white streetcar conductor was keeping.

They were over halfway to civilization now and the ground was firmer underfoot. He bulled through a bank of fern and stopped. Prue joined him in the waist-deep fern and said, "Oh, isn't it pretty?"

They'd come to a clear crystal spring set in a little Eden where the sun shafted down to warm the water and white sand all around.

The trees and bushes around the spring were free of the slimy moss of the deeper jungle. He spotted the smooth copper bark of gumbo limbo and licorice-scented umbrella trees. There were sugar apples and sour sops. Best of all, a couple of native avocado. He walked around the water's edge and reached up to pick some of the alligator-skinned fruit, saying, "These feel ripe, and the oil in them will, make us feel like we've really eaten something more solid than sweet goo."

Prue laughed and said, "I'll still have sour sop for dessert. This is such a lovely place, Dick. Can we stay here and rest a while?"

He started to shake his head. Then he shrugged and said, "I guess we can use a break. We'll rest half an hour or so and then make a beeline for the rail spur I told you about."

Prue threw her grass skirt down and waded into the pool with an avocado in each hand. She sat down in the water and said, "Oh, this feels heavenly. Lord knows I needed a bath. Why don't you join me?"

He leaned the shotgun against a kapok trunk, shucked off his pants, and splashed out to her. As he neared her she lowered her eyes and stammered, "Oh, I didn't mean naked."

He hunkered down into the water and took a bite of buttery avocado before he grinned and said, "You're being silly. You've been running bare ass through the woods for years."

142

"Women are different. They don't have those old *things* waving about so wickedly."

He said, "Hell, it's out of sight and out of mind." He put an arm around her and pulled her closer, adding, "Out of sight, anyway. You shouldn't have reminded me of how we first met."

She didn't really resist as she murmured, "I wish you'd stop. I've sort of left that back there with the Caribs, too. I'm a *missionary,* damn it."

"Well, let's pretend we're Adam and Eve in the Good Book. This time I killed the serpent and we don't know shame, right?"

She laughed and said, "Those serpents sure did mess things up for everybody, didn't they? It would be awfully nice if this was really Eden and we were really Adam and Eve, but . . ."

"But me no buts, Miss Eve. In the here and now of Eternity we're all alone in the Garden and maybe this time we'll do it right. God knows that other pair sure messed things up."

"I know. If this was real instead of 'let's pretend', what kind of a world would you build, Dick?"

"Call me Adam. I think I'd start by getting rid of mosquitos. God said we had Dominion and had to name everything. So let's just not bother with having mosquitos. We'd better not have lawyers or poison ivy, either. Your turn."

Prue snuggled against him dreamily and sighed, "I'd have everybody speak the same language and there'd only be one race and nationality."

"Black English-speaking Protestants?"

Prue laughed and said, "Pooh, I could do better than that if it was up to me. I think from now on everybody should be a nice shade of lavender. Lavender is my favorite color. We'd all start out even if everyone was lavender. Then maybe I wouldn't feel so mixed up about you and me."

He glanced up at the sky, saw it was still early, and threw his fruit away. He took her in his arms and kissed

143

her. Prue resisted as their clean wet flesh pressed together in the crystal water, and then she sighed, wrapped her arms around him, and opened her thighs as he faced her, kneeling on the sandy bottom. He slid a hand down her spine, cupped her tailbone in his palm with two fingers between her slippery black buttocks, and pulled her on to his underwater erection. Her eyes popped open as she gasped, "Oh, it's so *cold,* this time!"

Then she started going crazy and he was worried about drowning until he'd worked them into the shallows, where he could lay her flat on her back to do it right. She laughed aloud and said, "This is shameful! We're wallowing like hogs in the mud, but I don't ever want to stop!"

So they shared her first real orgasm, splashing like hell, and then he moved her up on the bank to do it some more as they dried off in the sunlight. By the time he'd sated himself, Prue was regaining her sanity and he thought when she started to cry again that she wanted him to stop. But as he half withdrew she hugged him to her damp dark breasts and crooned, "Don't move. Just hold me. I feel so happy I could just die. Listen, darling. My heart is beating so hard I can *hear* it! Can you?"

He cocked his head and said, "Yeah, but that's not your heart we're listening to, it's *drums!*"

Prue stiffened and said, "Oh my God, you're right! That's a cursing drum!"

"Never mind its manners. I make it two or three miles off, due south. We'd better get out of here. Pappa Blanco knows we've left home and wants us back."

He rolled off and shucked on his pants as Prue got to her feet and tied on her skirt of shredded leaves. As he scopped up the shotgun, she said, "That drum is aimed at *me,* Dick. I've heard them do that before. That Pappa Blanco is *mad.*"

"Come on. We've got a good lead. Screw the drums. Listen for branches breaking *closer.* Like I said, the drum is too far off to hurt us."

144

As he led out, Prue sobbed, "You don't understand, Dick. That's a Macamba *curse* they're sending after me."

"Prue, you don't buy any of that Voodoo crap, do you?"

She shuddered and said, "I don't know what I believe anymore, Dick. I've seen things that both science and the Good Book says can't happen. That beat is aimed to draw my soul back to Pappa Blanco. I feel scared and all watery inside."

"Oh shit, you've been swimming and you've just been laid. It's natural to feel weak in the knees at a time like this, even without a mess of cannibals and zombies chasing you. You'll be all right in a minute, doll."

He was wrong. Prue followed him another half mile before she sank to her knees and sobbed, "I can't go on. I have to go back. The drums are pulling and pulling at me and I can't hardly breathe."

He stopped and faced the sound of distant drums. He knew it was useless to argue. The civilized part of her mind would agree that superstition only worked on people who believed in it. But Prue had been part of that tribal bullshit for a good five years. As a Voodoo priestess, albeit an unwilling one, she'd picked up a lot of Voodoo, Macamba, or whatever. *He* still felt pretty shaky about those fucking zombies, however they worked. Prue had seen as much and more, and hadn't been as well educated as him to start. At best she'd washed ashore with a high school education, long on theology and short on science. This was no time to lecture her on auto suggestion.

He bent down and hauled her to her feet, saying, "Come on. I'll carry you piggyback. But you'll have to hold on so I can have my hands free with this gun."

She sobbed, "Leave me, Dick. I know I'm done for, but at least *you* can get away."

"Are you going to get on my back or not, damn it?"

"Honey, you can't burden yourself with me. Face it, Dick. You're nice, for a white man, but I'm only . . . "

145

He slapped her face and said, "Shut up, you mixed-up, pretty idiot. We'll talk about feelings of inferiority later. Right now, two *human beings* have to haul ass *out* of here!"

Prue covered her face with her hands and began to bawl, hysterically. He muttered, "Shit," bent, and picked her up to carry head down over his left shoulder as he made tracks, packing the Browning in his free right hand. Prue was a big gal and he knew Gaston would chide him for not being *"Practique"*. The rules of the game called for leaving the wounded and weak behind. But rules were made to be broken and he'd never forgive himself if he let *anyone* fall into the hands of those weird witch doctors.

Prue gasped, "I can't breathe!" as he lugged her through the jungle head down. He didn't answer. His own breaths were too short to waste on idle chitchat right now. He wasn't making good time with the big Negress slowing him down. Her hips blocked his vision to the left and he had to swing his whole body that way from time to time to guarantee not being jumped from that direction.

He cut a foot on something but kept bulling through. Branches whipped his face and Prue's bare bottom, and if they stepped in a tar pit that would be that. He was staggering on half-blind.

Another drum began to throb, closer and off to one side. He asked Prue what it was, and she gasped, "Directions. That's a talking drum."

"Do you know what it's saying?"

"Dick, I was reared in Baltimore. How am I to know what a fool Ibo drum is saying? I understand Carib and some Spanish. The inner circle powwows in West Africa lingoes. I reckon that talking drum is talking about us, but I don't know what it's saying."

Captain Gringo stopped, lowered Prue to her feet, sighed and said, "I do. It said to head us off."

He pumped a shell in the Browning's chamber as Prue screamed and pointed to the long ragged line of figures ahead. He wondered what else was new. They weren't the graceful shell-draped Caribs he'd been hoping not to run into. They were ragged-ass zombies. He hadn't wanted to run into them either.

He said, "Let's study this. Those whatevers don't move fast. We can outrun them. The question is which way to run."

Prue sank down to her knees again and covered her face. He muttered, "Oh shit," and glanced back the way they'd come. There was nobody there. But that was obviously the way Pappa Blanco figured they'd be heading. The innocent trees might as well have had AMBUSH painted on them in big red letters.

He nudged Prue as the zombies sleepwalked toward them and said, "*Listen* to me, damn it! I've got their tactics figured, even if I don't know how the details work. We have to blast through that skirmish line. None of them have any weapons but machetes and clubs. Pappa Blanco saves the good stuff for people who know what they're doing."

"Dick, I'm so frightened! I can't look at them!"

"So close your eyes. Hang on to my belt and, for Pete's sake, stay on your feet. I'm going to bust through a thin spot I hope I'm right about."

She didn't make a move to help herself. He swore, yanked her to her feet, and put her hand in place around his belt. Then he said, "Hang on, damn it," and moved forward to meet the zombies.

He saw they were starting to slowly close ranks as he headed for what had been a break in their line. He drifted sideways, looking for another while, beyond the zombies, he heard another throbbing sound. He growled, "Damn," but they were committed now. The nearest zombi was an almost white mestizo, holding a club. Captain Gringo said, "We're coming through, friend. If you can hear me at all, get the fuck out of our way."

The mestizo stared, slack-jawed, then slowly raised his club. Captain Gringo shot him in the face and ignored him as he staggered on, blind, thrashing the club in front of him. Captain Gringo crabbed to one side and got past the first one. Zombi number two was a Negro with a machete and wide, staring eyes. Captain Gringo blew his face off and cut the other way to avoid the blind rush. That was when Prue let go of his belt and fell sobbing to the jungle floor.

The Negro with the machete was bearing down on her, zeroing in on the sound of her sobs whipping his machete back and forth at waist level. Captain Gringo overhauled him and smashed the butt plate of his weapon into the base of the blinded zombi's skull. That did it. He went down near Prue, with his legs still moving mindlessly. Captain Gringo grabbed Prue's arm and hauled her upright while she babbled, "Oh, Lord have mercy!" and he said, "Shit!" They were circled now, so any way out was as good or bad. He only had three shells in the magazine. He dragged the hysterical girl after him and picked out a likely target, waited this time until they were almost in contact, and fired into the machete-swinging zombi's face. He was getting the hang of it now. A full charge of number nine buck at point-black range makes an awesome hash out of any skull, alive or dead, and the thing went down. He hauled Prue through the gap and yelled, "Move your Goddamned *feet!*"

Again they almost broke free and again Prue fell helplessly to her hands and knees, and this time if he didn't leave her he was done for. He turned, fumbling to reload the shotgun while they closed in on him from every side, and the drumlike sound from the north drew ever nearer. Someone was singing in time to the oddly metallic beat, and Captain Gringo's jaw dropped as he made out the words. Someone was singing, *"Marchon, marchon, aux Liberté . . ."*

It was Gaston, singing the Marseillaise off key to the chugging of a steam engine!

Captain Gringo picked Prue up and held her by the waist like a big football and charged to meet the sounds that made little more sense than anything else around here. He fired into a zombi's guts just as it grabbed the barrel of the shotgun and wrenched it from his grasp.

Then he saw trees parting like the Red Sea before Moses, and it really was Gaston, perched atop a monstrous steam tractor, holding a machine gun while Gordo drove.

Gaston spotted him and the girl at the same time and opened up with the Maxim. Not at them, of course, but at the zombies snapping at their heels. Gordo stopped the tractor and Captain Gringo shoved Prue up over the eight foot wheels and Gordo grabbed her other end without being told. Something clutched at Captain Gringo from behind. He kicked and started climbing while Gaston fired the machine gun over his shoulder and spattered him with hot, spent brass. And then they were all up between the wheels on the locomotive-like platform and he snatched the gun from Gaston, saying, "You drive and I'll shoot. I thought you were supposed to be in bed."

Gaston said, "I was, until Gordo staggered in to tell us the Caribs had you." He shoved Gordo away from the controls to say, "Attend this lady, who may be on our side. Where are we going, Dick?"

"Head toward those drums."

Gaston nodded and opened the throttle, swinging the big front wheels to run over a zombi as Captain Gringo peppered a couple too close for comfort, but said, "Forget these guys. None of them have guns. The sons of bitches we want are using them as a screen and I think they're over that way!"

Gaston shrugged, said, "Spoilsport," and ran over another zombi with the spiked wheels, and smashed a tree at the same time. The tractor was slower than the locomotive it resembled, but it still moved a good six miles an hour, and Prue, down on the deck plates with Gordo, was safe for the moment. They had left the skirmishing zombies behind before Gaston asked, laconically, "Who were those gentlemen back there, Dick?"

"I'm still working on that one. Watch out for real stuff. I've been wondering what happened to the guns and ammo they must have retrieved from all those raids. The Caribs have the usual witch doctors, but I smell a white man leading them."

From the floor, Prue protested, "Pappa Blanco is supposed to be a Macamba man, Dick."

"Sure he is. Only you've never seen him and these tactics are too neat for primitive tribesmen to dope out all by themselves."

Gaston asked, "Who is Pappa Blanco, and, while we are on the subject, who is this colored lady, Dick?"

"She's Mamma Macamba, née Prudence Lee from Baltimore. Miss Lee, may I present Gaston Verrier, late of the French Legion? How did you get Mab to let you out of bed, Gaston?"

"Mab? Ah, you mean the red-headed Irish nurse. She apparently left yesterday on the steamer."

"What do you mean apparently, Gaston? Did Mab leave or didn't she?"

"One must take certain things on faith, *hein*. Willie May, the black head nurse, said Miss O'Shay seemed upset by the primitive conditions and other perplexing qualities about this island. So, since she is not at the infirmary, one can assume she left on the steamer. I know *I* would leave on a steamer, if I had any place at all to go. *Regardez* those bushes over to your right, Dick."

Captain Gringo fired into the oddly swaying shrubbery and the clump exploded into running Caribs. One knelt to aim the rifle he was packing, but a second burst blew him to red froth. A bullet spanged in return off the big rear wheel at Captain Gringo's side. He elevated the Maxim to put a burst in the umbrella tree where he'd spotted gunsmoke drifting through the leaves. A tawny body fell limply out of the treetop to vanish with a big wet thump, and Gaston said, "To your left," as the machine gun tap-danced hot lead in that direction and a howl of agony told them they'd both been right about leaves that moved when the wind wasn't blowing.

They were coming to the marshy ground between rises now, and Captain Gringo warned Gaston to slow down. He fanned a burst of machine gun-fire ahead for effect. Then he said, "Hold it. Let's listen."

Gaston shut the throttle and the big machine

stopped chugging and clanking as it went on building boiler pressure. The drums they'd heard had fallen silent, and the tall American said, "Nuts. How much range does this thing have, Gaston?"

Gaston looked at Gordo, who shrugged and said, "It will plough a hectare on one load of firewood, my Captain."

Captain Gringo opened the firebox door, saw the coals on the firebed were three-quarters gone, and said, "We'd better pull back and feed this critter on the pressure we have."

"Don't you want to pursue the enemy, Dick?"

"I want to, but it's a big jungle and I don't know where they ran. Let's get our butts out of here before they stop running and come back for another round."

Chapter Eleven

"So, you've captured Mamma Macamba and put a crimp in the blighters' style, eh what?" said Colonel Gage at tea that afternoon. Captain Gringo hadn't wanted to come to tea, but what the hell, the old fart was the governor.

Prudence Lee was in the infirmary, balled up in bed with a blanket over her head to block out the sounds of drums that she alone could hear. The dumb question gave Captain Gringo a place to look at without blushing. The colonel's oversexed wife was simpering across the table at him. Their nymphomaniac daughter was seated next to him, with her husband, Burton, next to his nutty mother-in-law. Captain Gringo wondered if Burton had laid Mrs. Gage, too, but saw no polite way to ask. Dama Luisa wasn't there, damn it. She'd been tea and crumpetted the day before while he was out getting killed in the jungle.

He told the governor, "Miss Lee's not exactly what we thought she was, sir. They've been holding her captive, too."

"Burton here, explained that while we were waiting

for you, dear boy. The point is that they've lost their Momma and that you chaps gave them a good spanking."

Captain Gringo knew Gaston had been invited, but the Frenchman had been too smart to worry about appearing rude. He was nursing his grievous snake bite over at the cantina, the bastard.

Mrs. Gage said, "I understand you have the colored girl under guard, Dickie-bird. Why are you guarding her if she's as innocent as you say?"

Her daughter, Alice, nudged him under the table with her own knee as she purred, *"Is* she innocent as you say, Dick? I must say, a lot of people were startled when you drove out of the bush with a six-foot, bald Negress, naked as a jay."

Captain Gringo ignored the thrust and answered Mrs. Gage, "We're not guarding her to keep her from running away, ma'am. We want to make sure nobody *takes* her back. Your husband is right about her being sort of valuable to Pappa Blanco, and poor Prue is sure they're trying to get her."

Burton said, "I know. The other colored girls over there are having a time with her, even under sedation. That damned Mab O'Shay sure picked a bad time to leave us without notice. Do you realize we don't have a single qualified medical advisor on Nuevo Verdugo now?"

Captain Gringo said, "I know. And I haven't been able to pin down anyone who actually saw Mab board the steamer."

"Good Lord, are you suggesting she never left of her own free will?"

"I don't know. There's no way to make sure until the steamer puts in at its next port of call. I sent a cable ahead, but Mab won't be able to answer for almost a week, even if she's safe. So I'm being a pessimist and we're looking for her."

Alice nudged him again and said, "But, Dick, if she's still on the island, don't you see what that must mean?"

"Sure, it means she's been captured or killed by

153

somebody. Meanwhile the only nurse we have is Miss Willie May, and while I'm sure she's a nice girl, she isn't a doctor or even a registered nurse. So let's not anyone get hurt or sick, huh?"

"I don't like it," huffed the colonel, as if the others at the table were delighted. He saw nobody was going to argue about that, and said, "Strike while the iron is hot, I say. Now that you know where this Pappa Blanco's hideout is, you'll just nip back and machine gun the buggers, right?"

Captain Gringo shook his head and said, "No sir. For one thing I'm not sure I could find the camp they took me to. For another, Pappa Blanco wouldn't be there. He meets the witch doctors somewhere out in the jungle and not even a common Carib could lead us there."

Burton asked, "Do you still think he's a white renegade, Walker?"

"Well, there are a lot of those going around. Pappa Blanco doesn't have to be white. He could be a mestizo or Negro, but the point is that he's not a real primitive. He's not playing the game right for a simple savage."

Colonel Gage said, "I say, I'd hardly call the way the blighters have been acting *civilized*. They're rebuffed every attempt on our part to show good will. They've simply killed and slashed and burned since we arrived. I'd say that was pretty savage, wouldn't you?"

"No sir. I've met some savages, if we're talking about the old-fashioned kind. The guys I just tangled with may have started out as simple natives, but somebody's put some bugs in their ears and taught them basic infantry tactics."

He took a sip of his tea, repressed a grimace, and added, "I owe you and Pantropic Limited an apology. The island is bigger than I thought and there's still plenty of untouched jungle that ordinary natives would probably be satisfied with for now. So somebody has to be telling the Caribs that you plan to plough it all up, and so on. Somebody had to show them the old Napoleonic trick of sending a screen of useless cannon fodder out ahead of your trained troops, and somebody had to train the riflemen we ran into. Any Indian can pick up a gun and fire it. But a guy I blew out of a tree knew what he was doing. You don't hit that close at that range without instruction."

Burton said, "I'm not the expert you are, Walker, but I agree somebody with military training has been training those Caribs. But try it this way: Pappa Blanco used that negress, Prudence Lee, as propaganda. Some of our men are missing and presumed dead. What if they captured one of our trained guards and made him give instructions?"

Captain Gringo said flatly, "Your company guards aren't that good. Gordo is shaping up. Poor Sergeant Montalban was a nice guy, but a lousy soldier who walked right into a machete with a loaded gun in his hand. Whoever trained those Caribs we ran into did a better job than you guys did with your guards. No offense."

Colonel Gage shrugged and said, "That's why we sent for *you*. But let's consider motive. If some soldier of fortune is out there whipping up a cannibal army, what in the devil does he *want*? I mean, we call them rebels or guerrillas, but in God's truth, they've never contacted us to make a single demand. Isn't that the whole point of having a war?"

Captain Gringo nodded and said, "Yes sir. War is a strenuous form of diplomacy when you get to the small print. Even our Indians back in the States had some demands to make, if only to move back and leave them alone. *Real* Carib chiefs should have set a deadline by now. We know they tolerated Hispanic settlers before you people got here. So they'd obviously conceded at least part of the island. But you say they just attacked you right off. They didn't try to powwow. They ignored your gifts and overtures. In other words, they'd declared an all out war before they could have known who you were."

Gage frowned and said, "By Jove, that's true! Someone had to tell them we were coming and who we were. Someone who knew."

His wife said, "But my dear, everyone knew. It was in the London Times."

Gage looked disgusted and said, "Of course it was. In the financial section. How many bloody newsstands do you imagine there are in the bloody jungle, eh?"

Burton said, "All right, let's assume some adventurer is leading the Indians for some murky reason of his own. The point is, what are we going to do about it, Walker?"

Captain Gringo said, "I've already started to do something about it. Gordo is welding some chain from the warehouses into a drag, and we know tractors can move through the jungle. Our next step is to clear that cordon as we originally planned. Then we'll make a sweep through the half of the island we've secured, to make *sure* it's secured. That'll put your plantings on a paying basis."

"I see. Once that's taken care of, there'll be time enough to track down Pappa Blanco and all, and finish them off, eh?"

Captain Gringo smiled thinly and said, "I don't think we'll have to. He's going to order an all out attack on us. But I think we can stop him, zombies and all."

There was a puzzled murmur around the table. Gage asked, "What makes you think a trained soldier of fortune would risk a frontal attack against barbed wire and machine gun-fire, Walker?"

"He has no choice, sir. He was sent here to put you out of business. He can't do that if you're shipping sugar, can he?"

"I suppose not, but what do you mean he was *sent* here? How do you know someone sent Pappa Blanco to put us in the ruddy red?"

"That's easier than some of the other questions, Colonel. Ask yourself a simple question. Would *you* be out there scratching mosquito bites with a bunch of uncouth cannibals unless somebody was making it worth your while?"

They told him Prue was dead when he arrived at the infirmary after tea to check on her condition. The ugly Willie May was acting pretty hysterical about it, and the guards swore on their mother's honor that nobody had gone near the late Miss Lee. Willie May led him into the private room where Prue lay spread-eagled on her sweat-soaked sheets, staring wide-eyed up at the light bulb in the ceiling. Another colored nurse was standing over her, crying. Willie May said, "That's how we found her, Captain. Nobody touched a thing."

The other girl sobbed, "She kept saying the Voodoo drums were calling her. Only none of us could hear no sassy drums! I came in to see if she'd take some lemonade and, Oh Lord, I'm scared!"

Captain Gringo stepped over to the bed, closed Prue's eyes, and bent to smell her open mouth. He asked, "Did she have anything but those sleeping powders, Willie May?"

The nurse shook her head and said, "I never poisoned her, Captain."

"I didn't say that, Willie May."

But the nurse was obviously upset. She stepped to the bed table and picked up a half-filled glass. She said, "This is the medicine I gave her from the dispensary, Captain." Then, before he could stop her, Willie May upended the glass and swallowed every drop.

She put it down and said, "There, are you satisfied, Captain?"

"I never suggested *you* put anything in her glass. But we'll know damned soon if anyone else did! You'd better take an emetic medicine and try to upchuck, Willie May."

"Pooh, I 'spect I know what sleeping powders taste like, Captain. I've taken them myself many a time when I was feeling poorly."

157

He was too polite to ask if she meant the nights Charlie Burton couldn't make it. Jesus she was ugly, but he and Burton had agreed his pretty wife, Alice, was a bitch. Maybe Burton saw something in this black girl that he couldn't get at home. Willie May seemed pleasant enough and he knew another thing. Burton had been having tea with him and the others and, let's see, that eliminated bitchy Alice, too. But that was no big deal. None of the people in town had any motive for murdering a woman they'd never seen before.

Or was it murder? He knew Voodoo was supposed to scare folks to death and Prue had acted like she believed in it. She'd lost her survival instincts and common sense back there, just hearing the damned drums. The infirmary was out of range and nobody here had heard any drums. But she might have been listening to her own heart beat and . . . "Damn!" He swore, "If only I had someone here to perform an autopsy!"

"There's a book about poisons in Doctor Lloyd's office, sir," said Willie May, trying to be helpful. He smiled at her and said, "It wouldn't be much help, unless some obvious poison like cyanide had been used. How are you feeling, Willie May?"

"I feels a mite sleepy. I 'spect I'd best go lie down if it's all right with you, Captain."

He nodded but told the other nurse, "You stay with her. I'll take care of things here."

The younger, prettier nurse took Willie May's arm and led her out. Captain Gringo picked up the blanket Prue had cast off and covered her nude body with it. Then he went over to the wall and punched a dent in it. It didn't do a thing for Prue, but it made him feel better.

He went to the door and whistled in a guard. He posted the man at the door and said, "After I give this place a final check, I'm going for a priest. Nobody in or out, right?"

The guard nodded. Captain Gringo checked the window. It was screened and the latch was locked on the inside. He wasn't surprised. Just for the hell of it he stepped over to a wardrobe in the corner and opened it. Prue hadn't had any clothes. So he wasn't surprised to find the wardrobe empty.

Almost.

The little black doll lay on the bottom of the wardrobe like a big spider hiding from the light. He bent and picked it up. It was made of the native asphalt, and was as crude as a gingerbread man, except for two lifelike shell eyes, glaring up at him. A needle of palm frond had been driven through the doll's chest, where its heart would have been, if the doll, or the person who made it, had had a heart. He glanced at the still figure on the bed and muttered, "Yeah, finding this ugly thing could have been the last straw for a terrified girl with a weak heart. Pappa Blanco would have known if you had a heart condition, too."

That had to be it. He remembered how Prue had kept collapsing on him in the jungle. Jesus, what if she'd croaked while they were tearing off a piece! What had she said about hearing her own heart pounding after she'd come? Oh boy, he might well have contributed to her condition!

But, hell, she'd been acting pretty wild and spooky when he first saw her and . . . that figured, too. She'd been hopped up on something. She'd said she couldn't believe some of the things she'd seen and done while living among the Caribs. If they'd been giving her some sort of stimulants and hypnotics all those years her weak-kneed panic might have been withdrawal symptoms and . . . Okay, how the fuck had this juju doll gotten in here to frighten her?

It hadn't walked in. It had been left in the wardrobe for her to find, drop, and collapse across the bed, scared skinny. He knew it was a waste of time to question the nurses. If they'd seen it, they'd have told him. They'd have probably passed out, too.

He put the doll in his jacket pocket, told the guard

159

he'd be right back, and left. He ran into Gaston just outside.

Gaston said, "I heard somebody just died over here." Captain Gringo said, "You heard right. It was Prue. She was either poisoned or scared to death. Without a doctor on the island it's up for grabs. I have to notify the governor and round up a priest or something. She was a Protestant, but I can't see the local Anglicans planting a colored girl in the ever so *veddy veddy* churchyard."

Gaston nodded and said, "You march to the governor and I shall go talk with the priest. In the mood you are in you are not fit to discuss delicate religious matters, *hein?*"

"Right. We'll save time working as a team. It'll soon be getting dark and I want to get this detail settled and post a perimeter guard. The bastards are starting to play rough and might try hitting us closer to home."

They split up, and he strode on to the headquarters building making plans the whole time. Until he drove that sanitary cordon across the island it made sense to pull in the vulnerable field workers and thinly spread guards. The country was dry enough for burning again. But sugar cane could be replanted. It was more important to save lives and guns. He now knew the bush general he was facing knew how to use the guns they'd captured, and some of them were machine guns. He didn't mean to let them have any more.

Captain Gringo was a good strategist. He tired to put himself in the other leader's shoes. But Pappa Blanco wasn't acting like he wore shoes. The American tried to picture what he'd do if he was out in the jungle planning another attack on the advance of civilization. Civilization wasn't all that great an idea, so he started out all right. But it was hard to figure what he'd do with a zombi army, since he didn't exactly believe in zombies. He didn't know what the hell those things were. It made it a bitch to figure out how they could be used in a battle.

He knew the Black Caribs sent them in ahead as a screen and terror weapon. The hard-hitting mop up guys

160

were just normal cannibals armed with guns and led by someone who was either a magician or . . . what?

The guards presented arms as he went up the steps and entered the headquarters building. He walked down the deserted corridor to Colonel Gage's office and raised his hand to knock. Then he heard a silly high-pitched titter on the other side of the paneling. Someone was saying, "Oh, it hurts so good when you ram it deep, sir."

"Sir?" What the hell was going on in there?

Captain Gringo looked around and saw he was alone. So he did what anyone else would have. He squatted down to peer through the keyhole.

Colonel Gage was standing by his desk with his linen pants around his ankles and his fat rump moving fast. Another bare rump was presented to the colonel's thrusts by a figure bending over on the desk. The someone was a man. Captain Gringo couldn't see his face but every time the colonel moved back for another hard thrust you could see the guy's balls below the colonel's reaming shaft. The old boy had a big pecker and he was really shoving it to the guy bending over for him. Captain Gringo rose and moved away from the door with a grimace. Mrs. Gage had complained that her husband slept a lot while she was out screwing around. He knew now what made the colonel such a sound sleeper. He didn't think they wanted to be disturbed.

As he headed back to the infirmary he spotted Gaston crossing the green. They met near the doorway and Gaston said he'd arranged for a decent burial and that the priest had said he'd read a nondenominational service over poor Prue.

They went inside. A black girl, who seemed rather fond of Gaston, said that Willie May was up and around after a few scary minutes with the sleeping powder she'd swallowed. They went and found her in Doctor Lloyd's office. She said she'd taken a wake-up and felt fine. Captain Gringo said, "Dosing yourself can be dangerous, Willie May. What did you take?"

The girl pointed to a brown bottle and wet glass on the desk and said, "Doctor Lloyd took the same medicine every time *he* felt tired, Captain."

He picked up the bottle and read the label. It was strychnine sulfate. He whistled and said, "That'll wake the dead and poison coyotes. How much did you take?"

"Just a couple of drops, Captain. Doctor Lloyd said it was a strong tonic."

He said, "I believe him. If you're not going into convulsions, could you see about a coffin for Miss Prudence? Gaston here, has a priest lined up and . . . where the hell *is* Gaston?"

Willie May simpered and said, "If I know that sassy Lilly Belle he was just talking to, he's likely in her quarters doing things I'd blush to mention. But I'll see to the dead gal, Captain."

He started to follow. Then he let her go and helped himself to a couple of books from the shelf above the late Lloyd's desk. The old boy had gone in for heroic medicine indeed if he took strychnine for a pick-me-up. Could he have died of something like that instead of a mysterious snake bite? He hadn't died attended by a physician.

Captain Gringo sat down and leafed through a book until he got to strychnine sulfate. It said the stuff was a strong stimulant in small doses, but warned that it was toxic as hell in moderate amounts. The poisonous effects of strychnine were from overstimulation of the central nervous system. Every muscle started working at once and the victim could snap his own spine during the resultant convulsions. The forensic symptoms of strychnine poisoning didn't fit the way they'd found Prue, or the description of Lloyd's death. So that was that, what else had the silly bastard been dosing himself and the staff?

He got up and looked at the bottles and pill boxes haphazardly scattered around the small untidy office. He found lots of things he didn't know about. He found atropine, foxglove, and . . . *wolfbane?*

Back to the books. Wolfbane was a poisonous weed

162

and doctors weren't supposed to give it to *anyone*. So what the hell was it doing here? The effects of the crude herbal extract weren't well understood, but wolfbane had been used in the Middle Ages by devil worshippers. In large doses it killed. In smaller dosages it produced a dangerous stupor in which the victim felt he was floating or flying and invincible. Witches on their way to be burned had used it to face the flames with satanic glee. It sounded pretty sick. He wondered if a guy full of wolfbane could keep floating along with a face full of shotgun pellets.

He browsed some more, and then another nurse came in to say they had Prue boxed and ready to be delivered. So he put the book he'd been reading down and followed her. Gaston was waiting in Prue's room with a sheepish look. Captain Gringo saw that the pine coffin had been nailed shut and said, "Right. Let's get some guards for a burial detail and get this show on the road. I want you to stop screwing around, Gaston. We've got work to do."

"You accuse me of dereliction, Dick? You are most unjust. You know I always put duty ahead of my pleasures, *hein?*"

"Sure. It's still broad daylight and everybody but me seems to be screwing themselves silly while there's work to be done."

"*Merde,* you are just in a bad mood because you were left out. But who has been getting it besides me?"

"If I told you, you wouldn't believe it."

"Ah-ha, you have been snooping, *hein?* What have I missed? Was it pretty?"

"I don't know. I didn't see his face."

Captain Gringo and Gaston walked on ahead to the local churchyard while six guards and the weeping black girls from the infirmary slowly carried Prue's coffin into the Spanish quarter. They attracted attention, naturally, and others drifted in to see who was dead. There was a modest crowd around the young mestizo priest Gaston

163

introduced to Captain Gringo as a Padre Hernando. The stucco church was a ways off, outlined by the setting sun. Captain Gringo noticed stone markers closer to the church. The ones nearby were wood and many had weathered until one couldn't read any names that might have once been written on them. They were little more than pickets driven into the ground. He commented on this and Padre Hernando said, "This is hallowed ground, but you are right about signs of neglect. The *pobrecitos* buried here are strangers who left no relations to tend their graves. We try to keep the grounds neat, but you must understand this is a poor parish and I have little help."

"You mean this is a potter's field, Padre?"

"Yes and no, my son. As you see, we are still within the church grounds. But until Pantropic Limited came we had no need of graves so far out from the church. Most of these *pobrecitos* were imported laborers from other parts of the world. I assure you each was given a proper burial but, well, one must understand that the local Creoles prefer a modest distance be set from the graves of their own family members."

Captain Gringo stared across the slightly rolling greensward. There was no cruel fence, but he could see a twenty foot strip had been left between these newer graves and the older, crowded tombstones closer to the spartan stucco walls of the church and rectory.

A couple of the Padre's sextons had already dug a grave in the red soil, and he knew it would make for a pointless fuss if he suggested Prue would rest easier in the shadows of the bell tower. What the hell, she'd been a Protestant before she took up Voodoo and the Padre was trying to be decent all things considered.

He looked the other way and saw the little funeral procession arriving. A familiar figure in white linen was beating it to the grave site. It was Colonel Gage. He puffed up to Captain Gringo and said, "I just heard. I hate to sound stuffy, but one *would* think I'd have been

164

informed. I mean, dash it all, I am supposed to be in charge of things around here, Walker!"

"I was going to tell you, sir. But they said you were, ah, busy, just now."

Gage reddened and said, "Quite. That *was* you they said popped in to see me, eh? I was wondering why you didn't knock."

Captain Gringo didn't answer as he met the older man's gaze, poker-faced. Gage looked away first and muttered, "Well, if you must know, I was attempting to recapture my lost youth."

"That's between you and your lost youth, Colonel. I see he couldn't make it to the funeral, but we'll say no more about it."

Gage gasped, saw the priest was talking to Gaston at a safe distance, and said, "Don't be impertinent, Captain Walker. I heard about what goes on in Yankee military schools, too."

"I *said* it was your business, sir."

"You don't understand. My wife is getting old and cold and, well, variety is the spice, and all that rot. I wouldn't want you to get the impression I was, uh, strange."

Bisexual was the word he was groping for, but Captain Gringo really didn't give a damn. The guards carrying Prue's coffin were by the grave and one of them was having trouble with his corner. The man across from him gasped, "Don't drop it, for God's sake!" and the big American moved swiftly over to lend a hand. He grabbed the corner of the box and said, "Easy does it. I'll take this corner. Let's just work it over those ropes across the grave and . . . what the hell?"

The coffin was heavy. Too heavy. Prue had been a big woman, but he'd carried her and knew how much she weighed. He ordered them to put the pine box down and reached for his pocket knife while Gaston and Padre Hernando joined him, looking puzzled. He opened the screwdriver blade of his knife and started to pry open the lid as the priest demurred, "Is that really necessary, my son?"

Captain Gringo said, "Just checking, Padre," and opened the pine lid. There was a mutual gasp from everyone and a scream from Willie May. The box was half-filled with dirt. Period. There was no *body* in it!

Padre Hernando crossed himself and asked soberly, "Is this some kind of joke, my son?"

Captain Gringo said, "I don't think it's funny either." Then he stared thoughtfully at the guards and added, "All right, who's the wise guy? What happened to the dead woman in this coffin?"

None of the guards had an answer. Willie May was running away, screaming. Another nurse wailed, "Oh Lord, that gal was a *haunt!*" and followed Willie May.

Grimly, Captain Gringo explained to the priest and others who hadn't seen the late Prudence Lee prepared for burial. Padre Hernando sighed and said, "You know what my simple people are going to make of this, of course."

"Yeah. Don't tell me *you* believe in zombies, Padre?"

"Of course not. But we are civilized men. The native children already think this part of the grounds are haunted. This is terrible."

Captain Gringo frowned and said, "Back up and run that past me again, Padre. What do the kids say about these neglected graves?"

"Oh, you know. The usual nonsense about ghostly figures wandering at midnight. Zombies are supposed to rise from their graves and walk off to meet their masters and so forth. It's a ridiculous but all too prevalent superstition on these islands."

Captain Gringo saw one of the grave diggers had left a spade standing in the spoil heap of Prue's intended grave. He stepped over to it, picked it up, and looked around. The priest asked him what he intended and he said, "I'm looking for a fresh marker."

The priest crossed himself again and said, "You can't mean that! You can't open a grave!"

"Sure you can. You just stick the shovel in and dig 'til you hit bottom. I think we'd better clear the area though. This marker here, says a guy named Ferraro was buried a month ago. This might turn out to be a little stinky."

He started digging while the others edged back, save for Gaston, who stood by offering the observation that his big friend was being *trés* foolish.

Captain Gringo said, "The soil's moist and I noticed that other grave was only about four feet deep, so what the hell."

"Do you really expect to find a month-old rotting corpse, Dick?"

"I sure hope so," replied Captain Gringo. So Gaston sighed, found another shovel, and started to help. The sun was low and the sky was blood red by the time they'd dug down a good four feet, found nothing and kept going. The bottom of the empty hole was filling with water. Captain Gringo climbed out to find an ashen-faced Colonel Gage next to Padre Hernando. Everyone else had left.

Padre Hernando crossed himself again and said, "This is not possible. I distinctly remember the late *Señor* Ferraro. He died a month ago of a fever. I stood right here and read a funeral service over him."

Captain Gringo said, "Yeah. We'd better rustle up some workers. I'm not up to opening every grave in this section, but somebody'd better."

"Are you suggesting *all* these graves are empty, my son?"

"I sure hope not, Padre, but we'd better make sure."

Chapter Twelve

It took some persuasion and a lot of yelling by Sergeant Gordo, but the frightened guards dug by lantern light in the gathering darkness. Captain Gringo waited until six more graves turned out to be empty before he put Gordo in charge and headed for the company headquarters. Gaston, of course, tagged along, asking what was up.

Captain Gringo said, "Pappa Blanco's using diversionary tactics. We're all supposed to be in a flap over his black magic."

"We are *not* in a flap over his black magic, Dick?"

"Oh, I'm sort of *concerned,* but I'm not ready to start swimming for the mainland yet. They obviously have confederates here in town. So we'll let Pappa Blanco think he has us scared shitless, while we make a few moves of our own."

Gaston said, "That sounds *practique*. I, for one, *am* scared shitless. How did they spirit all those bodies out of all those graves, Dick?"

"If I knew that I'd have Pappa Blanco half whipped. Meanwhile I just remembered something a stage magician once told me. Do you know why professional magicians hate to perform for children?"

"Mais non, I went to few shows as a child in France."

"If you had, you'd have been a pain in the ass to the nice man pulling rabbits out of his hat. You see, kids don't look where the magician tells them to. He points his wand and all the adults look to see what he's pointing at. That's when some kid with a wandering attention span catches his other hand doing something sneaky."

Gaston nodded and said, "I see. Your plan is to ignore the occult dramatics while we search for the other hand, *hein?* It is dark and there will be no moon tonight. Perhaps if we fit lanterns on the tractor . . ."

"Forget it, Gaston. Listen!"

As they crossed the green the night was filled with the ominous sound of Macamba drums. Captain Gringo nodded and said, "Right on schedule."

They found most of the Anglo-American company gathered on the steps of the headquarters building. The women looked frightened. The men looked more frightened than they were letting on, and most of them were packing guns.

Charles Burton said, "I was just about to send for you. It sounds like the natives are getting set to attack."

Captain Gringo nodded and said, "I'm leaving Gaston here, in charge of you and yours. Gaston, you know the form. Get everybody forted up with clear fields of fire all around. Do any of you other guys know how to fire a machine gun?"

Burton and two men he didn't know by name said they did. Captain Gringo nodded and said, "Okay, I think the warehouses are your best bet, Gaston. You'll have stout walls, plenty of food and ammo. Agreed?"

Gaston said, "We could hold off the Russian Army from there. But where are *you* going, Dick?"

"Two places. First, I'm going to take the train out to gather in all the outpost guards."

Colonel Gage sputtered, "Egad, are you suggesting we abandon our standing crops to the savages?"

Captain Gringo looked disgusted and said, "What standing crops? There's not enough sugar out there to pay for one human life, and the stuff will grow back once we secure this half of the island."

Alice Burton pointed and said, "Oh, what's that over there to the south, above the tree tops?"

Captain Gringo stared at the red glow in the sky and said, "Burning cane, ma'am. The guards are staggering back along the tracks right now, if they're still alive. I'll see you folks later." As he turned to leave, Gaston asked, "What's the second place, Dick?"

Since it was Gaston, Captain Gringo shouted back, "Got to secure the native quarter, of course. We're not *alone* on this island, you know." As he jogged away he heard someone say, "By jove, he's right. We forgot the *natives* might be in danger."

He knew they'd forgotten. Queen Victoria's Empire wasn't going to make it through another century if the folks who ran it didn't shape up.

He picked up a machine gun and a young guard named Pedro at the guardhouse by the tracks. Pedro said he was afraid of the zombies but Captain Gringo said he didn't have to look, as long as he kept the engine stoked. He frog-marched Pedro aboard the puffing billy, checked the steam gauge, and opened the throttle. As they headed into the throbbing bush, Pedro asked why they didn't light the headlamp. Captain Gringo said, "There's plenty of light." Pedro looked up at the ruby sky throbbing with drums, and crossed himself.

They chugged a mile and he saw a trio of guards headed his way as if they were fleeing the hounds of hell. He slowed, yelled for them to jump aboard, and kept on going. One of the guards climbed over the tender to protest, "You are going the wrong way, Captain Gringo!"

The American said, "Get up on top of that fuel with

170

your rifle. It's just as spooky where we came from. First we pick up all our people. Then we talk about going back."

They rounded a curve and saw a long ragged line of cotton-clad machete men across the track. The guard atop the tender screamed, "Zombies!" and Captain Gringo opened the throttle. He ploughed through them, hashing a couple under the narrow gauge wheels, then he braced the machine gun on the sill, waited until they were past the skirmishers, and raked the dark trackside brush with a steady stream of fire. Pedro asked who he was shooting at as he released the trigger. He said, "Hopefully, the second line of Pappa Blanco's sneaky advance. I don't know if I got anybody or not. Do you know how to run this engine, *chico?*"

"*Poquito, Señor*. I have switched in around the yards."

Captain Gringo said, "Good. Take the throttle." Then he climbed up on the tender and told the guard, "Go down there and help with the fire. It'll be your ass if you let the pressure drop."

"The pressure shall not drop, Captain Gringo."

"I didn't think so. Leave your rifle and hand me up that machine gun, will you?"

He had a better view from atop the tender and once he had the Maxim braced across his knees he saw his field of fire covered a full circle except for the vulnerable boiler just ahead and below his knees. He could hose the track ahead with plunging fire if he had to.

He had to. They whipped around another curve and he saw a clump of oiled dark flesh trying to drag a log across the track. He fired into the Black Caribs and the clump exploded into screaming shot-up flesh as the train bored on, nudging the end of the log with its cowcatcher to send it boomeranging into those Caribs still on their feet and running. He figured, as they whipped out of sight, that about a third of them had survived, but what the hell.

They drove another mile and found some desperate

171

uniformed men lugging another machine gun, followed by frightened cane workers who'd been caught in the fields at sundown and holed up with the men who were supposed to protect them. He yelled to Pedro and the boy stopped the train.

As the survivors piled aboard, he yelled down to ask if the machine gun had any ammo. The noncom in charge yelled back, "No, my Captain. We used it all up getting away."

"Right. Everybody keep your heads down and hang on. Let's go, Pedro."

"You wish for to go *farther,* Captain Gringo?"

"To the end of the line. Then we cut across to the other terminals via the cross track and head back to town."

Pedro shuddered and opened the throttle. Captain Gringo nodded in approval. The kid was scared. He had a right to be scared. But he did as he was told under fire. Kids like Pedro were the real heroes in any battle. Those guys in the rear had held onto their weapons, too. The next twenty-four hours figured to separate the men from the boys.

And so they chugged, rattled, and fired their way on. They passed cane fields where Pedro's whistle drew no response. Other times a mess of relieved-looking men ran out to climb aboard. More than one cane field was a mass of fire, and once they stopped, signaled, and saw a long line of zombies staggering through the cane toward them. Captain Gringo yelled, "Aim at their knees!" and suited action to words by chopping through numb shinbones with hot lead as Pedro opened the throttle to haul ass. Some of the others fired. Things were looking up. The men were almost shitting in their pants, but now they had a leader and now they saw the zombies could be stopped.

Captain Gringo thought about that as the train bored on under a blood-stained sky. The zombies didn't fight or fall like humans, but not even black magic could make a leg work once the bone was shattered, and dead as their eyes looked, they couldn't see once you put them out.

Their vital organs seemed in a state of suspended animation. Could a dead body move without blood or something circulating through its revived muscles?

"Four or five minutes," he decided. One minute was a hell of a long time in any fight, and four minutes was a boxer's full round. If the brain could last four minutes without fresh blood, that could explain a lot of impossible stuff. Most men went right down when they were hit because the shock and pain *told* them they were dead. If a guy was too doped up to give a shit . . . but could a guy actually crawl out of his *grave* after he'd been declared dead?

"So who's to say who's dead?" he said and frowned, remembering even Prue had been placed in that coffin without a medical examination. *He'd* sure thought she was dead, but who was he? Damn it, he hadn't put a mirror to her lips or even felt for a pulse! He'd taken the word of a semi-trained nurse's aid. What if Prue was still alive? What if they'd made a zombi out of her? What would he do if he spotted a tall shapely form leading another attack on them? He sighed, patted the warm breech of the gun in his lap and tried not to think about that.

They came to a switch point. Pedro stopped the train and jumped down to switch them on to the cross track. One of the others yelled, *"Mirar!"* and Captain Gringo saw a line of figures outlined by the red skyglow. Pedro saw them, too, but he kept working the switch lever. The guard in the cab stepped over to the throttle. Captain Gringo said, "Touch that and you're a dead man! How are you coming, Pedro?"

The boy heaved the lever desperately, the switch clicked into place, and Pedro ran back to climb aboard without answering. But he'd heard the exchange and as he opened the throttle he called up, "I am called Pedro Herrerra y Valdez, and my people will remember this night if ever you should have need, Captain Gringo."

The man who'd panicked said, "Hey, I knew you'd make it, *muchacho*."

Pedro just shrugged and said, "Put some more fuel in the firebox."

Going back was much the same as going forward had been. In all, they saved thirty-eight men and three machine guns during the long running fight. About twelve company guards and workers were unaccounted for as they chugged back into town. Utopiaton was buzzing with excitement and everyone was running around like chickens in the ruby light, but the drums, and the attackers, seemed content to hover a mile or more away from the city limits. They were doubtless busy burning everything they could lay hands on out there.

He put Pedro in command on the guardhouse roof, leaving him the machine gun and some men who'd proven themselves, to cover the rail yards.

He found Gaston had herded most of the company personnel into the nearby warehouse and set up machine gun nests at each corner. Gaston and the colonel met him out front. He brought them up to date and said, "I don't think they'll try an attack on the town, just yet, but why take chances? I've got to scout up the alcalde and do something about the Creoles. They should be safe if we can just get them all behind some walls, and post some lookouts on the roofs. There's a good field of fire all around and those fires were a tactical error if the Caribs are really serious."

Colonel Gage looked defeated, sighed and said, "My God, do you call this attack anything *but* serious? We're ruined! They've completely destroyed our crops and by now they'll be tearing up our tracks as well!"

"Relax, Colonel. Your workers and equipment are safe here, where Pappa Blanco can't get at 'em. Those fields have been cleared and the right of way for your tracks are cleared and graded. In a few months you'll be back in business, and this time you'll have the bastards walled off on their own end of the island."

"That's easy for *you* to say, dear boy. But London

has cabled that the stockholders are not happy, and they haven't even *heard* about *this!* I'm afraid we've about had it."

"You're pulling out? Okay, who's buying your island, Colonel?"

"Buying the island? Surely you jest! Who the devil would offer two bob for the bloody island now?"

"You mean you've had no offers at all?"

"Of course not. Why do you ask?"

"Simple. Those natives may be in this for fun, but the son of a bitch leading them knows enough to send men to knock out tracks and switch points. I don't think Pappa Blanco is trying to put you out of business as a *hobby*, sir."

"I quite agree. Someone's put considerable thought and at least some money into this sticky business. But what are we to do?"

"*Fight*, damn it. Look, you haven't lost as much as it looks like. The sugar cane will grow like weeds out of those ashes. Tell your stockholders you burned the fields to get rid of cane borers or rats or something. Get them to give you another season."

Gage sighed and said, "I'll try. After this afternoon I'm surprised you take me for a fighting man."

Captain Gringo shrugged and said, "What you do for, uh, relaxation, is your own business, Colonel. But if it's any comfort, Julius Caesar shared your, uh, tastes. He never let it get in the way of a good scrap."

"By George, you are an understanding sort of chap. I *will* give the blighters a run for their money. Playing fields of Eton and all that rot, eh what?"

Captain Gringo nodded and moved on. He'd heard funny things about the lads at Eton too, but the colonel had probably been talking about the Duke of Wellington, who'd liked girls, according to official history.

Chapter Thirteen

Captain Gringo assumed Gordo and Padre Hernando would know who and where the alcalde was, so he went back to the church.

Gordo's detail was finished and scared skinny. They'd dug up over fifty graves and every one had been empty. Gordo said the dead had all been off islanders who'd died working for Pantropic. He had no suggestions as to how they'd gotten out of their graves, but Padre Hernando insisted there was only one possible answer. Someone had dug them up.

The young priest said, "I see now that the children who said they had seen ghosts must have observed graverobbers."

"That's a lot of graverobbing, Padre. How come so many workers were buried here? I was told this was a healthy island."

"It is, my son. Now that I think about it, most of the *pobrecitos* died soon after they arrived. You know the company recruits labor from all up and down the Mos-

176

quito Coast. Many of the impoverished *peones* must have been ill when they boarded the company boat. People who have lived here some time have no higher a death rate than anywhere else."

Captain Gringo stared across the open graves, black blobs in the scab-colored grass under a ruddy sky, and said, "Hmm. If a guy was on drugs before he got here ... yeah, you round up beach combers along the skid rows of a dozen ports, and you're likely to wind up with pretty weird people, Voodoo drums or not."

He turned to Gordo and said, "I've got to see the alcalde about a defensive perimeter. I've got another job for you, Gordo. Take some of these guys to the Anglican graveyard up at the far end of the green. Nobody's there, so they won't question what you're doing."

Gordo said, "I can see that, my Captain. But what is it that we are going for to do?"

"I want you to dig up Doctor Lloyd's grave."

Gordo and the priest exchanged nervous glances. Gordo asked, "You wish for to see the doctor's body, my Captain?"

"Not particularly. If he's still in his coffin, say you're sorry and cover him up again."

"*Nombre de Dios!* Don't you think he is really dead, Captain Gringo?"

"I don't know. That's why I want you to make sure. Do you know what he looked like, Gordo?"

"Of course. But he has been dead a while and ..."

"I'll take your word for it if the mess looks anything like Lloyd. I never laid eyes on him. People keep telling me he's dead. But they said Prue Lee was dead, too. I'm learning to take things with a grain of salt around here."

He turned back to Padre Hernando and asked, "Can you show me to the alcalde, Padre?"

The priest said, "If you mean an elected mayor, we don't exactly have an alcalde since the British came. Colonel Gage's assistant, Webster, more or less takes care of things."

"I know Webster takes care of the colonel's, uh,

interests, Padre. But surely you Creoles have someone you depend on, if only informally."

The priest said, "Well, when the people want advice about temporal matters they generally ask Dama Luisa what to do. I will show you where she lives."

Captain Gringo said, "I already know the way to Dama Luisa's, Padre. Isn't a woman an unusual boss down here?"

Padre Hernando nodded, but said, "You must understand that Dama Luisa's family is ancient and honored here on Nuevo Verdugo. Her grandfather was the last Spanish viceroy, back in the twenties. Dama Luisa is the last of her line, but the people hold her in great respect."

The tall American saw that the unexpected development offered possibilities. Dama Luisa seemed intelligent and friendly. But it offered unexpected questions, too. He asked the priest, "If Dama Luisa remarried, what would that make her husband?"

Padre Hernando blinked in surprise and said, "Such a fortunate man would be most important, of course. But I don't follow you, my son. Who is trying to marry Dama Luisa? I have heard no such gossip about the lady."

Captain Gringo smiled thinly and said, "I'll ask her. Oh, not to marry me, but if someone *else* has been working at it, that would answer a lot of questions." He elaborated no further but sent Gordo one way and legged it the other to Dama Luisa's nearby home.

The street out front was crowded with frightened but quiet people, who parted respectfully when he elbowed his way to the door. The footman who let him in was respectful, too, but armed to the teeth. As the footman led him back through the house, Captain Gringo saw that the patio was crowded; by the light of paper lanterns he noted mothers and children made up most of the mob. The kids were running up and down the patio, excited but unaware. Their mothers and some older men sat quietly listening to the distant drums.

He found Dama Luisa in a drawing room, presiding

over an all-male contingent from the town. She was seat-ed near the cold fireplace under the huge portrait of a man sporting a copper-colored spade beard and a chest full of medals. The family resemblance was obvious and the old viceroy looked pretty tough. His granddaughter looked pretty tough, too. She'd discarded her satin and lace for a whipcord riding outfit and two ammo bando-leers across her chest. Some of the armed mestizos in the room gave him dirty looks when he was shown in, but Dama Luisa smiled and said, "We were wondering when someone from the company would come. You *were* sent by the British governor general, yes?"

He nodded. It wasn't a flat lie and he could see they were feeling left out. He said, "We've secured the area around the green. This part of town is safe from attacks from the east and, of course, the sea to the north. Anyone crossing the open ground due south is subject to machine gun enfilade. So if they hit at all, it will be from the west, across the gardens and orchards you folks have over that way."

Dama Luisa nodded and said, "We were just con-sidering that when you arrived. Is the governor going to issue machine guns to us?"

Again it wasn't an out-and-out lie when Captain Gringo said, "No. Not unless some of your people are qualified machine gunners."

A dark man wearing a pistol on each hip shouted, "Bah! Anyone who knows how to shoot can shoot a machine gun. Those Anglos do not care what happens to us!"

Captain Gringo shook his head and said, "It's not that simple, Señor. Do you know how to set the head spacing on a Maxim?"

"Head spacing? Maxim?"

"That's what I mean. I haven't time to go into it, but if you fail to adjust the size of the breech in a hot machine gun it tends to blow up in your face. The brand name matters, too. No two makes of machine gun work the same way."

179

The mestizo patted one of the Colts he wore, and grumbled, "We have other guns." There was a growl of agreement. They were frightened but full of fight and Gage was being dangerously negligent. The Brits had screwed up like this in India during the Sepoy Mutiny. If you're going to ask natives to fight for the Queen it's a good idea to keep an eye on them. An armed man keyed up for a battle is going to battle *somebody*. The Sepoy troops had turned on their officers after a long series of false alarms had worked them up to itchy trigger fingers with lots of ammo. They'd have fought for the Brits if a serious enemy had been available. But since there hadn't been, they'd remembered a long list of insults from the Pukka Sahibs and figured, what the hell.

He saw Dama Luisa was with it when she asked, "Do you think we should cut down the fruit trees to the west?" and gave him the chance to be a nice guy. He shook his head and said, "No. I wouldn't advise that, folks, though it would give us an improved field of fire if they hit us with an all-out charge. But I think we have enough good fighters to stand them off and your people have invested a lot of time and labor on their gardens and orchards."

A Negro with a rifle slung on his shoulder nodded, and said, "By the bones of Christ, that is true."

Captain Gringo saw less resentment in the faces around him now, and said, "I do have a few suggestions, but only if you guys want them."

The mestizo with all the pistols said, "Of course we want them, Captain Gringo. You are a professional, no?"

Dama Luisa was smiling at her American guest with her eyes and he knew what she was thinking. He said, "All right. I'm going to write a note and we'll send a detail to the warehouse. My friend, Lieutenant Verrier, will issue a machine gun and some rolls of barbed wire."

"But you said we could not have a machine gun, Captain Gringo."

"I said I wouldn't issue one to an inexperienced gunner. I'm going to man the Maxim."

"You will fight with us, at our side?" The mestizo grinned and another man shouted, "*Viva* Captain Gringo!"

Dama Luisa rose and went to a secretary against the wall, opened it and said, "We have paper, pen and ink, Captain. How many men do you want to send for these things?"

He sat down and started to scribble and suggested, "A couple of dozen, as long as they're going. We'll build our defenses on the walls of the houses along that side of town, with wire between and a line out between the houses and the gardens. If I set up the Maxim on a corner rooftop I can sweep either way. We'd better build a bonfire out along the tree line if there's time. That way they'll be visible to us before we're visible to them."

He finished his short note to Gaston and handed it to one of the men, who took off shouting for some strong backs.

Captain Gringo got to his feet and told Dama Luisa, "I'm going out to start putting things in shape. You'd better stay here and take care of the women and children."

She patted the S & W .38 on her shapely hip and said, "My servants will show them where the bathroom is. I'm going with you."

He didn't argue. Dama Luisa was obviously used to having her own way. The two of them led the others out into the semi-darkness where the drums seemed louder now. The sky was a red-echoing bowl of swirling blood as the trade winds mixed sea mist with the rising smoke from countless fires. Dama Luisa glanced up and said, "*Mirar!* They are burning closer to town now."

He said, "Yeah. They have a lot of railroad ties to play with. But that's Pantropic's problem. Are these friends of yours the bigger frogs in this puddle?"

"They are the leading men of the Creole community, if that's what you mean."

He said, "That's what I mean." He stopped to turn and yell, "Each one of you fan out and gather eight or ten

181

peones you can order around. I'm making each of you a squad leader. Meet us at the south-west corner of the quarter and we'll take it from there."

Then he started legging it to his planned command post with Luisa matching his stride in her whipcord skirts. By the ruby glowing sky, he saw the last house down the street. It was a one story flat-roofed cube of stucco and baked brick. Luisa said the family who lived in it were huddled on her patio. So he tried the door, found it locked, and kicked it in. She asked, "Are you always so direct, Captain?"

"Call me Dick. There ought to be a ladder to the roof and . . . hold it, someone's coming."

The fat sergeant, Gordo, was running toward them, panting and shouting Captain Gringo's name. The American yelled back, "Over here. What's up, Gordo? You look like you just saw a ghost."

Gordo joined them, leaning a hand against the door jam, wheezed for breath and said, "I think I did, Señor. You remember you told us to open that English doctor's grave?"

"Yeah. What did you find?"

"You are not going to believe me, Captain. You had better come and see for yourself."

"I'm busy, damn it. Get to the point."

"It's insane, Captain. We did not find Doctor Lloyd in his coffin when we pried open the lid. We found somebody else!"

"Jesus, don't tell me it was that black girl, Prue!"

"No, Señor, it was the white girl, Mab O'Shay! She was in the doctor's grave, where the doctor was supposed to be. We could not find a trace of *him!*"

Captain Gringo felt sick to his stomach and as if his head was screwed on wrong, but he muttered, "Jesus, Mab's dead too?"

"I sincerely hope so, Señor. She looked most dead and her features have started to discolor, but lately one never knows."

Luisa tugged Captain Gringo's sleeve and said,

"This is all most confusing, Dick. What is going on? Why are you digging up the dead?"

He said, "Somebody's playing musical graves. Let's see if there's a way up to the roof and I'll tell you all about it."

"I certainly hope so. Nothing I've heard so far makes any sense."

Captain Gringo sighed and said, "Welcome to the club."

Captain Gringo and Dama Luisa had been on the roof about an hour, when one of the other Creoles stuck his head up through the trap door to say, "Our people are getting tired of this waiting, Captain. Have you any suggestions?"

The American said, "Yeah, get back to your post. You're *supposed* to get tired of waiting. Nobody ever attacks when you're expecting them to. Tell the others to hold out as long as they can. Then hold out fifteen minutes longer. That's how Wellington won at Waterloo."

The man went back down the ladder, muttering. Captain Gringo stared out across the gardens at the bonfires burning low along the tree line. He was pretty sure there'd be no attack too. The drums had fallen silent and the trade wind had rain on its breath. The barbed wire entanglement midway to the fire line looked hasty and sloppy, but nobody was going to walk through it half asleep. He was half talking to himself when he muttered, "It doesn't add up. Pappa Blanco has more of those whatevers than the empty graves can account for."

Luisa had been brought up to date on the weird happenings, although she didn't seem to buy much of it. She said, "I think those so-called zombies must be beachcombers and drunks they recruited on the mainland. There are many coves where a schooner could unload in secret."

He said, "You're right. That ties in with outsiders being in on the deal. I've been trying to figure out a nice way to ask you a rather delicate question, Luisa."

183

She asked, "Is it a question having anything to do with all this Macamba business, or are you just curious about local color?"

"It's important. It's not very delicate, but . . ."

"Ask anyway then. I'm old enough to tie my own laces, Dick."

"Okay. Have you been sleeping around with anyone important?"

Luisa blinked, recovered, and said, "My, you do get right to the point, don't you? To answer you as bluntly, anyone I was sleeping with would *have* to be important, at least to me."

"Don't spar around, doll. I have to know."

"All right. Since my husband died I've had one affair and I didn't like it. It made me feel cheap. Since then I've been trying to control my natural desires until the right man comes along."

"That sounds reasonable. I'm not asking you to play kiss and tell, but answer me this. Was the guy connected in any way with Pantropic Limited?"

Luisa laughed incredulously and said, "Of course not. If you must know, he was a Creole. First officer on an island freighter. My foolish mistake was over a year ago and he hasn't been back since."

She looked away and added, "I was trying to forget, damn it. Now I suppose it will be all over the Anglo-American community."

He said, "Not unless *you* tell them, Luisa, I didn't mean to pry. I had a reason for asking. I thought at least one other guy had made a play for you."

She looked back at him with a puzzled smile and said, "A play? You mean flirtation? Heavens, everybody *flirts,* Dick. We don't have an opera house or other entertainment on Nuevo Verdugo."

He said, "I noticed. So somebody *has* been rubbing knees with you at Mrs. Gage's tiffens?"

"Of course. I'm not deformed, you know. Poor Charles Burton has been almost slavering at me since we met. But I assure you I've never even been alone with him."

Captain Gringo nodded thoughtfully and said, "I believe you. But that could answer for the attack on your carriage. Hell hath no fury, and the gossip has Burton playing footsie with a local belle."

"Well, I assure you *this* local belle wants no part of Charles Burton, even if he was single and from a good Creole family! Who could he be involved with among my people?"

"I don't think he is. I could tell you who he *has* been fooling with, but you'd laugh yourself silly and us gents have to stick together. Just one more question and we'll drop it. Has Burton acted like he had honorable intentions, or is he just out for sex on the side?"

"Good Lord, nobody's ever talked to me that way! What do you take me for, Dick Walker?"

"A lady, Dama Luisa. I'm trying to eliminate Burton, but I can't if you keep acting coy. I have to know if he's just a rotter with a roving eye, or a guy trying to marry into the local aristocracy."

Luisa grimaced and said, "As I understand it from the few words he offered as an excuse to peer down my dress, Charles and his wife, Alice, have an understanding about his, uh, needs. One gathers Alice is frigid or something. I shut him up before he could elaborate."

He nodded and said, "I'll have a chat with Alice about her suspicious nature. She's not nearly as understanding as her husband says."

"You mean *she* sent that young man to attack me? How could she have gotten any man to act so foolishly?"

"Oh, she has her own methods, and the guy was a drug addict anyway."

"What do you mean she has her own methods, Dick? Is there something I don't know about sweet little Alice?"

"No. I don't intend to tell her about your sailor either. Let's get back to this machine gun belt. I've shown you how to load for me, as long as you insist on hanging around. But we'd better go over it again."

"I know how to feed you ammunition, Dick. What on earth does all this nonsense about the Burtons have to do with me?"

He shrugged and said, "I don't think it has anything to do with you now. Somebody is trying to run Pantropic Limited off the island. I've cabled a guy I know on the New York stock exchange to see if outside interests are bidding on the property. So far I keep drawing blanks. A company man trying to work his way into the Creole community would add up, if I could catch one doing it. You just poured water on my prime suspect."

"I see. You don't think Charles married Alice for herself alone, eh?"

"Not unless he was a glutton for punishment. Burton married a *job*. A better job than he'd have ever gotten on his own."

"Do you suppose he could be working with this Pappa Blanco to eliminate his father-in-law so that he could be the big boss?"

"No. He's too useless for Pantropic's board of directors to consider for top spot. Besides, if he only wanted to get rid of the colonel, he'd have done it by now. Why mess around with dozens of murders when one would have done the job? The minute the old boy dies, Alice plans to divorce him."

He realized he'd said too much even before Luisa smiled and said, "You *do* know Alice pretty well, don't you? I take it Charles fibbed when he said she was frigid?"

"I wouldn't know. I've been sleeping with her mother."

It worked. Luisa laughed at the outrageous picture he'd thrown as a quick curve. He knew it was time to change the subject. But as he was about to ask an innocent question about the local economy they heard a thunderous boom coming from *behind* them. Luisa gasped and said, "My God, what was that?" He said, "I

186

don't know," then yelled out down the line, "Heads up, *muchachos!* Forget that noise to the rear and watch your *front!*"

Luisa shouted, "Look! They're coming!"

Captain Gringo said, "I see them." Then he yelled out again, "Hold your fire, everybody! Let those guys out front hit the wire and don't fire until *I* cut loose!"

The ragged line of tattered men were outlined by the fires behind them as they half stumbled toward the town. Luisa gasped, "There must be hundreds of them! Why don't we shoot?"

He said, "I make it about three dozen. Stay cool. The real rush is planned to hit us after we waste a lot of ammo on those poor clowns."

One of the villagers fired without orders and a zombi staggered but kept coming. Captain Gringo yelled, "Hold your fire, damn it! Can't you see they don't have firearms? Watch the tree line!"

The first zombies had reached the wire. They kept walking numbly in place, and piled up stupidly, waving their machetes and clubs. Captain Gringo saw the glint of firelight on steel, in the shadows of the trees, and said, "Here comes the real show."

The Caribs waited until their zombie screen was windrowed on the sagging wire before they broke cover, bounding gracefully forward while others opened up with small arms from the trees. Captain Gringo knew better than to traverse wildly with a single machine gun. He started at one end, slowly swung the barrel and opened up with short-aimed bursts. The villagers started firing their rifles and shotguns. The Caribs started going down like any other human being with a bullet in him.

Their leaders didn't like it much. A bullet spanged off the bricks near Captain Gringo and the girl. He'd seen the rifle flash. So he elevated the muzzle and lobbed a burst of thirty rounds into the treetop where the sniper had been perched. Then he depressed his aim to blow a clump of men near the wire to hash.

The savage machine gun-fire, added to some quite

187

good shooting on the part of the Creoles, broke the back of the attack. The Caribs left their dead and wounded with the hung-up zombies and ran back to the tree line. The Creoles started cheering. Captain Gringo bellowed, "Reload your weapons and get set for another charge, Goddamn your eyes! This isn't a football game!"

He saw his own belt was about used up. He ripped it out and asked Luisa to hand him the end of a fresh belt. She did, but asked, "Are they really liable to try again, Dick?"

He said, "Not if they have any brains. But always assume the other side is crazy enough to do anything."

One of the zombies had worked its way through the wire and was wandering in. He yelled down, "Don't anybody shoot that guy! He's lost his machete and he's hit bad. I want to talk to him if anyone down there has the balls to grab him!"

A trio of macho Creoles broke cover to run out and wrestle the zombi to the ground and hogtie him. Things were looking up. The locals were learning not to be afraid of the unknown.

Another machine gun woodpeckered off to their rear. He grinned and told Luisa, "They've decided to try from another angle, the poor bastards. That'll be a kid called Pedro, atop the guardhouse."

He cocked his head as a nearer Maxim coughed and added, "That's Gaston. He always fires in morse code for some reason. Our guys have them in a cross fire, over by the railroad yards."

Luisa said, "It sounds like they're taking a dreadful beating. But what was that explosion we heard?"

"A diversion. The Anglo-American side of town is deserted. We pulled everyone in to strong points, so they could be dynamiting empty housing over that way. It's nothing to worry about. Windows can be replaced."

Luis asaid, "But you worked hard to save our native quarter, Dick."

"That's different. Pantropic can afford new tin houses. You folks have your life savings tied up here."

"I see. You put my people above your own!"

"I'd like to take a bow for that, Luisa, but I gave up walking picket fences for pretty girls a long time ago. I put human life, any human life, first. The company people are safe and in Gaston's good hands. Property comes second, and this part of town west of the green is more valuable than the temporary structures to the east. War is a matter of saving what you can. Nobody can save everything."

"Just the same, I am grateful, and my people will be too."

He didn't know how to answer that. There was only one thing she could offer him that he really wanted. But he wasn't sure she'd go for that.

Chapter Fourteen

It was a long night. The cold gray dawn brought rain and a little sanity as the survivors surveyed the damage. Utopiaton had gotten off a lot lighter than the Caribs and their zombie allies. The captured zombi died just before dawn, staring blankly and muttering something about its mother while Captain Gringo tried to question it. The ones hung up on the wire had been caught in a lot of cross fire and were all dead by the time the villagers moved gingerly out to gather them. The wet grass was liberally sprinkled with dead Caribs, too. It made for a grisly line of corpses while some peones dug a mass grave across the tracks and under the cover of Pedro's gun.

Padre Hernando insisted on giving the last rites to the enemy dead, pagan Caribs and whatever the zombies were, alike. It came as no great surprise to Captain Gringo that the priest and villagers failed to identify any of the bodies. He didn't hang around to see them buried. Gaston had send a messenger from the infirmary.

What was left of it.

He found Gaston and Colonel Gage staring morosely down at the splintered wreckage of one whole wing of the infirmary. Gaston looked up and said, "Willie May and Lilly Belle. They must have been in the doctor's office. You're not going to believe who must have simply walked in on them, holding a lit dynamite bomb."

Captain Gringo stepped around a pile of debris Gaston indicated and swallowed hard. The lower half of Prudence Lee would have simply been that of a tall black woman to anyone who hadn't known her rather well. The rest had been blown to bits. The grotesquely twisted, still shapely legs attached to the shattered pelvis looked like an obscene parody of giant frog legs, lightly fried. A shoe with a human foot still in it lay in the red mud a few feet beyond. Gaston said, "Willie May wore shoes like that. The rest of her and Lilly Belle are sort of mixed with everything, but there are features here and there one can recognize."

"What about the other colored girl?"

"Susan? She was with us in the warehouse. She seems a bit upset, but I can get her, if you think it's worth talking to her."

Captain Gringo said, "Forget it. If she wasn't here, she doesn't know anything."

Colonel Gage said, "It's ghastly. It's unreal. First that Mamma Macamba vanishes from her coffin. Then she comes back with a bomb and blows everything to smithereens! How on earth do they *do* it?"

Captain Gringo shrugged and said, "I don't know. The guys we found on the wire are going to surprise the shit out of me if they get up *again*. They look like they've been drugged to the eyebrows, and some of 'em took a lot of killing. But this time they bled real blood."

"What about the black girl, and the Irish lass in Lloyd's grave?"

"Yeah, what about 'em? I just looked Mab over. She was just plain dead. I'd say she was poisoned. We reburied her. As for Prue over there, she might have walked in with that bomb. Somebody might have just tossed her body in, on top of it. She's in no shape to tell us now."

"Dash it all, we know she escaped from her coffin, don't we?"

"No sir, we don't. She might have been in some kind of trance. She might have really been dead and somebody snatched the body on us."

"Ridiculous! The others would have seen anyone mucking about with her closed coffin!"

"They'd have seen her open it and climb out, too. And Willie May tended to be excitable. Don't you suppose she'd have mentioned it?"

Gaston considered and said, "I like the doctor, Lloyd. If one must worry about missing dead people, I can't think of anyone more likely to be useful to a witch doctor than a real doctor, *hein?*"

Colonel Gage sputtered, "See here, damn it, I *saw* Lloyd die. I was at his funeral. I saw him buried."

Captain Gringo said, "I'll take your word for that, Colonel. But he sure as hell wasn't in his grave the last time we looked. He had a lot of drugs at his disposal, too. We'd better keep an open mind about Lloyd."

"Good God, are you suggesting he's out there alive in the jungle, plotting more black magic?"

"*Somebody* sure is. Let's get a head count and see if anyone else we know is missing."

He spotted Webster crossing the green with a quartet of guards and hailed them over. Webster was pale and looked like he'd had a hard night. Captain Gringo said, "I want a detail here to clean up this mess and bury what's left of the girls. Do you really need those guys?"

Webster said, "Rather. We're under siege and I'm not very handy with a gun."

"Hell, by now the Caribs are halfway home. That rush last night was a last ditch effort to stop us from starting our sanitary cordon, and it didn't work. Pappa Blanco won't want any of his people caught on our side of the deadline. Stick with us if you're nervous."

Webster said, "Righto, tight as a tick and all that. But what's next on the agenda, old bean?"

"Head count. Couple of Creoles and some glass were hit by stray shots over in the native quarter, but nobody on our side was killed or seriously hurt. Gaston here, says everyone holed up with him in the warehouse made it, and Pedro's guys guarding the rail yard only had one guy lightly creased."

"Then why do we have to call the roll? All present and accounted for, eh what?"

"I'm not sure. I don't even know half the company men on sight and Padre Hernando is missing a couple of Creoles."

"Are you suggesting the Caribs slipped in and carried off some of our people?"

Captain Gringo stared soberly at the ruins of the infirmary and said, "No. We shot the piss out of the guys trying to move in from the jungle. Some son of a bitch working *inside* our lines blew this place up. A Black Carib is just a mixed breed wearing no pants. A Creole is just a native who says he goes to Church. Pappa Blanco has confederates moving back and forth."

"Good Lord, cannibal intelligence agents?"

"That's about the size of it. They know about our plan to seal them off. They've been moving corpses around like peas under a carnival shell. So let's line everybody up and start asking questions."

He turned and ordered the guards to get to work on the ruins. Gaston waited until he was finished before he nudged Captain Gringo and said, "Dick, the colonel and M'sieu Webster can record the details of who was with whom, doing what. I will feel more like playing policeman once I run a perimeter patrol. So, with your permission, my old and rare . . ."

Captain Gringo glanced up at the pale sun peeking back at them through the gray rain clouds and said, "When you're right you're right. I think they're long gone, but we'd better make sure."

He turned to Colonel Gage and added, "You and Webster here, get a picture of where everyone was last night on paper. Gaston and I are going to take a tractor out for a drive in the country."

Colonel Gage frowned and asked, "Since when have you been giving the orders around here, damn it?"

"*You* want to patrol the jungle while Gaston and I count noses here?"

"Well, since you put it that way."

Captain Gringo took Gaston, Gordo and Pedro along with two machine guns and plenty of ammo aboard the mammoth steam tractor. They chugged out along the trackside trail, expecting to find the narrow gauge tracks torn up. But the tracks were still there, gleaming wetly in a soft drizzle that had set in for the morning.

They came to the first sugar field. It was a black carpet of char, steaming wetly. The next one was the same. Gaston said, "Ridiculous. I thought you said this Pappa Blanco was an old hand at guerrilla warfare, Dick."

"I did. I expected them to tear up the tracks, too."

"*Trés* bush league. Why burn crops that grow back like weeds while one ignores expensive installations?"

"Maybe to spare the expense of rebuilding them? The colonel says Pantropic is about to give the island up as a lost cause. I doubt like hell that the Caribs have any need of a rail network across a third of the island. So the scam has to be a takeover."

"Perhaps. But you cabled Wall Street and no other sugar company has shown interest in Nuevo Verdugo, *hein?*"

"Yeah. How about that? United Fruit isn't bidding either. I cabled New Orleans. United Fruit looked into conditions here before Pantropic rented it from the Crown. They say it's a lousy place to grow bananas."

"Perhaps. But big businessmen have been known to fib, Dick."

"So what else is new? But Nuevo Verdugo *is* a lousy place to grow bananas. The island's half rock and Pantropic was advised against its sugar operation by old hands who know this part of the world. Some know-it-alls in London rammed the project through without ever looking at the place. As a crown colony the island has never shown a profit, so the rent is cheap. Pantropic's ninety-nine year lease would be a bargain, if only they could *grow* something here."

They smashed through some brush and started chugging across another expanse of ash. Captain Gringo asked Gordo about the buried roots of the burned off cane and Gordo said, *"Si,* my Captain. The sugar will sprout back in a week or so. One plants cane by ditching in lengths of rootstock saved from the previous crop. These fires will have burned off all the insects and weed seeds, too. I agree Pappa Blanco has most peculiar ideas about destruction. He kills peones and cane, but both are easily replaced."

"I'll have to point that out to the colonel when we get back."

Gaston nudged him and said, *"If* we get back, Dick! Over there, near the tree line. What the devil *is* it?"

Captain Gringo stopped the tractor out on the charred field and raised his field glasses. A human figure stood in an odd position between two scorched tree trunks. He lowered the glasses and said, "One of the workmen who didn't make it to our rescue train. They've impaled him on a gumbo limbo stake."

"He's dead?"

"Wouldn't you be dead with a sapling in your ass and out your mouth? I hope they had the decency to kill him first, but I doubt it. They seem to be trying to send us a message."

Pedro asked, "What is the message, Captain Gringo?"

"They don't like us. But we can't leave that guy here like that."

195

He opened the throttle and drove toward the tree line at an angle. Gaston said, "That impaled body is the other way, Dick."

"I know. You're going to have to switch places with me once we hit cover. I'm dropping off with one of the Maxims. Do I have to draw you a picture?"

Gaston grinned and said, *"Merde alors,* I was at this game before you were born. One gathers you wish much smoke as well as noise?"

"You're learning. Pedro, empty your canteen on some of the greener sticks and shove them in the firebox when I drop off."

Gaston took the throttle and wheel, speeded up, and said, "Gordo, brace that other machine gun in line with our boiler and get ready to commence fire."

"Señor Gaston. I know how for to shoot a machine gun, but I don't know how for to hit anything with it."

"Sacré Goddamn! Who can expect to hit anything in the middle of a tossed salad? Do as you are told."

The tractor nosed into the brushy tree line and Gaston swung the wheel hard over as Captain Gringo dropped off the far side with the other Maxim cradled in his arms. He hit running and headed for a fallen log in the forest gloom as, behind him, all hell broke loose.

Gaston drove up the tree line, one big spiked wheel out in the open while the other smashed the growth edging the field and Gordo fired blindly ahead at the falling tree tops. Gaston cut a fifty foot gap, swung out in the open, then swung back to chew up some more green-ery before whirling around and churning out to the mid-dle of the field, gun silent. The tractor drove in a circle, raising a cloud of ash, then suddenly tore back toward the trees, machine gun flashing as if Gaston had suddenly spotted something. From behind his log, even Captain Gringo had to admit the guys on the tractor looked like they'd gone a little crazy.

The Caribs must have thought so too. They'd been set to ambush a foot patrol coming across the open field to retrieve its dead. A mechanical monster driven by an obvious maniac had not figured in their plans. So, as Gaston hit the tree line on the far side of the impaled body and proceeded to knock down trees and spray lead with abandon, they did what any other sensible cannibals would have done. They started moving away from all the wild excitement, hugging the tree line where the brush was thickest and the cover best.

There were a dozen of them, naked save for strands of sea shells, but packing Remington repeaters. They retreated in good order and with more grudging common sense than panic. They came to the messy gap Gaston had made with his first apparently wild dive into the jungle. Their leader grinned and pointed. Captain Gringo watched while they darted across the gap and stopped to take cover behind the jackstrawed timber the leader had spotted as a likely place to make a stand. The Caribs crouched and got set for the oncoming tractor with their rifles braced across fallen logs. They had no way of knowing they'd presented an open flank to Captain Gringo until he rose with the Maxim braced against his hip and opened fire!

It was like having them in a bowling alley. As the machine gun sprayed them, some rose right into his hosing lead. Others tried hugging the ground, but he simply had to drop the muzzle between bursts to spatter them. The recoil rode the gun up with each short savage burst and Captain Gringo used that to good advantage as he watered his garden of spurting blood until, unlike other gardens, it stopped growing.

His ears still rang when he lowered the smoking muzzle. But he heard the sound of chugging machinery and falling trees. So he ran out in the open to keep from getting run over or shot by mistake. As he passed the line of dead Caribs he recognised a couple from the clearing where they'd tried to feed him to that snake. It made him feel better about the guts and brains spattered all over the logs where they lay.

Gaston spotted him, swung out of the tree line and stopped the tractor. When he climbed aboard, he saw they'd pulled the dead man off the stake and lashed his stiff body to the tender box. He told Gaston, "It worked. We nailed a squad of the bastards, but they were all natives."

"One expected to encounter Queen Victoria, my old and rare friend?"

"No, but I was hoping to nail the son of a bitch who wants her colony. But I think Pappa Blanco has pulled in his horns for now. The moron leading those guys was a wild type I saw by Prue's cave. He was jerking off then too. I'd say the main bunch has pulled back for now, and we're pretty far from town. Let's head back. I want to start that sanitary cordon before noon. We'll pick up a good crew and use the rails to carry the tractors and gear most of the way. We can bull through to the narrows and use the results as a road later."

Gordo said, "Forgive me, my captain, but it will soon be time for La Siesta."

"Let me put it this way, Gordo. Would you rather work in broad daylight or fight off attacks like we had last night?"

Gordo sighed and said, "Screw La Siesta. It is a rather old-fashioned tradition in any case, now that I think about it."

Chapter Fifteen

The trouble with tropic days is that they are all the same length. North or south of the tropics of Cancer and Capricorn the summer days are longer than the nights. Nearer the equator you get twelve hours of daylight and twelve hours of darkness all year long.

So while Captain Gringo's chain drags worked better then he'd hoped, and his men ignored La Siesta with the enthusiasm of beavers, they'd only cleared a quarter section by the time he blew his whistle and yelled out, "Knock off, *muchachos. Mañana* is another day."

Gaston joined him with a puzzled frown and asked, "Why are you quitting so soon, Dick? There is another two hours of daylight left."

"I know. I want to get our people clear before the elves move in at twilight."

"*Merde alors,* we are abandoning all of this to the savages? I thought we'd set up camp and . . ."

"Are you crazy? What's the point? Our guys will

199

work better in the morning if they're rested at home and start out with a good breakfast and maybe a morning quickie from mamma."

"But who is to guard our work here?"

"What's to guard? We're not building. We're tearing down. Do you really think black magic can grow all those trees back in a night?"

Gaston stared soberly at the huge gash of uprooted timber and sighed, "I must be getting old. You are right, of course." Gaston laughed and added, "Pappa Blanco is probably planning a night attack on this work site right this very minute. *Sacré,* he will be *trés* confused, *hein?*"

"I hope so. Up to now, everybody's just been reacting to his moves, and letting *him* choose the whens and wheres. Two can play at razzle-dazzle. Let him worry about what *we're* going to do next."

As they walked toward one of the tractors to unhitch the drag chain and use it as a vehicle çum machine gun nest, Gaston said, "I see now why you chose to ignore all the occult goings on."

Captain Gringo nodded and said, "Sure. They've had everyone going crazy trying to figure out how he worked his Voodoo shit and what his plans were."

"You, of course, have it all figured out?"

"No, I just don't give a shit. We were hired as soldiers, not detectives. You were around when we had our Civil War, Gaston. Did you follow old U.S. Grant's career?"

"*Mais non,* I was having my own civil war in Mexico, on the losing side. What has U. S. Grant to do with Pappa Blanco? I fail to see what they might have in common."

Captain Gringo laughed and said, "Grant would agree. He was probably the most unimaginative officer in the Union Army. That's why the Union started winning every battle, once they got rid of the bright boys and put old Rummy Grant in charge. You see, the Confederates had made all the other Union leaders look like assholes by springing flashy razzle-dazzle surprises. Lee had Stuart and Moseby tear-assing all over hell, and the Union guys went crazy trying to figure out what they'd do next."

"Ah, I begin to see the analogy. What did your Grant do about the ingenious tactics of M'sieu Lee and all?"

Captain Gringo helped Gaston aboard the tractor and looked around before he answered. He saw the others were moving out, well-guarded by Gordo's flank guards, and decided to wait and follow up with the tractor-mounted Maxim. So he told Gaston, "Grant ignored the flashy stuff. Scouts would dash in to report a rebel column doing something noisy somewhere else and Grant just puffed his cigar and went on planning his *own* moves on the map. He wasn't a brilliant general, but he had common sense and he saw what more imaginative men had missed. He, not Lee, had the bigger army, the supplies and the guns. So he just went by the book and took the positions all the time-tested rules said he ought to take. At Shiloh he marched into a brilliantly set up Confederate ambush. His advance reeled back while Grant was having breakfast at a country tavern. He wasn't a very excitable guy, and ham and eggs beat running around inspecting things."

Gaston said, "Wait. Even I know that Grant was not beaten at Shiloh."

"Most other generals would have been. The rebels shot the shit out of his advancing columns and had him in a pincers with half his army on one side of a river and half on the other. Grant got up, wiped the egg off his face, and wandered over to the battlefield. He saw some units retreating and told them they were going the wrong way. A brigadier galloped up to warn him they were about to be surrounded. Grant said that was bullshit. His army was four times the size of the rebel army, so, no matter what they *looked* like they were doing, they *couldn't* surround anything important. Grant cussed and fussed everybody back into position and the Union advance went on. It was a blood bath for both sides, but the Union had the weight and numbers, so that was that. He crossed the river where he'd meant to cross. He marched up, taking position after position, until, one day, the war was over."

Gaston said, "I see. We have the men and the guns. Pappa Blanco has a bag of tricks. We pay no attention to his black magic. We come back again and again, in strength, until he is walled off to the south. I agree it should work, Dick. But are you not even *curious* about how Mab wound up in Lloyd's grave, or where all those other corpses went?"

"Sure I'm curious. Grant must have wondered about Moseby's Gray Ghost act too. But first we put the son of a bitch out of business and *then* we figure out who he was and what he wanted."

"Who he *was*, Dick?"

Captain Gringo's eyes were grim as he nodded and said, "Yeah, past tense. The son of a bitch killed a couple of people I was rather fond of. So he's already dead. He just doesn't know it yet."

The governor general and his wife gave a garden party that night. Captain Gringo thought a victory celebration was premature, but he went anyway. Gaston said he'd rather act as O.D., and keep the guards on the ball as darkness fell.

The rain had let up. The trade wind dried everything to the clammy, damp stage people from England seemed to find comfortable. So again the tables were set up under paper lanterns above the terrace. At Captain Gringo's suggestion, Pedro and a couple of the other guards were set up on the roof with a machine gun and Mrs. Gage was gracious enough to send them up some refreshments.

Captain Gringo's main reason for coming was Alice, and she wasn't hard to corner alone near the punch bowl. She asked him why he hadn't been back to "see" her, which was a rather *veddy veddy* word for hot and heavy screwing, if he was reading her eyes correctly.

He made certain nobody could overhear them before he said, "I've been busy. Listen, you have Charles and Dama Luisa wrong."

She shrugged and said, "I don't think adultery is wrong. I rather enjoy it."

"I noticed. The point is that Luisa is an innocent bystander. Old Chuck hasn't been able to get near her."

"How unfortunate for poor Charles. I gather she told you all this when *you* were making love to her?"

"I've been unfortunate too. The dame Chuck was seeing on the side is dead. So you can make up with your husband if you want, or throw the bum out if that's your pleasure. Just don't send any more boyfriends to work Luisa over. You've been barking up the wrong tree and the local peones would tear you limb from limb if they found out you were after one of their favorite people."

Alice looked like butter wouldn't melt in her mouth as she sipped punch and said, "Darling, I have no idea what you're talking about. I don't assassinate my rivals. I out-fuck them, as who but you should know? Why don't we find some place where we can lie down and talk about it?"

"Maybe later. I have a couple of errands to take care of tonight."

"Oh? I hope they're both pretty."

He saw she didn't want to talk about anything but her twat, so he excused himself to mingle his way toward the colonel on the far side of the garden. Mrs. Gage caught up with him and whispered, "I saw you flirting with my daughter. Why don't we nip over to your quarters and discuss your naughty ways, Dickie-bird?"

He repeated, "Maybe later. I want a word with your husband."

"Heavens, you're not bisexual too, are you, Dickie-bird?"

203

He blinked and asked, "You know about the colonel and Webster?"

"Heavens, he's been sodomizing my son-in-law for years too. But don't tell Alice. She and Charles are already having trouble and . . ."

"Jesus H. Christ! You people are *weird!* Burton gets his job and your daughter from his nibs by bending over, and you try to patch things up by . . . I'll talk to you later."

As he moved away, she said, "Talking wasn't what I had in mind." He wondered where he *was* going to sleep tonight. At the rate things were going he could wind up with mother and daughter under him and dear old Dad trying to climb on top!

He found the colonel talking to his male harem, Webster and Burton. They didn't act like two bisexuals and a fag. They were talking business as usual. Captain Gringo assumed the casual sodomy of exclusive boys' schools had its own rules of public behavior. West Point hadn't taught him the form. He was glad. If Americans were unsophisticated by international standards, he was willing to live with that.

Colonel Gage said, "Ah, there you are, Walker. We were just talking about you."

Captain Gringo felt his asshole tighten, but he kept a straight face and said, "I just made a final check with Gaston. The Caribs must know we'll soon have them cut off. So they've pulled all the way back. We've secured the area, but I don't think they'll hit us again, now that they're on the defensive."

The colonel nodded and said, "So Webster here, was just telling me. You know, of course, that they'll try to do something about the ground you cleared this afternoon?"

"Yes sir. I'm sort of hoping they'll burn some trees for us."

"The more the merrier, eh what? The farm workers assure us the sugar will grow back good as new, too. How long do you think it will take you to set up that entire defense cordon?"

Captain Gringo shrugged and said, "About a week, at the rate we're going. Pappa Blanco doesn't have a week, if he values his hide."

Burton frowned and said, "I don't think I follow that, Walker."

Captain Gringo saw the others didn't either. He said, "We have the Caribs pushed back and probably having second thoughts about their Macamba man's magic. Don't forget he's an off-islander, whatever his race. There are always sub-chiefs jealous of the big cheese, and lately Pappa Blanco's magic hasn't worked out so hot."

Webster asked, "Oh, do you think his followers might turn on him?"

"If they don't, *I* intend to. I've got some cabled feelers out and we'll soon know who's been bidding to replace Pantropic here as leaseholder."

Colonel Gage said, "Not bloody likely! *I've* just cabled the stockholders that we have the blighters whipped!"

Burton said, "Besides that, no other sugar trust has *bid* on Nuevo Verdugo."

Captain Gringo nodded and said, "I know. It's an oil company. Three of them, as a matter of fact. Two American oil trusts and a Dutch outfit. I think we can assume the Dutch are innocent. I've got a guy in the states digging into it and . . ."

Webster cut in to blurt, "Oil? What oil are you talking about?"

"Come on, the shit is seeping out of the ground all over the island! The two main bulges of Nuevo Verdugo are classic anticlines like the ones they've started drilling in Texas."

"But we *had* our own geologists look for signs of petroleum, old bean."

"Sure you did. British geologists brought up on the old textbooks. Drilling for oil is a new science and it pays to keep up to date. Those first oil fields in Penn State seem to be a fluke. No oil strikes since Drake's well back in the fifties has ever been found in the classic rock

205

formations of the Ohio Valley. But your geologists, who've never found an oil well in England, looked for the rocks and fossils the books said should be there, and when they didn't find them, they ignored their own eyes and went home. Don't take my word that we're sitting on two oil domes. I told you I checked with Wall Street. Three of the biggest petroleum trusts have been secretly bidding against each other with the Crown."

Colonel Gage looked like he was about to vomit. He gasped, "See here, damn it, we were here first!"

Captain Gringo nodded and said, "You're right. Pantropic has a ninety-nine year lease. That's why somebody has been trying to drive you out of business *before* you found out there was something better than sugar you could ship from here at a tidy profit."

Gage said, "I see it all now. But once I cable London, the board of directors will never sell out and . . ."

"And that will be the end of it," cut in Captain Gringo with a nod, adding, "by now the mainland operators know the game's up, too. My questions were discreet, but word gets around when a guy starts asking about oil wells."

Burton said, "If *I* were this Pappa Blanco, I'd try to overrun this town and drive everyone off the island tonight!"

Captain Gringo shook his head and said, "No, you wouldn't. It wouldn't do any good. They could butcher us all in our beds and burn Utopiaton to the ground, but Pantropic would just send in another bunch of us. The scheme called for the company abandoning its lease. Would you abandon a lease on an oil field?"

Colonel Gage said, "By George, I'd better cable London right away!"

Captain Gringo said, "You don't have to. I already cabled Sir Basil Hakim that I had a handle on the situation and explained the plot. He's got stock in Pantropic, but he'll probably buy more before he tells your board of directors and rockets the price out of sight."

Colonel Gage said, "I know you're trying to help, but I rather resent your high-handed way of taking charge without informing me, old chap!"

Burton snapped, "Goddamnit, you might have let *us* in on it before you cabled! A guy could make a killing on the exchange if he knew Pantropic's stock was about to go up!"

Webster looked annoyed, too, as he said, "Obviously you and your friend, Gaston, have already placed your orders for a few shares, eh what?"

Captain Gringo's smile was bitter as he answered, "No. We don't have permanent mailing addresses. You guys still have time to get rich. The London exchange is closed for the weekend. So don't get your shit hot. You've got plenty of time to wire your brokers. They'd be home in bed, right now. But . . ."

"By Jove, all is forgiven!" Colonel Gage laughed and said as visions of sugarplums danced in his head. Burton was grinning like a shit-eating dog, too. Captain Gringo knew his next moves, as if he'd spelled them out in a fireworks display. Burton stood to make a killing on the stockmarket and leave his bitchy wife. He probably hadn't enjoyed getting cornholed by the colonel either. It was nice to see a fellow American so happy, even if he was a fat stupid bastard.

Webster said, "I can see why you're so optimistic, Walker. How do you imagine these sneaky oil chaps will contact their man here on Nuevo Verdugo to tell him the show is over? We control the only cable outlet."

Captain Gringo said, "I know. It's my guess they've given him a timetable, so he'll know when it's time to leave. That's when we'll nail him."

The three of them looked blank. So he explained, "The guy can't stay here now. If the other witch doctors don't eat him or something, it's only a matter of time before we find out where he's hiding. There's another steamer due in a couple of days. We just have to watch and see who's anxious to leave . . ."

"Are you suggesting Pappa Blanco is hiding out

among *us* here in town?" asked Webster. Captain Gringo nodded and said, "He has to be. That girl, Prue, told me he met the other witch doctors away from the Carib camps, somewhere in the jungle. For a guy living in a tree, he also had a pretty good grip on our plans. Somebody, a worker, a guard, a harmless-looking Creole, or whatever, has been slipping back and forth. Meanwhile, I've got Padre Hernando, Gordo and some other people, asking questions and comparing alibis. If we don't uncover him before the ship pulls in, he ought to be nervous enough to try and board her."

Webster frowned and said, "You make him sound like a rather crude criminal, Walker. Have you forgotten he has, well, certain powers?"

Captain Gringo snorted and said, "Sleight of hand, you mean. Those so-called zombies were just vagrants they recruited, doped up with painkillers and strychnine, and used for cannon fodder. They probably were landed from a schooner further down the coast."

"But that beheaded black corpse, full of embalming fluid when it attacked you . . ."

"Bullshit. The guy I beheaded was drugged to the stage where neither one of us knew what he was doing. Later, Pappa Blanco's confederate at the infirmary just switched corpses on us. One dead Negro looks like any other, if you cut off his head."

Burton gasped, "Someone on the medical staff was working for Pappa Blanco?"

"Yeah. Willie May. Sorry about that. She was the one who murdered Doctor Lloyd so we'd have no professional medical advice when they tried to spook us. Poor Mab O'Shay knew her job, so they murdered her too, and tried to hide her in Lloyd's grave."

Webster looked sick and asked, "Then where on earth was Doctor Lloyd when you dug the nurse up?"

"Under the earth, of course. They put Mab in his grave on top of him. When Gordo dug as far down as her coffin, he saw no reason to dig deeper. He opened the coffin, found the wrong body, and wet his pants like he was supposed to."

Burton said, "I can't believe poor silly Willie would do anything like that!"

Captain Gringo nodded and said, "Yeah, she did act pretty silly. But it has to have been her. Process of elimination. She was the only one who could have put that snake where Lloyd could step on it, after switching his anti-venom labels. Gaston was sort of, well, chummy with the other colored nurses, so they have alibis."

"But Willie May was murdered by that zombi girl, Miss Lee."

"No she wasn't. Prue was poisoned by Willie May, just like Mab. Then Willie May moved her body at the last minute. She was the only one who had a few moments alone with Prue's coffin. She rolled Prue under a bed or into a closet or something. Pappa Blanco or his Carib assistants were supposed to come and carry it off. Only they delivered a bomb instead. They blew up Willie May and that other innocent nurse because Willie May was getting dangerous. She was involved with a white man and maybe talking about a bigger piece of the action. Anyway, the dead Prue's corpse was blown up in the process, and you can figure out the rest."

Burton said, "Jesus, we knew they played rough, but Pappa Blanco must be a real son of a bitch."

Captain Gringo shrugged and said, "I'm a real son of a bitch, too. People playing for high stakes don't hire pussy cats. We'll never know what sort of a hold he had on the late Miss Willie May. He uses people like toilet paper. But his zombies fizzled and his Caribs have found out that a Maxim beats black magic and drums at scaring people. So now I figure he'll be out to save his own ass. I've wired the steamship company. Even if he somehow slips past us on the docks, they'll let us know if he tries to book passage on the Q.T."

Webster said, "You keep saying *he,* Walker. How do you know we're not dealing with a woman?"

"*You're* not dealing with the motherfucker. *I* am. Prue Lee said he was a man and the Caribs say he's a man. They met him bare ass, wearing spooky paint, but he must have had a pecker. None of them wear so much as a fig leaf. He may be black. He may be brown. I'm betting on white. The big oil companies are hung up on racial superiority and they wouldn't trust an operation this size to anyone but a company man."

"Couldn't some American pass himself off as a mestizo?"

"Sure he could, for a while. The Indians didn't know *what* the fuck he was. But it's a small town you've got here. He can't stay hidden in the woodwork forever. Right now he's probably sweating bullets trying to figure a way out. The trouble with islands is that you can't just walk away."

He took out his watch and added, "You guys know as much as I do now. I've got a date with a lady. So why don't you play the stock market or something? Nothing's going to happen tonight."

He turned to go, but Webster said, "Not so fast, dash it all! I see how they tricked us about a lot of things, but they must have a huge gang of confederates right here in town!"

"How do you figure that, Webster? I told you how Willie May and maybe a couple of beachcombers rigged the spooky shit around the infirmary. By now the mastermind will have eliminated all his stooges who could point a finger at him. The *Caribs* left are back in the Stone Age, where I'd leave them for now, if I were you. They'll eventually get used to the idea of civilization if the company shares some of the oil and sugar revenues in the form of pots and calico. Without outsiders stirring trouble, the island will go back to status quo."

Webster said, "Willie May could have killed Lloyd, Mab and that Macamba priestess with a little help from her friends. But, dash it all, you've forgotten that someone dug up a whole graveyard, if we assume the zombies didn't dig *themselves* out!"

"Oh shit, nobody can revive a corpse if it's really dead. The folks buried over there were just innocent workers who died of natural causes."

"Then where in blazes *are* they tonight?"

"Right where they were buried, of course. I'll admit Pappa Blanco's simple trick gave me a turn until I had time to think about it."

"You *know* how all those corpses left their graves?"

"Sure, they never left them. Willie May's white uniform was spotted by some Creole kids while she carried out Pappa Blanco's instructions."

Burton blurted, "That little skinny negress never dug up fifty graves in one night by herself, Goddamn it!"

Captain Gringo said, "I'll take your word for how skinny she was. She didn't dig them up. She just moved the markers. She pulled up each stake and drove it back in the soft earth a couple of yards to the side. If you dig where nobody's been buried, you don't find anyone there. Haven't any of you guys ever played poker with a stranger on a train? Pappa Blanco's not even a good stage magician. He's just a con man with a nasty imagination."

Webster frowned and said, "It's all so simple, once the obvious is pointed out. But I confess he had me frightened with all that mumbo-jumbo!"

"That was the plan. Between shipping no sugar and sending wild reports about Voodoo bullshit, you guys were supposed to be recalled to London as either worthless, crazy, drunk, or all three. That was when another outfit meant to make Pantropic an offer that would pay off their losses here and let them forget the whole deal. I've really got to be going, guys. The lady is expecting me."

Chapter Sixteen

They jumped Captain Gringo as he was cutting through a dark alley on the way to Dama Luisa's. There were four of them. That was a mistake. The ideal team for ganging up on a man is three. So the fourth bumped into the third as they closed in from all sides and the tall American took advantage of the confusion to fall flat and roll as he went for his gun. He rolled under two pairs of legs and a guy fell on top of him as a comrade swung his club and hit the wrong head. Captain Gringo fired, laying on his back, and that was that. The other two scrambled for cover as the gut-shot mestizo fell screaming across his unconscious comrade and Captain Gringo's legs. The American got out from under them and braced his back against a wall to slide to his feet, gun in hand. Doors and windows were opening all around. He walked on through the alley and met a man running the other way, who wanted to know what was up. He said, "I'm not sure. Somebody either wanted my life or my shoes back there. Would you see if you could find one of the guards? Tell him I'll drop by the guardhouse later to question the one that's still breathing."

Another Creole ran up and the first one explained, "Some *cabrones* tried to kill our Captain Gringo! Help me deal with them."

The American walked on. He knocked on Luisa's door and a servant let him in. But when he was shown into the patio where Luisa sat alone, she seemed surprised to see him.

She rose from her seat by the fountain, a vision in the soft lantern light, as he said, "I got your note, but I had a little trouble getting here."

"My note, Dick? I don't understand. I am happy to see you, of course, but I sent no note."

He sighed and said, "So they weren't after my shoes."

"Your *what*, Dick?"

"Never mind. Some kid ran up to me as I was on my way to the governor's. I should have known the note was a ruse. Some guys just never learn. I'm sorry. I didn't mean to disturb you."

But she said, "Wait, for heaven's sake, sit down and tell me what this is all about. I'll ring for refreshments."

He said, "Never mind. I just filled up on gooey pastries." Then, as she sat on the edge of the fountain, he joined her and told her what had been going on. She waited until he was finished before she nodded and said, "So your job here is nearly over, isn't it?"

He slipped an arm around her waist and said, "Oh, we'll have time to finish those defenses before the steamer arrives. By the time it pulls away we ought to have Pappa Blanco in a box and, yeah, I guess that'll mean there's not much reason to hang around, unless . . ."

She didn't try to move his hand as she said, "Please don't, Dick. You're just teasing us both."

"Both, Luisa?"

"Of course. It would be easy to fall in love with you. But then what? I'm not the sort of woman you're used to, Dick."

"I know. I'm trying to improve my habits."

She laughed and he moved his hand up to cup her breast. Again, she didn't struggle. But she said, "Please control yourself, dear. I don't want to remember you with distaste."

He moved his hand down to her waist and just sat there like an old friend and nodded, saying, "You're right. I'm bigger than you, but you're stronger than me."

She patted the hand against her waist and said, "You're wrong, Dick Walker. You're a very strong man indeed. That's why I feel so safe with you. It's the weaklings who whimper and wrestle. I *like* you, Captain Gringo. So I'm going to tell you something I could only tell a friend."

"What's that, old pard?"

"I really want to make love to you. You're handsome, you're strong and you're decent."

"But what?"

"You know the answer, dear."

He looked away and said, "Yeah. It wouldn't work. You're a lady and I'm a roving guy with a price on his head. Any guy who makes it with you will have to be a Spanish Catholic with a steady job. Can I say something, kid?"

"Of course, dear friend."

"Whoever gets you is going to be one lucky son of a bitch."

"Why, thank you, dear. That's the nicest compliment I've ever had."

She got to her feet, bent, and kissed him on the cheek. He knew she wanted him to leave. So he stood up too, put a hand on each of her shoulders, and started to draw her closer.

She turned her head away and he asked, "Not even a good-bye?"

She shook her copper curls and sighed, "No, dear, I told you this was hard on me, too. Please don't make me cry."

So he didn't. He let go of her, turned around, and walked out of the patio and Dama Luisa's life.

It was the least a knock around gent could do for a lady.

Morning found Captain Gringo, Gaston, Gordo, and Pedro putting along the mangrove-haunted shore in the steam launch. The American had two machine guns braced side by side in the bow. As they rounded another bend, hugging the shore, Gaston said, *"Merde alors!* Another empty cove. Why do you insist there has to be a schooner? Has anyone *seen* your thrice-accursed schooner?"

Captain Gringo said, "Quit your bitching. Those vagrants everyone thought were zombies never landed off an inter-island steamer. Pappa Blanco has been shipping in enough arms and narcotics for an army, and I *have* heard rumors about a schooner."

"Bah, even if the other side has a fleet of them, what makes you think we'll find one this morning, *hein?* If I were this Pappa Blanco, I would have left as soon as I saw my black magic was no longer winning."

Captain Gringo said, "So would I, but we're wise asses. We've taken the wind out of his sails, but he had to hang around and eliminate some people to cover his tracks. I know he was still on the island last night because he sicked some spooks on me in a last ditch effort to stop me."

"True, but the unconcious thug died without ever regaining consciousness. So you didn't get to question him. Ergo, you have no idea who Pappa Blanco might be."

Captain Gringo's eyes were hard and his grin was wolfish when he said, "You're wrong. I talked to him and threw a good scare into him by pointing out how close we were to nailing him."

"Last night you talked to Pappa Blanco? You know who he is?"

"Yeah, it's that fruitcake, Webster, but I can't prove

215

it unless he takes my suggestion about sudden departures."

Gaston's jaw dropped as he gasped, "Webster? The colonel's silly catamite? That's insane!"

"So's Webster. He enjoys his work too much to be considered completely rational. He's been the colonel's right hand man all this time, as well as his occasional change of pace. Who else had his opportunities to run all over the fucking island like a twittering sparrow? I've accounted for where everyone else has been at important moments in time. So . . ."

"Wait a minute. You saw the colonel sodomizing his little playmate at a time Pappa Blanco must have been planning his all-out attack!"

"No I didn't. That was Charlie Burton getting in good with the boss by letting the boss get in him good."

"Burton is that way too?"

"Not really. He just doesn't like working for a living. I don't think Burton cares who he has sex with, just so he advances his career. Some guys are like that. The point is that Webster, not the colonel or Burton, was unaccounted for that afternoon. Nobody remembers standing next to him during the Carib attack the other night. Everybody else I asked has an alibi. Jesus Christ, do you need a signed confession?"

"Only if you mean to see him go to trial, my old and rare friend, but one gathers we did not bring these machine guns to make a citizen's arrest."

By this time they were approaching another point of land and Gordo, at the tiller, swung wide to pass it. At that moment a sixty foot schooner tore across their bow with a bone in its teeth, sails furled and running on auxiliary power, fast!

Captain Gringo snapped, "Gaston! Take the helm!" as he dropped behind the twin guns, teeth bared. Gaston ran back, shoved the willing but inexperienced Gordo out of the way, and steered an interception course, with the bow swinging to cover the schooner.

The men aboard the schooner saw them too, and gunsmoke blossomed along the bulwarks of the faster vessel as it swung its stern to them, obviously planning to easily outdistance them.

Captain Gringo said, "Thanks, chumps," and opened up with both machine guns, a hand on each trigger. A slug from the schooner wanged off the launch's rail to his left. He ignored it with cold glee as he tap-danced machine gun-fire into the enemy vessel's stern. Gaston shouted, "More elevation, Dick! You're hitting too low for the bastards in the cockpit to feel the effects!"

"They'll feel effects, the sons of bitches," growled Captain Gringo as he fired another double burst into the schooner's waterline. Another bullet whizzed past his right ear and he fired once more before he yelled, "Fall off, Gaston. There's no sense getting shot this late in the game."

Gaston swung the launch hard alee but marveled, "You are letting them go? Why did we come all this way if . . ." and then he saw what was happening, and added, "Oh, Dick, that was *trés* dirty!"

The schooner was sinking by the stern, of course, after having its rear end shattered by massed machine gun-fire. It lay dead in the water now, white vapor gushing from its stack as sea water hit its engine. The men from the cockpit were moving forward to the one and only lifeboat. Gaston asked if he wanted to move in and dust them some more. Captain Gringo said, "No," and reached for a bucket under the thwarts. He started chumming chicken entrails as they bobbed quietly just out of rifle range. The boy, Pedro, started to ask why he was throwing bait in the water, then a dark fin started to circle them and Pedro paled and crossed himself. Gordo said, "I think our captain must be very angry."

The men aboard the schooner were desperately trying to launch their one remaining chance, and Captain Gringo was about to suggest moving in to smoke up the lifeboat. Then he saw what was happening aboard the other vessel and smiled. He said, "They let the fittings rust while the yacht lay hidden under wet brush. I don't think they're going to work it loose in time."

He was right. The schooner was sinking faster and the men aboard gave up to run up to the bow. There were seven of them. One he recognized as Webster threw his rifle in the drink and started waving at them.

Captain Gringo said, "They want to surrender. Let's move in within hailing range."

The other cutthroats were tossing their guns overboard while Gaston moved the launch closer. A dozen shark fins were now circling, as the brainless appetites they were attached to searched for the source of the blood in the water that they'd followed in from all around.

Captain Gringo said, "Close enough, Gaston," as they drew alongside the sinking schooner. Webster yelled across to them, "You win, you bastards! We give up."

Captain Gringo smiled across the water as the schooner kept going under, gurgling in protest. Webster spotted a shark fin cutting between them and shouted, "I said you win, damn it. Take us off this thing before it sinks."

Captain Gringo shook his head and said, "No. Fair is fair. You tried to feed me to a boa constrictor, so . . ."

"You can't be serious! This is inhuman!"

"Yeah, there's been a lot of that going around lately."

One of the other men with Webster yelled, "Hey, look, Webster is the one you want." But Captain Gringo said, "I don't want any of you. I'm feeding you to the sharks. I wish I could think up something nastier, but I don't have as much imagination."

Webster screamed in utter terror as something gave and the schooner started sinking faster. Captain Gringo turned and said, "Let's get out of here, Gaston. This isn't as much fun as I thought it would be."

Gaston nodded and swung the tiller while Webster begged and pleaded. Captain Gringo didn't look back as the schooner went under and the sharks moved in. He didn't have to. You could hear the screams for a mile or more.

Captain Gringo stood smoking at the starboard rail as the ship steamed through the night. A new moon was rising and he could have seen it if he'd wanted to walk around to the port side. But what good was a rising moon over tropic waters to a guy who faced a long voyage on a slow boat, alone?

He wasn't *exactly* alone. Gaston was working on a pair of touring flamenco dancers in the ship's saloon, but they were both pigs. Gaston could and probably would wind up with both of them. He'd recovered nicely from his snake bite.

Just how he'd been bitten aboard that other ship would probably never be known. Both the British government and the much more frightening Sir Basil Hakim had chided a certain international oil trust about that sunken schooner registered in their name. They'd assured everyone that the late Pappa Blanco Webster had exceeded his instructions, and that they'd never never do it again.

So the job was done. Sir Kakim had cabled them enough to live on for a year, they were headed for a port where nobody was after them, and why did he feel so shitty?

Maybe it was because he hadn't pulled the chestnuts out of the fire for anyone he gave a damn about. Sir Hakim and Pantropic Limited were no better or no worse than the outfit that had been trying to take over Nuevo Verdugo. The colonel and all were safe and secure, but still pretty weird. Alice had promised not to sick peon lovers on her rivals, and since Burton had taken off with a tidy profit, she'd probably be too busy screwing to break her promise.

The employees of the company and the natives of Nuevo Verdugo would be safe too, and probably better off, now that the island's economy was about to boom. Even the Black Caribs would come out ahead in the end.

The Brits tended to leave primitive religions alone as long as nobody got hurt, and the last gifts of baubles and blankets left on the tree line south of the new fence had been accepted, stolen or whatever. The Caribs would be won over in the end and their grandchildren would probably wind up working as dishwashers in London.

So Captain Gringo knew he should be feeling better. But he just felt drained. He didn't want a drink, he didn't want either of the pigs his sidekick was lining up, and he was too keyed up to go to his cabin and sleep. Maybe booze and babes *were* the answer. The flamenco gal with the moustache had a nice ass. But it was just as much fun, and just as pointless, to have a smoke.

He fished out a cigar, cupped his hands around a match to light it, and someone asked, "May I have a light, too?"

It was Luisa. Her eyes glowed warmly in the flickering matchlight as he held the flame to the tip of the little claro held between her moist lips. He said, "I didn't know you smoked in public. What are you doing aboard this slow boat to nowhere?"

She took a drag, let it out, and said, "We're not in public. We're on a ship where nobody knows me. I thought a sea voyage would help me forget."

"Oh? I thought everybody knew Gaston and I were leaving on this tub."

"Everybody did, Dick. I meant I wanted to forget all the horrible happenings back in Nuevo Verdugo. You know I never wanted to forget you."

He wanted her so bad he could taste it. But he said, "A lady could get in trouble following a wandering star, Luisa."

She said, "I know. It hurts as much to wait for one in a sleepy little backwater, too. Where is this ship going, Dick?"

"I think it stops in Rio and turns around. I'll be getting off somewhere along the way, alone. You've got to understand something about me, honey."

But she put a finger to his lips and said, "Hush,

don't explain. We don't need explanations or false promises, do we, dear?"

He started to put his arms around her. But he saw she was frightened too, so he didn't. The night was young and they had a long voyage on a slow boat ahead of them. There was no need to rush things. So he took a long deep drag on his cigar as he smiled down at her. It was funny how good the smoke tasted, all of a sudden.

DIRTY HARRY by Dane Hartman
Never before published or seen on screen.

He's "Dirty Harry" Callahan—tough, unorthodox, no-nonsense plain-clothesman extraordinaire of the San Francisco Police Department...Inspector #71 assigned to the bruising, thankless homicide detail...A consummate crimebuster nothing can stop—not even the law! Explosive mysteries involving racketeers, murderers, extortionists, pushers, and skyjackers: savage, bizarre murders, accomplished with such cunning and expertise that the frustrated S.F.P.D. finds itself without a single clue; hair-raising action and violence as Dirty Harry arrives on the scene, armed with nothing but a Smith & Wesson .44 and a bag of dirty tricks; unbearable suspense and hairy chase sequences as Dirty Harry sleuths to unmask the villain and solve the mystery. Dirty Harry—when the chips are down, he's the most low-down cop on the case.

5 EXCITING ADVENTURE SERIES
MEN OF ACTION BOOKS

__NINJA MASTER
by Wade Barker
Committed to avenging injustice. Brett Wallace uses the ancient Japanese art of killing as he stalks the evildoers of the world in his mission.
__#3 BORDERLAND OF HELL (C30-127, $1.95)
__#4 MILLION-DOLLAR MASSACRE (C30-177, $1.95)
__#5 BLACK MAGICIAN (C30-178, $1.95)
__#6 DEATH'S DOOR (C30-229, $1.95)

__THE HOOK
by Brad Latham
Gentleman detective, boxing legend, man-about-town. The Hook crosses 1930's America and Europe in pursuit of perpetrators of insurance fraud.
__#1 THE GILDED CANARY (C90-882, $1.95)
__#2 SIGHT UNSEEN (C90-841, $1.95)
__#5 CORPSES IN THE CELLAR (C90-985, $1.95)

__S-COM
by Steve White
High adventure with the most effective and notorious band of military mercenaries the world has known—four men and one woman with a perfect track record.
__#3 THE BATTLE IN BOTSWANA (C30-134, $1.95)
__#4 THE FIGHTING IRISH (C30-141, $1.95)
__#5 KING OF KINGSTON (C30-133, $1.95)
__#6 SIERRA DEATH DEALERS (C30-142, $1.95)

__BEN SLAYTON: T-MAN
by Buck Sanders
Based on actual experiences, America's most secret law-enforcement agent—the troubleshooter of the Treasury Department—combats the enemies of national security.
__#1 A CLEAR AND PRESENT DANGER (C30-020, $1.95)
__#2 STAR OF EGYPT (C30-017, $1.95)
__#3 THE TRAIL OF THE TWISTED CROSS (C30-131, $1.95)
__#5 BAYOU BRIGADE (C30-200, $1.95)

__BOXER UNIT—OSS
by Ned Cort
The elite 4-man commando unit of the Office of Strategic Studies whose dare-devil missions during World War II place them in the vanguard of the action.
__#2 ALPINE GAMBIT (C30-019, $1.95)
__#3 OPERATION COUNTER-SCORCH (C30-128, $1.95)
__#4 TARGET NORWAY (C30-121, $1.95)
__#5 PARTISAN DEMOLITION (C30-129, $1.95)

"THE KING OF THE WESTERN NOVEL" IS MAX BRAND